The Highland Lass

Rosemary Gemmell

*"This finely layered novel evokes place with vivid
realism, both in contemporary Scotland
and in the past."*
A Woman's Wisdom Reviews

Opal Scot Books

Originally published by Crooked Cat Books
Cover Art Design: Courtesy of Crooked Cat Books
Original Editor: Christine McPherson

New Edition Copyright © Rosemary Gemmell 2019
www.rosemarygemmell.co.uk

The Highland Lass is a work of fiction. Names, characters, places and incidents are the product of the author's imagination except where used fictitiously. Any resemblance to actual events, locales, or persons, living or dead, is purely coincidental, or fictionalised.

ISBN: 978-1-9162577-8-8

*In loving memory of my wonderful mother,
Mary, who first introduced me to
Highland Mary's grave so many years ago*

The Highland Lass

Prologue

"Nae gentle dames, tho' e'er sae fair,
Shall ever be my muse's care;
Their titles a' are empty show,
Gie me my highland lassie, O."
(R. Burns: *The Highland Lassie*)

The young girl grasped her mother's hand as they left the open pathways and began the long walk through the well-trodden, winding paths of the old part of Greenock Cemetery, past weathered moss-covered tombstones with almost indecipherable writing.

Daylight flickered on and off through the overhanging branches of trees, as ancient as the graves they shadowed. On they wandered, past the resting place of infants with stone guardian angels, up beyond the large family vault surrounded by everlasting iron rails of privacy, and finally to the furthest away path beside the cemetery wall. They usually stopped at this particular spot on their way to granny and grandpa's grass-covered resting ground in the modern part of the cemetery.

"That's where she's buried, Eilidh, my namesake and ancestress, Mary Campbell. Highland Mary."

Eilidh gazed at the old, high gravestone standing within a semi-circle of tall trees. It looked neglected, forlorn. The chiselled name had worn over time, the grass slowly creeping over the lowest edges of the stone.

Yet, more than any other grave in the vast cemetery, this one never failed to fill her with a sense of awe, a strange knowledge that this Mary Campbell had been someone important, but almost forgotten in this dark place. Perhaps it was the way her mother stopped as if in homage, the way they both gazed at the tomb as though in fond remembrance.

On that final childhood day, as she stood at Highland Mary's grave several months before leaving the old country for the new, Eilidh sensed that the spell cast by these visits to this dark but strangely comforting memorial to the past would be woven in some way with her future.

Chapter One

"The lazy mist hangs from the brow of the hill,
Concealing the course of the dark winding rill.
(R. Burns: *The Lazy Mist*)

Eilidh gripped the arms of the seat, psyching herself up to endure the transatlantic flight. She would be fine once actually in the air when the disconcerting changes of speed and engine sound had ceased. She closed her eyes, using the time to think. So much had happened over the past month that she was still amazed at her ability to change her life in such a short time. But if she wanted to discover her father's true identity, she had to do it now.

She'd long been disturbed by dreams of Scotland and a need to revisit her roots, especially after her mother lost her fight with cancer. Now, after selling her share in the second-hand book shop, her own apartment and her mother's, she was on her way back home. Or a temporary home, until she decided what to do with her life and how to find out the truth of a past her mother had kept hidden.

Finding the memory box had only added to her questions. Apart from the old black journal handed down through the years, and the photograph of her mother with an unknown naval man, it was the note hidden inside a small book of Robert Burns' poems that convinced her she must return to Scotland. Part letter, part verse, the words were branded on her mind.

To my own Highland Lass,

Although I loved you deeply, I never loved you wisely,

And though we now must part, you are ever in my heart.

I'll never stop thinking of you, or loving you both. It was never meant to happen this way. You are so much stronger than I am.

Yours for aye and aye,

R

At first, she thought it was a rare letter from Robert Burns. Then she studied the flowing black script; it was too modern, the verse too amateurish. But there seemed little doubt that whoever wrote the letter may well have been her natural father.

"You do know we're in the air now, don't you?"

Hearing the amused, rich Scottish accent, Eilidh frowned and opened her eyes. She hadn't paid much attention to her travelling companions, apart from a cursory glance to acknowledge they existed; she'd been too busy worrying about take-off. She glared at the owner of the voice, indignant at her thoughts being interrupted. For all he knew she might have been in a deep sleep.

"Yeah, thanks, I was quite aware of that."

He had the cheek to grin. "Oh, that's fine then. I could see you obviously didn't like the take-off and I only wanted to reassure you."

How did he know she was nervous? Then Eilidh realised she was still gripping the armrest on either side of her and blushed at taking up so much of his space. Not that he seemed bothered. She noticed his deep blue eyes and slightly greying black hair that betrayed his Celtic heritage, as well as his vaguely unshaven look, relaxed manner and seeming good humour. She smiled despite herself.

"Thanks, it's kind of you to care." This time she was rewarded by a devastating lopsided smile.

"Lewis Grant. Pleased to meet you."

Eilidh glanced at his outstretched hand and hesitated. She didn't particularly want to strike up a conversation with a complete stranger. Then she felt a bit churlish. What harm could it do? She could always lose herself in her book if he threatened to talk too much.

"Eilidh Campbell. Likewise." As her small hand disappeared in his large one, she felt strangely comforted and relaxed some more.

"Let me guess. A Scot by birth, but American by adoption," he said.

Eilidh nodded. "How observant." Was it that obvious?

"I can hear your faint Scottish accent, and your name kind of gives it away." His voice still teased. "Is that Eilidh with an 'E' or an 'A'?"

"The Gaelic spelling with an 'E', like ceilidh without the 'c'. You're right of course. I'm glad the accent is still discernible." She didn't offer any more information and was pleased he took the hint and settled back into his own seat. She was not going to be too friendly.

By the time the meal had been served and cleared away, she relaxed enough to give some thought to what awaited her in Scotland. She'd seen some of the in-flight movies before and while her companion read a book, she closed her eyes and tried to remember childhood haunts.

The memories took her straight to the central area of Greenock where she'd spent her early years; part of the industrial working class where the men worked hard and drank deep while the women kept a clean home and a firm hand on the pay packet. She recalled one incident before they left Scotland for what would be her mother's one and only time. Her Auntie Elizabeth had paid them a visit. She was married to a tugboat captain, had one son, Rory, and had managed to get herself a secretarial job at the local school, so they were what her mum had called "well-to-do".

Compared to her mother, her aunt had seemed a bit snooty and well-dressed. She'd glanced around the flat with a good sniff now and then, as though it was all a bit beneath her. Although Eilidh had never been in their house, she knew it was in the west end of town, near the grand Esplanade.

That particular day stuck in Eilidh's mind, for her aunt had never called before. She'd seen her briefly at Granny's funeral, along with a tall man and a thin boy of about her own age, whom she presumed was her cousin. They'd left immediately after the service and hardly glanced their way. Yet now her aunt was suddenly visiting Eilidh and her mother.

"Now, you know, Mary, you don't have to leave the country; that seems a bit drastic. And what about Eilidh? She's at a terrible age to uproot to another culture. Or if you're so set on going, why don't you consider leaving Eilidh with us? You know I'd look after her, and she'd get on with Rory since they're nearly the same age. I'm sure William wouldn't mind."

Eilidh had stopped breathing for a minute. Stay here? With Auntie Elizabeth and an uncle and cousin she didn't know? She'd rather take her chances with America; at least she would be with her mum. She waited to see what her mother would say.

"I know you would look after her. And how would I know that, Elizabeth, since we've hardly set eyes on you while she was growing up? I don't know what you think you're playing at, but I don't think your husband and son would be very happy."

The atmosphere had cooled and Eilidh listened for Auntie Elizabeth's reply, but was stunned when the woman turned and walked out of the house never to be seen again. The silence had continued all through the day and Eilidh couldn't bring herself to mention her aunt. It was enough she wasn't being left behind with strangers. Suddenly America had seemed an exciting idea…

Eilidh started suddenly as she felt a hand on her arm; she'd been miles and years away.

"Sorry, didn't mean to startle you but they're bringing the drinks trolley."

"Thanks. I could do with some water."

She was wary when he took her smiling answer as an invitation to start a conversation. Yet, why not? It was hours until they reached Glasgow and she didn't sleep well on planes. It wasn't every day she got to have fairly intimate conversation with a handsome stranger – in respect of their nearness to each other. She listened politely at first as he told her he was a lecturer at a local college, but her interest caught when he mentioned a special interest in old books and first editions.

"Sorry, what did you say you teach?" She was ashamed to admit she hadn't been giving him her full attention.

"Oh dear, and here's me thinking you were hanging on my every word! I teach history, or at least I try to impart some meagre knowledge of the past into enquiring minds."

She had to laugh; at least he had a sense of humour and certainly didn't fit the worn-out stereotype of a dour Scot. But he was also impressively broad of chest and dark of hair, with penetrating eyes, and just for a moment she could imagine him striding across some heather-clad hill in a kilt. Heavens, what on earth was she thinking? She'd obviously been away too long if she was starting to think like a tourist.

The remainder of the flight passed more quickly, largely due to Lewis Grant.

"So, what brings you back to the old country?" he asked.

"A need to find my roots, I guess. When I found my mother's memory box with so few reminders of our life in Scotland, I couldn't resist trying to fill in the blanks. I've no ties in America." She didn't look at him, hoping he wouldn't take it as a hint she was available. "I also want to find out more about the story of Highland Mary and Robert Burns. I remember seeing her grave when I was a child, and my mother had an old book of Burns' poems."

"I hope you find what you seek," he said, but didn't ask further questions.

She held back from telling him about the photograph of the American naval officer and her young mother that she'd found in the box, taken in Dunoon when the American Navy had been based at the Holy Loch. Or about the ink-penned letter signed with the initial *R* from a lover of Burns and hidden in the treasured small book of poetry. Her unknown father?

Her mother had often talked about being descended from the same branch of Campbells as Highland Mary, one of Burns' great loves. Growing up with her mother and granny, Eilidh had never questioned when the adults told her that her father had died. But she did know she was a bastard, though she hadn't known what it meant when a boy had called her that at school one day.

Lewis Grant proved a good listener and Eilidh was surprised she told him so much about herself and her life in America. Perhaps because he was a stranger she was hardly likely to meet again? That thought seemed to lodge somewhere and take root, as though it would grow in significance. Then she called herself all kinds of fool and remembered she didn't need a man in her life.

Yet, she responded to something about this particular man, almost as though she had met him somewhere before. Once she forgot her reservations and followed her natural inclination to be friendly, she couldn't look away. As far as she could see, he was every bit as keen to speak to her. When he had to go and stretch his legs at one point, Eilidh stood in the aisle to allow him to pass and his arm accidentally brushed hers. Their eyes met for a second and they smiled at the same time.

"Thanks, Eilidh." It was all he said, but as she sat back down, she thought of the way he'd said it.

Her name had never sounded so... *right*. She closed her eyes. She must be far more fanciful than she supposed. Of course, instant attraction was entirely possible, but she wanted to get to know this man. And they were going their separate ways when the plane landed.

Before she had time to take the thought any further, Lewis returned and she went for a walk and a tidy-up herself, stretching on tiptoes at intervals to avoid the dreaded DVT. By the time she returned to her seat the lights were being dimmed for the next part of the journey and they busied themselves opening their complimentary blanket and little pack with an eye mask. Eilidh dispensed with the pack but snuggled under her blanket, ready to try and doze for part of the way. She kept her earphones handy in case she had to resort to watching a film in the end.

Lewis had already stretched out his long legs as far as possible and was reading his book.

"Do you want to change seats, so you can stretch out a bit more?" she suddenly thought of asking, keeping her voice low.

"Thanks, but don't worry, I've been in worse seats than this and I probably won't sleep much anyway."

His whispered reply was oddly conspiratorial and for one single, ridiculous moment as she looked up at him from her comfortable position, she had the urge to be kissed.

She looked away at once, glad the cabin was almost dark. What on earth was she playing at? This just wasn't her. She'd never lusted after a man in her life, and especially not someone she'd only met. How weird! She whispered goodnight and turned her back on him slightly, determined to put him out of her mind as he'd soon be out of her life. Unbidden, she remembered reading once about a woman who'd left her husband for the man she sat beside on a transatlantic crossing, and they were eventually married. Real life really was a lot stranger than fiction sometimes.

When she awoke, Eilidh couldn't believe she'd even been to sleep – she usually couldn't relax when out of her bed. Then she sat up with a start. Her head was against Lewis Grant's shoulder while he calmly read his book.

"Oh, I'm sorry…"

"Don't be, we were both quite comfortable." He

smiled at her confusion.

The lights came back on and the announcement warned them of breakfast being served soon before making their descent into Glasgow. The sudden queasiness in the pit of her stomach was more than the fear of landing safely. She was coming home, to Scotland.

By the time they landed, and were gathering their belongings together, Eilidh had reconciled herself to saying goodbye to her companion. He made a thing of making sure her book was in her bag and that she had everything from the locker. Already, she felt bereft.

"Thanks for your company." She didn't know what else to say and held out her hand.

"It was a pleasure, Eilidh. And I mean that."

Instead of taking her hand, he opened his arms and she willingly gave him a hug. It felt as though she belonged there and she was horrified to feel the threat of tears. She was *not* going to blub in front of this man, this stranger.

She checked her handbag and lifted her jacket and small extra bag. How was she going to say goodbye? Then the doors opened, and in the ensuing flurry of movement, Eilidh found herself carried away down the aisle to the steps.

She walked to the baggage reclaim, hoping to catch up with him yet not sure what they'd say. The place was too busy with everyone trying to get their cases from the carousel once it started up. Then she remembered he'd been on a business trip so probably had only taken cabin luggage on the flight. Maybe it was for the best. He hadn't told her that much about himself, so no doubt he was married. Of course, he was. He was tall and broad enough to stand out among the other passengers, yet he had seemingly disappeared already.

As she walked past the green "Nothing to declare" sign and made her way through the arrivals lounge, she had a sudden moment of self-pity that there was no-one to meet her. She hadn't even told her aunt she was coming to Scotland as they'd never kept in touch. She hadn't yet decided how to approach her remaining estranged family, if they still lived in the same place.

The only person who knew she was coming home was Kirsty, her childhood friend. She had promised to try and get away from work to meet her, but it wasn't a firm arrangement and Eilidh could see no sign of her.

She planned to go straight to Dunoon, where she would play the tourist properly and pretend it was her first visit to the country; try and recapture some sense of belonging, if possible. She could stay a couple of nights at a hotel then take it from there. She had no timetable to follow and no-one else to consider.

Joining the taxi queue outside the airport building, she inhaled her first breath of Scottish air in twenty years. Even the fine drizzle of rain was a welcome she'd longed for, and she smiled at the feel of it on her hair. The other people waiting would think her mad to be happy at the weather, when some – like her – had left the Californian sunshine behind.

She was about to move along the taxi line when she heard her name called. At least she presumed it was her name being yelled from the terminal door, and she turned around in surprise.

Kirsty!

"You didn't think I'd let you arrive without coming to meet you, did you?" The admonition was light-hearted and accompanied by a great whoop of joy.

Before she could look at her friend properly, Eilidh found herself enveloped in a great big hug. She should have guessed Kirsty wouldn't miss the chance to see her as soon as possible. Their letters to each other had continued to fly across the Atlantic all these years, and it was as though they'd skipped the awkward years of teenage friendship and twenties' dating, to arrive at this supposedly more mature stage of their lives together.

"Oh, Kirsty, I'd have known you anywhere, you've hardly changed a bit! It's so good to see you. I thought perhaps you hadn't managed to get time off. We nearly missed each other."

"Och, you know me. Last minute as usual. I checked the arrival time and trusted I'd catch you somewhere, since the airport hasn't grown that big yet. Only problem is I'm still hopeless at timing myself. The car's over in the short-term car park."

Eilidh studied her friend with interest. Always small and neat, Kirsty had kept her trim figure along with the short dark hair, though Eilidh suspected a different shade had been added at some point. Her personality hadn't changed, from the way she chattered excitedly and obviously still did things impulsively at the last minute.

They had reached the entrance to the car park when a car slowed down enough for Eilidh to see the driver. Lewis Grant. Risking the anger of the drivers behind him, he stopped the car long enough to call to her.

"Have a good visit, Eilidh. Give me a ring once you get the chance."

"But I don't have your number."

The driver behind tooted his horn as Lewis

replied, "Look in your book." Then he drove away with a wave.

Eilidh finally became aware of Kirsty's voice.

"Who was he? What was all that about? Did he come over with you?"

Eilidh laughed incredulously. "Well! That was unexpected."

Kirsty waited impatiently until her friend recovered from her shock, then started again. "So, are you gonnae tell me, or are you no'?"

Eilidh laughed at the sudden slip into broad dialect and satisfied Kirsty's curiosity as far as she could.

"So, you are going to call him, right? He's a looker, isn't he, in a rugged kind of way?"

"I suppose he is. I can't believe he put his number in my book. I had no idea."

"But you are going to ring him, aren't you?" Kirsty's voice was wistful.

"He's probably married. Anyway, I'm not here for romance."

Even as she spoke, Eilidh knew she wouldn't be able to resist looking for his number. She would decide then whether or not to act on it, although she couldn't deny the obvious attraction between them. But she wasn't looking for any complications. She had enough to keep her occupied and a strange man, however attractive, was not part of the plan.

"So, you'll come and stay with me for a while then?"

Kirsty broke into her thoughts and Eilidh started to protest when she heard what her friend proposed.

"I can't possibly expect you to put me up. I was going to go straight to Dunoon for a few days."

"Och, you don't think I'm going to let you escape

that easily! After all this time? You've got to stay with me until we catch up properly on all the years we've missed. Anyway, I live near enough to the ferry so you can go back and forth to Dunoon as much as you need."

Eilidh recognised the determination behind the words and gave in gracefully, and gratefully. Kirsty's flat in Gourock would be convenient for trains and ferry, and it would be good to catch up with her friend and not feel so alone for a few days. She gave a fleeting thought to Lewis Grant's parting words and resolved to forget him for the moment. After all, they were only strangers passing the time on a flight. Or so she told herself.

Slinging her large holdall and flight bag into the boot of the small red car, Eilidh sat back and prepared to enjoy the ride through some of the most beautiful scenery in the west coast of Scotland, feeling unexpectedly homesick. She'd missed the country more than she realised.

She knew Kirsty was still single after an engagement had ended in tears and that she shared a flat with another nurse, but she hardly knew anything about the friend. She closed her eyes for a few minutes while Kirsty negotiated the traffic to take them onto the M8 towards Greenock. She'd be glad to get a good night's sleep to rid herself of any jetlag.

Eilidh opened her eyes just as they reached the exit from the Paisley roundabout and headed down the motorway.

"So, you awake okay, Eilidh?" Kirsty glanced towards her friend. "I didn't want to disturb you. I know how tiring these transatlantic flights are."

"Sure, sorry. I closed my eyes for a moment and

was away! How rude, after you being so kind. I managed to get a little sleep on the plane but I guess the time difference takes a while to catch up."

"Don't be daft, of course you'll be tired. I promise I'll try not to talk you into the ground today. They say it's best to adapt to the clock of the country you've landed in, so if you manage to keep awake until evening then you'll probably sleep fine."

"Don't you have to go to work? I hope you didn't take time off especially for me."

"Had some days due, so thought I'd make the most of the chance to catch up with you."

Eilidh kept quiet while Kirsty pulled out and overtook a slow car on the inside lane. Then a movement just beyond and above the windscreen suddenly caught her attention and she was amazed to see a jet climbing clearly into the cloudy sky, right above the motorway.

"Wow, did you see that? I'd forgotten how close the airport is to the road. It's kind of scary, isn't it?"

Kirsty laughed at her expression. "You get used to it, though I often wonder if any driver has become so distracted that he loses control. Now you've got to stay awake until we reach the most stunning view you'll see for a while. It won't be long."

As they drove on in companionable silence, Eilidh was content to watch the countryside go by, marvelling at the shades of green. Due to the amount of rain, of course. As they were about to pass under a bridge, Kirsty broke the silence.

"Just a few moments over the brow of this wee hill and you'll see it."

Eilidh sat up with interest. Then she saw why it was worth looking. The rain had stopped and the sky was becoming clearer. Just ahead, and to the right side of the road, the River Clyde was laid out like a painting, stretching far off into the distance. Although the sky still held a few clouds, she noticed the outline of hills and mountains that bordered the scene and added to its beauty. She wished she could capture it at once, either in paint or a photograph.

Kirsty slowed the car a little and Eilidh saw Dumbarton Castle perched on its rock just across the stretch of water from them. The tide was out and, with the sands visible, it looked as though she could walk across.

"See the Holy Loch away down at the 'tail o' the bank'?" Kirsty asked.

As far as the eye could see, mountains reached into the sky in all their glory, and Dunoon and Argyll were almost visible at the furthest end of the long river. Dunoon, where her mother had probably met her American and where Highland Mary was born. Eilidh fell silent again, watching the river and hills go by. Even on such a dull day the colours changed from the lightest green to almost black, with every shade in between, including the muted fawns and browns of fields. She was truly home again and was surprised to feel a lump in her throat.

"Beautiful." It was all she could manage and was glad when Kirsty concentrated on her driving and allowed her to watch the scenery.

As they reached Gourock, Eilidh couldn't believe all the changes in such a relatively short time. Soon they were in the west end of town and Eilidh remembered the Esplanade was on the right, parallel to the main street.

"Could we maybe drive along the Esplanade?" she asked, longing to see the river again.

"Of course we can, I should've thought of it

myself. We can turn down the next street."

And there it was: the wide esplanade with its grand old Victorian houses on the left and the river on the right. Her aunt and uncle had lived somewhere around here. Not on the Esplanade itself, but on one of the many streets branching from it.

"Oh, it's so good to see it all again!" She'd have to spend time exploring old haunts and appreciating all the best parts of the area again.

"Not far now," Kirsty said.

They passed the Battery Park, where Eilidh had spent many a warm summer's day, and were now turning round by Cardwell Bay. Eilidh couldn't believe it when Kirsty pulled up in front of an impressive old house.

"We're here. We've got one of the upper flats."

The view was incredible. Across from the house the river stretched for miles in all directions and hills formed a backdrop. Several boats moored off a small jetty and, to its left, a swing park invited children to play. Around a corner into the distance she could even see Gourock Station and knew one of the ferries to Dunoon left from that area.

"Wow, how did you get this? And you weren't kidding when you said it was near the station and ferry!"

Kirsty laughed at her reaction. "Come and see the inside. It might be a flat but it's got plenty of space, like all these old buildings. And it's so convenient for the hospital where Sarah and I work, just over the Larkfield hill."

A main door flat occupied either side, but Kirsty led the way round the side of the building to the back of the house. Eilidh's eyes widened at the sight of the delicate black, wrought iron spiral staircase leading to the upper flats. It looked so Mediterranean with all the potted plants and little courtyard with table and chairs. But that was nothing to the view from the front windows of the flat – an even better version of the one from street level. She was going to enjoy her unexpected stay here.

"You can have the bed settee, if you don't mind. It's quite comfortable. Sarah's out a lot and we both work shifts, so you'll have the place to yourself sometimes."

Eilidh hoped the other girl wouldn't mind having a stranger foisted on her.

As though reading her mind, Kirsty continued, "I've warned Sarah you're coming, and she's fine. You might find her quiet at first; she's a bit intense but she's great really. We muck along well. She'll be home for something to eat later."

The two bedrooms, bathroom and kitchen were a good size, but Eilidh was happy to sleep in the living room with a view. She was in the middle of unpacking her meagre clothes and fitting them into the space Kirsty had left for her when she heard a name from the past.

"You remember Jamie, of course, don't you? He was always sweet on you at school."

Eilidh stopped what she was doing to look up in surprise.

"Jamie Kilpatrick? You mean you've kept in touch all these years? How come you didn't talk about him in your letters?" He had hung around with them both at school, ignoring all the teasing from the other boys.

She saw Kirsty's face flush before she turned to shrug at Eilidh.

"Oh, well, I used to go out with him for a while

then we fell apart and I put him out of my head. He went off on his travels with his camera and we kind of lost touch again. But apparently he's back for a while."

The last few words were quieter and Eilidh wondered just how well her friend had been able to put him out of her mind. But it was a pleasant shock to find her old schoolmate still around these parts, and she might even get the chance to meet him.

"Anyway, we can talk later. I'll get you a cup of tea while you finish organising yourself. You do still drink normal tea, don't you?"

Eilidh laughed at her friend's expression. "It's a hard custom to break and I'll be glad of a hot cup."

Once she had hung up what she'd brought and made a mental note to buy some new clothes, they spent the rest of the day catching up on their years apart. She told Kirsty the real reason she had come back, and about her growing fascination with Highland Mary who was buried in Greenock cemetery.

"That's a great idea to do some research." Then Kirsty grew more serious. "But how are you going to find out about your father?"

"I'll have to play that by ear. My aunt doesn't even know I'm in Scotland."

Eilidh was amazed at how quickly the two of them returned to their old bantering chat and how all the intervening years seemed to be of little importance now they were together again. It was a measure of their friendship that it had lasted through distance and time and she was grateful for it.

Eventually Kirsty stood up. "I'm cooking tonight in your honour."

"Can I help?"

"Course not, you must be shattered after the flight. Don't worry, there'll be plenty of chance to help out on other days. Put your feet up and have look through the magazines.

Eilidh had a desultory read through one, then got fed up sitting and wandered through to the kitchen to carry on chatting while Kirsty prepared the meal. They heard the front door open and close. Sarah must be home.

"In here!" Kirsty shouted.

Eilidh's first impression was surprise, for there was nothing memorable about Sarah for someone who was meant to be so intense. Her medium brown hair was of medium length, half hiding her small face, and she wore frameless spectacles that threatened to overwhelm her. Even her size and shape were average, hardly enhanced by the shapeless skirt and top she wore. Then she smiled.

"Hi, I'm Sarah. It's lovely to meet you, Eilidh. Hope you don't mind sleeping on the sofa."

Eilidh warmed at the girl's friendliness and noticed that the smile brightened her whole face. She felt less nervous about being foisted on her.

"Good to meet you, too, Sarah. It's great of you both to let me stay here. I didn't expect this when I arrived at Glasgow."

When Sarah excused herself and left them to finish making the meal, Eilidh set the table by the window in the sitting room, glad they would be able to look at the view while they ate. She hadn't tasted minced beef cooked this way with carrots and onions since she was a child, and by the time the three of them had finished every drop she felt right at home.

It was a perfect end to the day when Kirsty suggested a short walk along the bay to the park. It was good to stretch her legs after the lengthy flight.

Nearing the end of July, the air was still warm enough for a light cardigan now the rain had completely gone. The slight tang of seaweed from the bay hung on the air. It was cleaner than she remembered, but everything else was close enough to what she had known as a child. When they returned to the flat, Kirsty insisted Eilidh got some sleep.

"It's fairly comfortable so hopefully you'll sleep all right," Kirsty said, as she put sheets and light blankets on the sofa bed. "Sarah's away to bed already as she's got an early shift tomorrow and I'm sure she'll be quiet in the morning. I'll take the chance to have a lie in, so you can sleep as long as you like."

"Don't worry, I'm ready to crash!" Eilidh stifled a yawn. "Thanks for the great welcome, Kirsty."

"I'm just glad to see you after all this time. Sleep well."

Eilidh waited until Kirsty finished with the bathroom, then brushed her teeth and had a quick shower, before snuggling down under the soft sheet and blankets. Just before she switched off the light, she drew aside the curtains to take one last look over the river. It was dark now but the moon lit up the still, black water and the faint outline of hills visible in the distance.

She lay back down and wondered where Lewis Grant lived. She couldn't quite get him out of her thoughts and knew she'd have to call him if she could find his number. She would get up and look for it right now but was so comfortable and tired; instead, she tried to remember every detail of their meeting. But sleep took over before she had time to form thoughts of what tomorrow might bring.

A faint sound had woken her. At first Eilidh couldn't think where she was, then gradually awareness returned. It was barely light but she could hear someone moving quietly between the hall and the kitchen and realised Sarah must be getting ready to go to work. She'd slept soundly but would probably need some more to fully catch up on the jetlag.

It was great not having to worry about going to work. She could look forward to getting to know her homeland again. Just being here was enough for now, and all the questions could wait until the right time. When she heard the front door close quietly, she got up. Kirsty wouldn't mind if she made herself some tea to quench her thirst.

Bringing the cup through to the sitting room, Eilidh switched on the lamp beside the sofa. Too awake to go straight back to sleep, she thought about all the places she wanted to see. Such blessed silence – apart from the occasional birdsong – felt like a gift. No sound of traffic, or early morning voices, or banging of doors like back home.

She pulled back the curtains again and stared at the river, just visible in the early dawn light, one or two small boats bobbing peacefully on the tide. She would sail on that river today, anxious to make her first visit to Dunoon after all these years.

How strange that two different girls called Mary Campbell had spent time there, separated by three centuries, and Eilidh was interested in them both. She took the empty cup back to the kitchen then lay down again on her makeshift bed, wondering what kind of existence eighteenth century Mary Campbell had lived.

Chapter Two

1785

Ma and Pa have been discussing my future. I am sure of it. They break from their talking whenever I appear in the room, trying to pretend they did not mention my name. I play along with them usually, for I fear what they will tell me. I suspect I must leave this place soon, to earn my keep; the little ones can take over my jobs here. I've scarcely been further than Dunoon where I was born on the farm, and Campbeltown where we now live, for there is nowhere else to go. We seem to be on the very tip of the land here and they say that across the Mull of Kintyre lies Ireland. There is little to do except tend the farmland.

Father escapes on his boat to travel up and down our river, and often I wonder what lies beyond these shores, what adventures there might be. Even he plies his trade only as far as the Ayrshire coast but still it's away from this place. Not that I mind living here, for it must be one of the most beautiful places on God's earth. The hills are green the whole year around – though some turn purple with the heather in the summer – and they are firm for walking, with only the sheep for company. The river flows deep and dark at times then is calm and blue, reflecting the sky and the hills on its surface.

They say our land is so green because of the vast amount of rainfall but that's a small price to pay for such perfection. Besides, I love the rain and its softness against my skin. One of my favourite games, when I have time, is to kirtle up my long skirts and run against a light downpour, letting it finger my hair until the strands lie flat against my scalp. Ma thinks I am soft in the head for liking the rain so much, but it makes me feel clean inside out.

"You'll be catching your death of cold one of these days, my girl. I've never seen such nonsense. I'll be finding you more work to do if you have a notion for wasting time." That's what Ma says most days.

There is always more work to be done. With milking the cows, cleaning out the byre, feeding the pigs and hens, or helping Ma with the baking or looking after the little ones, it is a rare thing to find a bit of peace. Is that not the trouble with families? Maybe it would be good to escape for a while, to see what it is like somewhere else. My brother, Robert, is to go away soon, to the town of Greenock away down on the side of the River Clyde where he will learn his trade in the great shipyards. At least distant family members live there and he'll be glad to be doing men's work in a busy town. Perhaps I'll be able to visit him once he is settled, and become part of the busyness for a time.

"Mary! Where are you, lass? We have need of you in here for a moment."

There! I am summoned to be told my fate. What shall it be? A dairymaid or such like, I have no doubt.

"Yes, Ma, I'm here."

They are sitting at the big wooden table in the kitchen where Pa is drinking his wee dram of whisky and Ma is sorting through her sewing cotton and needles for the never-ending mending. We all grow so quickly that hems are always being taken up for the younger ones or let down for Robert and me.

"Pa has secured a post for you, Mary, at a big house in Ayrshire, where a Mr Hamilton has need of a nursemaid. It will be good for you to get away from these small parts and mayhap you'll make a life for yourself down there."

Ma's voice is brusque, but I'm not deceived. That's her way when she does not want to show too much emotion, and I hear the slight wistfulness in her voice as though she wished she could have such a chance to escape.

As usual, Pa does not say anything but looks up and smiles in his gentle way, content to let his wife do the talking for both of them. I sometimes wonder how he ever managed to ask for her in marriage, and suspect he needed a push from Ma.

I'm determined to be as matter of fact as my mother, for I know there's no choice and in some ways I long to see other parts of my country, meet new people, perhaps even find love. The boys around here are of farming stock and most have the manners of the animals they tend. Some are as foolish as the sheep that blindly follow the flock, some are as lumbering as the cattle, and one or two are more spirited and independent like the horses. There is also one who is as sly and cunning as the fox and is just as likely to steal what does not belong to him. Most have tried to kiss me and the other girls at some time, especially when the harvest has been gathered and work has slackened, but I've managed to ward off their clumsy attempts at exploring further. There is none here for whom I'd give up my maidenhood.

Father is going to take me to Ayr in his boat, and that will be exciting since I've never been on the river before. He has warned me the boat is dirty and noisy, but it's of no matter for it will be something new and strange to experience.

One day I walk to the great stones near Saddell Abbey. Some say the graveyard is haunted, but the only ghostly presence I feel is that from the sculpted figures of the knights and the great stone standing crosses. A few of the figures seem poised for war with their swords and highland armour, yet others are in an attitude of prayer. The great cross tells a story of times past and the people who lived in these parts, and if I concentrate very hard, I can sense their presence and hear their voices. As well as the Celtic knot and other strange symbols, one depicts a sword and something that might be a stag and hounds.

There is even an old ship that makes me think of father and the boats that sail on these waters. It's a link with the past this place, yet it fills me with excitement about the future and a wonder for all the things that are possible in this world. Who can imagine that people from long ago lived and loved and worshipped here and now leave their evidence for those of us who live in this century? I have no fear of ghosts, for they leave their footprints in the essence of time and remind me that these people once drew breath as I do. Would that we might all be remembered by the people who will live after us.

Now I must return home and prepare to leave this quiet shore at the edge of our land. But I go willingly to whatever God has prepared for me, and trust only that I may see my family again one day.

Chapter Three

"Nightly dreams and thoughts by day
Are aye with him that's far away."
(R. Burns: *On the Seas and Far Away*)

The sun streaming through the window wakened Eilidh from her strange dream of standing stones and Celtic crosses, and that same feeling she'd often had of someone calling to her through the mists of time. She'd been accused of romanticism before and suspected it might become worse before her trip was over.

"Morning! You're awake at last." Kirsty put a mug of coffee on the table. "Thought you might be ready for this. If you want to get showered and dressed, I'll fix breakfast. Cereal and toast okay?"

Eilidh glanced at the clock on the mantelpiece, shocked to discover it showed 10 o'clock. She had obviously needed that extra nap after Sarah left and couldn't even remember falling asleep again.

"That's great, thanks. I'll need to start lending a hand. I can't have you waiting on me hand and foot."

"Don't you worry about that, I've no intention of keeping this up!"

Eilidh laughed and was happy to go and bathe away the deep sleep. Over breakfast she mentioned the possibility of going to Dunoon.

"Good idea. It's a fairly clear day for a sail and we could have lunch over there."

Eilidh was glad she'd thought to pack some

warmer clothes for the west coast breeze and dressed in comfortable jeans and light sweater with a t-shirt underneath, should the sun prove warmer than expected. Packing her notebook, pen, camera and money into a little shoulder bag, she picked up a light waterproof jacket to cover every eventuality.

A short walk round the bay and along by the water side took them to the ferry terminal, past ducks and swans and a variety of small boats moored to an assortment of buoys. Just in time to catch the next boat.

Eilidh stood on deck so she could watch Gourock gradually disappear as the boat set sail down the River Clyde.

"See the Cloch Lighthouse? Remember it used to throw its beam out at night when we were small?" Kirsty said. "Would you believe it's been turned into flats? Mind you, that'd be cool living in a lighthouse, though some of the accommodation is at ground level."

The greyish white lighthouse stood on a point at the corner of the road towards Lunderston Bay, where Eilidh had once searched for crabs amongst the rocks in the summer months.

"Want to go round the other side?" Kirsty asked. "Then we'll be able to see the approach to Dunoon."

Eilidh was content to stand anywhere on deck. The sea air lifted her hair and cleansed away all the intervening years and minor cares. All around, the hills bordered the river and seagulls cried their lament. A pang of sorrow pierced her when she remembered her mother had never returned to enjoy all this.

It hardly seemed any time until the boat approached the wooden pier at Dunoon. A small crowd waited patiently for the return journey: no doubt some of them would be off to the bigger shops at Greenock or Glasgow.

Eilidh and Kirsty joined the other passengers walking along the pier towards the exit. Then she saw it, on a trajectory overlooking the river: the statue of Highland Mary.

To the right of the incline, a path wove up through gardens to the Castle Museum. Kirsty didn't even have to ask. They made straight for the figure, clambering over the uneven path until they stood by the base of the statue to read the plinth: *Erected in 1896 to commemorate Mary Campbell, Burns' Highland Mary, born in Dunoon in 1764.* Eilidh noticed the eighteenth-century style of dress, the kilted-up overdress, and the sweet face depicted in stone.

Was she an ancestress, this Mary Campbell? It didn't matter really; Eilidh was fascinated by the girl's story whether or not she had any real connection to the family. Inside the museum, she discovered bits and pieces about Mary's life and a replica of the small thatched Auchamore Farmhouse where she'd lived as a child. A display of when the Americans had lived in Dunoon caught her eye before she returned to the gardens.

"Well? Any good?" Kirsty asked hopefully.

"I think so. I've some more information on Mary's life and it was also useful for the scenes of the 60s and 70s. Just think, my mother and her friends used to come over to Dunoon when they were girls." And maybe met my father here, she added to herself.

They wandered along the High Street past the assortment of small shops, many unashamedly selling the Scottish touristy wares of tartan and shortbread. It had the unmistakeable air of a seaside town, with the river down to the right. Eilidh recognised its charm, though the Americans had long departed from the area, giving it an excuse to rediscover its identity. When they came to a small bookshop, she couldn't resist having a browse.

"Look, this is perfect!" She held up a wide paperback and showed Kirsty the cover. It was about the very years she was interested in; the years when her mother would have enjoyed the company of the Americans at some of the many dances. It was written by someone who'd been a child at the time and might give her more of a feeling for the time and place. When they finally left the shop, Kirsty stopped a few doors down the street.

"This is a great place for lunch, I've been before and the food's good; hearty Scottish fare."

Eilidh's eyes lit up when she saw the large selection of hand-made chocolates at the counter of the downstairs shop, and the old-fashioned jars of sweeties on the shelves. The restaurant was upstairs but she determined to stop on the way down again.

They managed to get one of the tables at the lattice-pained window and Eilidh ordered Scotch broth with crusty bread. While they waited to be served, she watched the people wander along the street below. There was such an old-fashioned feeling about the whole place, inside and out, that she shouldn't have any trouble imagining it all those years ago. She couldn't wait to read through the book, and only wished she'd questioned her mother more closely instead of worrying about upsetting her with memories she would rather forget.

"So, what d'you want to do next?" Kirsty asked, as their steaming bowls of soup arrived.

"Have a walk along the promenade? Then we can go back, if you like. It's given me a lot to think about, especially after finding the book."

Eilidh insisted on buying chocolates for the three of them to enjoy later, and was amused when Kirsty bought some soor plooms.

"Rot the teeth, but they take me straight back to childhood," she laughed.

"I remember them well, and aromatics and flying saucers and macaroon bars!" Eilidh was suddenly transported to the school playground as she spoke, and all those times she'd spent her pennies at the local shop.

On the way back to Gourock, Kirsty shared her great idea.

"There's a charity dance at the town hall in late August in aid of the local hospice and I've got several tickets. We should go, to welcome you back to Scotland. Jamie is going to be around for a while and I'm guessing he'll be delighted to meet up with you again."

Eilidh couldn't hide her pleasure. "That's really kind of you, and I'd love to meet Jamie again after all these years."

She wondered if he might be the shadowy figure haunting some of her dreams. Who else would give her such a sense of someone calling her home? She shivered slightly. This country was definitely getting to her. She turned her attention to Kirsty's plans then realised she'd been only half listening when she heard the next words.

"Why don't you invite that gorgeous man from the plane? I'm sure he's waiting to hear from you."

"You've got to be kidding! He's a stranger. How can I just ring him out of the blue and invite him to a dance? I don't want him to think I'm that desperate. Anyway, Lewis Grant will have forgotten me by now," she added as an afterthought.

"Not the way he was looking at you," Kirsty assured her. "And I see you've remembered his name."

Eilidh didn't say any more, but as they stood watching the hills go by, she couldn't help thinking of him. He had been easy to talk to and good to look at. But she couldn't do it. He probably wouldn't have given her another thought. That decided, she watched their approach at Gourock and resolved to throw away his phone number. She'd look forward instead to seeing Jamie again.

Later that evening, after Kirsty and Sarah had gone to bed, Eilidh remembered about the phone number. Picking up her paperback, she rifled through the pages. Only her bookmark fell out. She searched more carefully but nothing was jammed between the pages. Shrugging, she determined to put the phone number, and the man, out of her thoughts once and for all. It had been nothing more than a chance meeting of strangers passing time on a plane. She tried to deny the pang of regret, but what could she do if she didn't have his number?

She lifted the book on Dunoon during the American Years and began to read of the impact made on the small seaside town by the secret decision – between the British Government and President Eisenhower at the height of the Cold War fear in 1960 – to allow an American Polaris base in Scotland. She could imagine the huge change such an influx of strangers must have caused, and she quickly flicked through the pictures in the book which recorded what those changes had meant to many people, Scots and Americans. She would take time to read the stories outlined over the thirty years of American presence. Maybe somewhere there would be hints of the kind of things her mother had seen and done.

She could also check back through old copies of the local newspaper, the *Greenock Telegraph*, to read the local view of the times when the girls went across the river to follow dreams of Hollywood-type glamour among the suddenly accessible American males. Thinking about it all reminded Eilidh that she couldn't put off seeing her aunt and uncle indefinitely. She didn't know their exact address, only the area, but she might find them in the telephone directory if they hadn't moved. What exactly had happened all those years ago to cause such a permanent divide? She shrugged. She'd make the first move to finding the answers soon. But not quite yet.

Would she ever see Lewis Grant again? She couldn't quite get him out of her head, and hoped he gave her a thought now and then. But there was nothing she could do to find him. She didn't even know where he lectured, and could hardly phone up every college and university to ask. Well, she could, but wouldn't. *Unless she became desperate*, a small voice said.

Still restless, Eilidh picked up her mother's ancient black writing journal, now so worn that some of the pages hardly held together. It dated back to the previous century, originating with one of her mother's great-aunts, and had been passed down through the ages to subsequent female family members. Most of it contained childish scribbles: a short verse or two, a joke, the occasional recipe or autograph from a willing adult. Occasionally, a more reflective mind had written innermost thoughts in an elegant, flowing hand. Eilidh loved the drawings. Among the odd pages of cartoons were turn-of-the-century fashions, exquisitely drawn and delicately coloured.

She turned to one of her favourite parts. The journal had no white pages; each was a pastel colour of either beige, fawn, mint green, dusty pink, primrose yellow or dove grey. The "Cure for Love" on one of the fawn pages, written with a fountain pen in the early 1920s, was now well marked with fingerprints. Eilidh smiled as she read the spidery words; if only it were that simple.

The Cure for Love
Take 12 ounces of Dislike; 1 pound of Resolution
2 grains of Common Sense
2 ounces of Experience; a large sprig of Thyme
3 quarts of the cooling waters of Consideration

Set these over the gentle fire of Love. Sweeten with the sugar of Forgetfulness. Skim it with the spoon of Melancholy. Put it in the bottom of the Heart, cork it with the cork of a clear Conscience. Let it simmer and you will quickly find relief and be restored to your senses again.

These things can be had at the apothecaries at the House of

Understanding next door to Reason in Prudent Street in the Village of Contentment. Take a drink of the above whenever the symptoms are troublesome.

How often had her mother read these same words? And why had she never told Eilidh the identity of her father? She stared at some of the drawings, remembering how much her mother would have loved to attend art school. But her illegitimate baby daughter had become her most precious creation instead.

As sleep threatened to reclaim her, Eilidh lay back down on her makeshift bed. She would do more research on Highland Mary and visit Ayrshire at some point, where Mary eventually met Robert Burns. She already knew some of the skimpy 'facts' that had been recorded by many a Burns scholar or admirer, but it would mean more if she could stand in the very streets Mary had trod and see the same villages, sky, and farmland that probably hadn't changed very much.

Mary's story eventually ended in Greenock, but Eilidh wanted to keep that part until she was ready since it was tied up with all that the area meant to her. In the meantime, she would find out all she could about the Highland Lassie of Burns' famous poem, the one who had caused him to record such a heart-felt sense of loss.

Chapter Four

1785

It is a strange new experience being away from the edge of the sea to live among these lowlands and farmlands. Everything is still as green for, truth to tell, it is as rainy here as at home but the hills are not so high and there is more of a bustle about the villages. The people are friendly and it's good to have other young company when we have a moment to spare.

I have settled into my work as an under-nursemaid to the grand family of a Mr Hamilton, who lives in the little village of Mauchline. It's a pleasant house and the little boy, Alexander, is a delightful child with a lively spirit and enquiring mind. Meggie, the older nursemaid, treats me well and teaches me much. She is the source of all local knowledge and tells me what is happening and the people I should know. She also helps me to understand the different manner of speech here and why I have heard whispers of 'highland lass' as I pass by.

"It's only their way of identifying ye, lass, for ye speak with such a soft Gaelic lilt to your voice, a musical sound that's missing in the lowlands here," Meggie kindly tells me one day.

"I never thought about it before now, for we speak more Gaelic than English where I used to live." I laugh with relief that it was not meant as an unkindness, for I am happy in this place.

Meggie makes sure I mix with the other young lads and lasses here, as she calls them, and it seems there's dancing and such like in the village. Ma and Pa would likely frown at such frivolity but I long to dance the reels and jigs. I am minded though of my Christian duty and shall also undertake to attend the Kirk, which should please them.

It is not only duty, for I love to hear the stories from the Bible, especially those of women like Ruth and Naomi. One of my favourite verses is when Ruth tells her dead husband's mother that she will never leave her. "Where you go I will go, and where you lodge I shall lodge; your people shall be my people and your God my God, where you die I will die."

To love another person that much, to be willing to go anywhere they go at whatever cost, that is what I wish for myself one day. Ma, or Meggie, would say I am a foolish child with too many dreams in her head, but one day I'll understand what it means to love that way.

There is no-one special here thus far, though many handsome young men swagger about the streets, but mayhap they are content to tease the maidens without serious intention. A few have less savoury reputations, but I know to be careful, for I've no wish to be left with a babe and no husband. The Kirk is hard on such a sin and I would not want to bring disgrace on Ma and Pa.

I shall work hard and take the chance to attend the country dances, if offered. What energy that's left after working needs an outlet and there are not the same hills to climb around here, though we have lovely walks by the river and fields. The others say they've never seen such a lass for walking as I am. They are content to laze and gossip when work is finished. Except on the evenings when they attend the dancing, where they hope to find a lad. Some of the lasses are lewd in their talk, boasting of the kind of sinful things they'd like to do, but they are of kind heart and I'm sure they like to tease me, thinking I know nothing of life.

Perhaps, one day soon, I will find someone who makes my spirit sing with recognition and my heart quicken with joy.

Chapter Five

"Follies past, give thou to air,
Make their consequence thy care."
(R. Burns: *Written in Friars' Carse Hermitage*)

She had to return to Dunoon. After reading part of the book about the American Years, Eilidh wanted to walk along the promenade, to try and identify the places in the photograph. She would visit Ayrshire another week; give herself time to absorb the Greenock and Gourock area first, and to find out more about the period of the American Navy at the Holy Loch.

She would also need to think about finding a flat of her own – rented probably, until she decided how long she was remaining in the area. She didn't want to take advantage of Kirsty's kindness for too long. A small car would be useful, especially if she had to live further away from transport.

Before Eilidh had a chance to discuss her ideas, Kirsty shouted from the hall.

"Phone, Eilidh!" Kirsty winked as she handed the handset over.

For her? Eilidh was bemused. Who would be calling her? No-one knew she was here at Kirsty's home.

She took the receiver. "Hi, this is Eilidh."

"Hello, Eilidh."

She recognised the deep tones at once.

"Lewis   Grant?"   She   couldn't   keep   the

astonishment from her voice. How on earth had he managed to track her down? She'd lost his phone number and hadn't given him hers.

"I'm glad you remember my name." He laughed at her puzzlement.

"But how–?"

"Did I know your number?" he finished. "You have a very enterprising friend."

"Kirsty! She found your phone number?" Eilidh didn't know whether to be angry or pleased.

"I'm hoping you'd have got around to calling me yourself eventually, but I decided to take a chance you'd want to see me again."

Eilidh laughed, appreciating his good humour. "Oh, I think I might manage that." She decided he was well worth seeing if he had the nerve to contact her like this.

"Why don't we meet for coffee on Friday about half past ten, if that suits you? There's a good hotel on Union Street, The Tontine, where we can relax and chat. Then we can take it from there."

"That sounds perfect. Look forward to seeing you then."

"See you, Eilidh. Bye for now."

Eilidh glanced at Kirsty dancing about in the background.

"You're not too annoyed with me, are you?" Kirsty asked.

"I can't believe you did that! I had no idea you were so devious." Eilidh turned on her friend. Then she smiled, as Kirsty backed away. "But thank you. I might never have bothered."

Kirsty's face brightened in a huge smile and she hugged Eilidh. "I could see he was keen at the airport, and you can't let someone like him get away. You needn't kid me that you don't fancy him. There're few enough decent men around at our age."

This last was said ruefully, as though their early thirties was beyond hope, and Eilidh wondered why Kirsty wasn't in a serious relationship herself.

"Anyway, do you think I might have his phone number now, please?" Eilidh asked. "And how did you come by it, might I ask?"

Kirsty grinned and fished the number from her bag. "I found it under your bed when making it into the sofa again. Figured it must have fallen from your book and I didn't want you to miss your chance. You can thank me again after you meet."

Eilidh had two days to decide what to wear and she'd need every minute. Two days to think of what to say to a handsome stranger she had only met high above the Atlantic. Yet she really did want to see him again. He didn't feel like a stranger and he'd been easy to talk to before. It would be interesting to see how they got on this time, in real life.

Over the next two days, Eilidh enjoyed exploring her immediate area, reacquainting herself with places she'd known as a child. Kirsty took her to the garden centre at Lunderston Bay and she was amazed at how big a place it had become, with a restaurant, shops, and a seemingly endless supply of plants. The bay itself was more unchanged. How she'd loved to come down here with her mother and gran in the summer. As well as the shingle shore that turned to sand as it reached the river, rocks tumbled down towards the sea at one end where she had loved to climb. Near the water's edge they became stones, under which were crabs and other interesting creatures.

"Oh, I just have to paddle in that water," Eilidh

said longingly.

Kirsty laughed and shivered. "You do know it'll be fairly cold?" Although dry and still, it wasn't exactly a hot summer's day.

"I don't care. I want to walk barefoot along the edge of the Clyde again." Eilidh had her sandals off and her cotton trousers rolled up before Kirsty could say another word.

"Och well, if you're that daft, then I'm going to join you." Soon both girls were dipping their toes in the cool water, trying not to gasp.

As they wandered along the sandy edge, with the tiny waves lapping against their skin, Eilidh felt about ten again. It was good for the soul being next to the sea, and the cry of the gulls delivered a shot of nostalgia that made her stop to look out across the river. She could see all the way across to Dunoon and the surrounding area where yachts and small boats sat on the river. It was all so peaceful and familiar.

"Think it's time to walk over to the garden centre for a shot of caffeine," Kirsty said eventually.

The café was busy but they found a quiet table and in between their conversation, Eilidh watched the people wandering up and down past the hundreds of plants for sale in the open-air gardens.

"So, tell me about the guy you left behind," Kirsty suddenly said, taking Eilidh by surprise. She'd only mentioned her previous boyfriend as an afterthought in one letter.

"Not much to tell: medium height, powerfully built, a hot-shot lawyer; we'd been seeing each other about two years before we called it a day."

"D'you miss him?"

"Not at all. That's how I know he was never the one. Anyway, what about you? How have you escaped matrimony so far?"

Kirsty didn't reply right away and Eilidh wondered if she was being intrusive.

"Hmm, where to start," Kirsty smiled ruefully. "You know I was engaged once, but it didn't work out.

"Jamie?" Eilidh asked.

Kirsty nodded. "Then he realised he didn't want to be tied down yet. He had itchy feet and needed to travel. So I stayed here and got on with a career I love, and he saw the world. I've had a few short-term relationships but I've yet to meet 'the one' everyone talks of but few find."

"And now that he's back?"

"Ah, well, that's a big question! I can't see us taking up where we left off, because we've both moved on too much. I don't think I could trust him not to let me down again."

They were both thoughtful as they finished their coffee and chatted about their childhood days.

Later, Eilidh thought about her mother and how she would have felt being back in Scotland if she'd had the chance. Was there anyone who might know about her mother's old life, apart from her aunt? Only one of her mother's friends had kept in touch off and on but she had no address. Grace, that was her first name.

Eilidh took out the black writing journal, as she had a feeling Grace had written in it one time and might have signed her surname. She carefully flicked through the pages. Yes, on a pale pink page, there was a fun little rhyme:

"*Love is like a violet, crush it as you may,*

It only yields a sweeter scent that cannot fade away."

It was signed Grace MacAulay. Eilidh had a vague recollection of her mother's friend and knew they had hung around together when teenagers. The woman might know about their trips to Dunoon and her mother's boyfriends. But how to find her?

When she mentioned it to Kirsty, she was quite hopeful.

"We can try the phone book first, it's maybe not that common a name and chances are she's still in the area. If that's no use, we can always try a message in the *Greenock Telegraph*. Absolutely everyone reads that for the 'hatches, matches and despatches', especially the despatches. It's a wee bit insular here and you usually find everyone knows someone else."

That was a positive step, Eilidh decided, but she would leave it until after she'd had her 'date' with Lewis Grant.

On the Thursday evening, Eilidh surveyed her meagre wardrobe with Kirsty in attendance.

"It's only coffee, but I don't want to be conspicuous." She'd got used to dressing casually most of the time.

"Jeans and a pretty top then," Kirsty said, picking up a blouse in greens and blues. "This is perfect for your dark auburn colouring."

For a moment, Eilidh didn't say anything. "You know, that was Mum's favourite top." She didn't want sad memories tomorrow. She picked up a jade, fitted, short sleeve blouse. "This'll do. The colour makes me feel confident."

"At least you have some colour in your wardrobe," Kirsty pointed out. "I'm fed up with all the blacks and greys and browns we see here. The dreich weather, of course. But it's better during the height of the summer months when everyone gets out their pretty clothes. We have to be quick: blink and we miss the sun!"

Eilidh laughed at that, as the west coast of Scotland had a reputation for more rain than sun.

"Right, the jade top it is," Kirsty agreed. "Try it on and I'll give my verdict."

Eilidh stripped of her sweater, knowing she'd get an honest opinion.

"Hey, I like your wee birthmark. Looks like a crescent moon," Kirsty said.

Eilidh paused and tried to look at the silver mark on her left shoulder. "I always forget it's there." She pulled on the top and stood back. "Well, will I do?"

"Perfect. That vivid colour suits your healthy skin."

On the Friday morning, Eilidh felt ridiculously nervous. He was only someone she'd met on a plane, she reminded herself again. But it was no use. It was more than that, as though they'd been meant to sit beside each other out of hundreds of people. And it seemed important, this second meeting.

She arrived at the hotel ten minutes early. Kirsty had insisted on dropping her off on her way to town and Eilidh said she'd find her own way back since it was such a good day. It would give her the chance to walk the whole length of the Esplanade. She'd got used to jogging in the States and was way behind with her exercise since she arrived.

The hotel looked graciously old, maybe Georgian. Once inside, she noticed the stunning staircase twisting up from the foyer. The coffee lounge was to the left and a bar made a semi-circle at the back wall. She looked around for a restroom and finally found one through the doorway to the side of the reception desk. Opening her shoulder bag, Eilidh gave her hair a quick comb and slicked some gloss across her lips to keep them from drying out completely. She took a couple of tissues from the provided box in case of emergency, and looked at her watch. It was time to see if he'd arrived.

She had no sooner sat on one of the armchairs when the door opened and Lewis Grant walked in. He saw her right away and came straight towards her, a wide grin on his face. She stood up.

"Eilidh, great to see you again."

"And you."

She was wondering if she should shake his hand when he put his hands on her shoulders and planted a brief kiss on both her cheeks. She was surprised but pleased; it seemed just the right thing to do.

As they sat down at the table in the window bay, Eilidh admitted he was very pleasing to look at, the smattering of grey in his unkempt hair giving him an almost rakish air. He had that confidence she appreciated in men who had nothing to prove, and she already knew he had a sense of humour. He was dressed more casually than on the plane – trim in dark jeans and a petrol blue sweatshirt that emphasised the deep blue eyes. *Careful, you don't know that much about him yet.* But she was bemused again by the effect he had on her.

A young waiter approached to take their order.

"Cappuccino, please," Eilidh said with a smile.

"Make that two, please, and some scones and jam if you have them." Lewis said the last with a questioning glance at Eilidh.

She shrugged. She hadn't tasted scones for years but it would keep her going if she was planning to walk the few miles back to Kirsty's. The lounge was quiet apart from a couple of women at another table, too deep in their own conversation to be interested in anyone else in the room. An ideal place to talk, Eilidh decided.

"Are you pleased to be back in Scotland?" Lewis asked.

"Absolutely. I've really missed the area but I can't believe all the changes I've seen so far."

"I've lived through them and hardly recognise some of them."

"You live in this area?" For some reason she'd assumed he lived in Glasgow. Yet why should he?

"In Inverkip now, but Gourock originally. And I teach at the local college."

It was a good start as they were soon reminiscing about the areas she remembered. They had gone to different primary schools and it turned out he was almost six years older, making him thirty-nine. Eilidh recognised many of the places he mentioned.

When the coffees were placed in front of them, Eilidh stirred hers and licked the chocolate-sprinkled foam from the teaspoon. She was amused to see Lewis stirred the foaming mixture completely into his before he drank. The scones were delicious but Eilidh found them a bit too doughy for her tastes now. She was used to eating fewer carbs and wondered if she'd be able to keep that up over here.

Their conversation soon turned to her reason for coming home. She hesitated at mentioning her quest for a father, but talked again about her fascination with Highland Mary.

"I can understand that. After all, Burns is celebrated by Scots all over the world. I've always loved his work."

Eilidh was pleased he was a fan and she told him about her idea to research her Campbell background and the Burns and Highland Mary story.

"You should give it a go. There's the Watt Library just along the road from here. They have many old documents and newspapers on microfilm, as well as books, so you might find some details you don't already know. Lots of local people research their family tree there. It's something I keep meaning to get into, but I believe it's addictive once you start."

"That might be a good place to explore," she agreed. Then she heard Lewis suggesting another option.

"We could also try the Mitchell Library in Glasgow. They have a dedicated Burns' room and I'm sure someone there might be able to help."

"That all sounds very promising, thanks."

She was pleased to find him so eager to help, then she registered the matter-of-fact way he had said 'we', assuming they could do this together. The idea filled her with anticipation. There was no denying her attraction to him and he seemed keen to pursue their acquaintance. But she knew few details about his life and a little voice cautioned, *get to know him some more*.

They were in the middle of talking about literature when Eilidh was aware that the two women had stood up, ready to leave. Then one of them glanced their way. Eilidh saw her look at Lewis while the other woman paid their bill. Sure enough, they walked towards Eilidh's table.

"Hello, Lewis. Enjoying your break from college? I was speaking to Jan the other day."

Eilidh noticed the different expressions on his face: shock, annoyance, and guilt, perhaps.

He stood up. "Sue. I didn't realise you were here. How are you?"

"Fine, thanks." Eilidh could feel the tension and wondered if Lewis was going to introduce her. The other woman stood by, probably thinking the same.

"Oh, this is Eilidh, a friend from America," he said.

"And this is Rhona, an old friend from school. She remembers Jan, too." Sue seemed determined to mention Jan, whoever she was.

They all shook hands politely and conversation ceased.

"Well, we'd best be going. I'll tell Jan we saw you." With a meaningful glance at Eilidh, Sue led her friend out of the lounge.

Lewis sat down again. "Witch!" he said quietly. As Eilidh stared at him, he smiled sheepishly. "Sorry, but I've never liked that woman and she was obviously trying to be as embarrassing as possible."

"Jan?" Eilidh decided to get the question out in the open.

He nodded. "My wife."

As Eilidh's heart flipped with disappointment, he added swiftly, "No, I mean ex-wife now, but some people won't accept that."

Eilidh was silent. Of course, he'd be married, or would have been. Men of his age and looks would hardly be single, unless they were gay or had been in a monastery.

"I'm sorry, that's spoiled the morning a little. But contrary to what that Sue woman was insinuating, I am well and truly divorced. And I have no children. Or girlfriend," he added quickly.

"You don't have to explain to me," Eilidh said, although it helped to know he was available. Otherwise she'd have hesitated to see him again.

"Changing the subject, have you any plans for the

rest of the day? Unfortunately, I have a meeting this afternoon or I could have shown you around the old place."

"Don't worry about that, thanks. I'll walk back to Kirsty's – she's round at Cardwell Bay. It's a good day and I want to enjoy the Esplanade."

"That's quite a walk. I can at least drive you down to the beginning of it as it's on my way."

He insisted on paying for the coffees since it was his invitation, and Eilidh promised it would be her turn next time. Then she hoped she wasn't being presumptuous that there would be another time.

His car was the same one from the airport. She was pleased when he held the passenger door open for her. Not for her the kind of equality that did away with old fashioned courtesy; she liked to be treated like a woman, albeit one with a brain.

"I'll go down Campbell Street which will take us to the beginning of the Esplanade. Do you remember the old Arts Guild Theatre? They've built a new one down by the waterfront, after all this time. Shame. I saw many a pantomime there over the years."

Eilidh remembered it. "Didn't it used to be a swimming pool once?" She was sure she'd heard that long ago.

"I think you're right. I suppose it doesn't owe the town anything."

After crossing several junctions, he turned onto the Esplanade and pulled in at a parking space on the river side. A few people wandered along, many with dogs, and Eilidh was looking forward to stretching her legs.

"May I see you again soon, Eilidh?"

His voice was suddenly serious and she glanced across at him. There was a definite connection between them, even stronger than on the plane, and she couldn't imagine not seeing him again.

"I'd like that." Their gaze held for a few seconds, neither breaking the silence. Then she remembered the charity dance and wondered if that was too formal, or too soon. Oh, well, no harm in asking.

"You wouldn't care to go to a charity affair with me, would you? Kirsty has persuaded me into going. I think it's in aid of the local hospice." She rushed the words out.

He was thoughtful for a moment. "You know, I think I've heard about that. What's the date?"

"I think it's the end of August, but I'll need to check exactly."

"Sounds good, if I'm free that evening. Once you let me know the date, I can get back to you on it, if that's okay?"

"Sure. And don't feel any pressure to go!"

"I'd love to go with you, really. I just hope the date fits."

"Well, I'd better let you get on if you have a meeting," Eilidh said at last. She was comfortable sitting here with him.

"Suppose I should." He seemed equally reluctant to end their chat. Then he got out of his side of the car and opened the door for her.

"Thanks for the coffee and scones," Eilidh said, and wondered if she should hold out her hand. But that was way too formal, considering how they'd got on.

"Thanks for meeting me, Eilidh. You know, I'm looking forward to helping you find out more about Highland Mary. I'll call you later and we can arrange where to meet next." He leaned towards her and kissed her cheek.

It was a chaste kiss but seemed to promise much more, and she looked forward to their next meeting. She watched as he got back into the car and drove away with a wave.

She was about to set off along the stretch of promenade towards Gourock when a church on the corner caught her eye and she went over to have a look. The Old West Kirk. She'd seen that name somewhere but couldn't recall where. It seemed quite an age and the mellow brickwork brightened up the corner of the grey street, while the well-tended garden bloomed with a variety of plants and flowers. She could imagine the peace such a place must offer and hoped it was as beautiful inside as it was on the outside. Then she laughed at such thoughts; it sounded as though she was philosophising about a person.

She crossed the road again to the water side and set off briskly, relieved she'd worn comfortable shoes with her jeans. The clear blue sky allowed her to enjoy the backdrop of hills across the river. Several yachts were dotted here and there, and an aura of calm surrounded her. She nodded to a couple of people walking past in the other direction.

Glancing over to the other side of the wide road, she admired the big, old houses that had stood there since the late nineteenth century, now interspersed with more modern blocks of flats. What a view these home owners have, she mused. It had always been one of the most expensive places to live in the town, and no wonder when they had all this beauty on their doorstep. Some of the largest, more gracious buildings had been divided into upper and lower flats, and a sprawling low-level complex for older people sat a little further along.

As she walked, she tried to remember exactly where her aunt had lived, as there was a good chance she would still be there. The name Bentinck Street came into her head. Was that it? It was definitely one of the streets that ran up into the west end from the Esplanade. She noticed a large yellow pole about halfway along the promenade which seemed a bit familiar.

A little further on, a woman and a man slowly walked towards her. Eilidh glanced briefly to smile a good day but the woman was turned towards the man, as though talking to him. Eilidh stood against the rail, staring into the deep water below. Something seemed familiar about that man and woman. No, she was being fanciful because she'd been thinking about her aunt. She surreptitiously glanced after the couple, still walking slowly in the opposite direction.

Surely if it was her aunt she would have recognised her? But such a long time had passed and she'd been concentrating on the man beside her. Everyone had changed to some degree, and her aunt had no advantage of knowing her niece was in Scotland, much less a few yards away. Yet, the man too had looked vaguely familiar. Could that be her uncle? She'd hardly known him all those years ago, so there was no way she could tell from such a fleeting glance.

It was too late to do anything about it now – she could hardly run after complete strangers and ask, 'Are you my aunt and uncle?' She laughed at the thought, but she'd have to find them sooner or later.

She continued on her way, admiring the scenery while thinking about her aunt. She'd be in her late sixties or early seventies by now, as she'd been older than Eilidh's mother. She wondered if her cousin,

Rory, still lived around these parts. How sad that she'd completely lost touch with her only family. Yet her mother had never mentioned them, as though she had wiped her former years from her mind. Had her mother told her only sister about her illness? When it was too late, Eilidh hadn't known where to contact her aunt. And if her mother hadn't wanted anything to do with her when she was alive, it was hardly appropriate, or likely, that the aunt would care now that she'd gone, sad as it was.

Rory was around her own age and probably married with children of his own, but she suddenly wished she could talk to this estranged family, to have people she belonged to in some tenuous way, who were part of the past even if they had no wish to be part of her present or future.

Eilidh stopped again near the end of the promenade and looked down the river towards the tail of the bank. She would go back to Dunoon, to get a feel for that time in the photograph when her mother had been happy with someone she cared about, however temporal it had been.

Turning away from the sea and the hills, she carried on walking past the old sailing club and on to the Battery Park. So many memories these places conjured up; most she'd long buried in her new life. She walked along the inside wall of the park, next to the busy road, pleased they had left so much of the green for children to play their makeshift games of cricket and football.

As she reached the end gate and strolled round by the bay towards Kirsty's flat, Eilidh finally allowed her mind to dwell on Lewis. She was really looking forward to seeing him again. Then she remembered the woman who had talked so much about his wife, and felt a moment's concern. How divorced was Lewis Grant? She realised the answer mattered very much indeed.

Chapter Six

1785

I saw him today! At the Tarbolton Kirk of all places. Perhaps it is some kind of sign. There I am reading the Scriptures and listening to the minister, when I look up and across the pews. And there he is, smiling at me when he catches my eye.

I quickly look down at my Bible then glance up again to see him still watching me. I recognise his dark, handsome looks at once, for his name is often mentioned, in one way or another, and he shares the same Christian name with my own brother, Robert.

The lassies glance after him longingly and the women warn against him, for his reputation is well known. Yet there must be other sides to him, for he sits in the Kirk and listens to the word of God. And I've heard my master talk of him with admiration at times. How the young man struggles to keep his farm going along with his brother, and of his writing and verses that are filled with intelligence and wit and great insight into human nature. I admire him long before I ever properly meet him.

Risking another glance, I see he has turned away to look at the preacher. His dark hair is smooth and curls in below his neck, and his profile is strong. He is smart in jacket and neckerchief and he has not the air of a farmer. As I remember I'm still staring, he looks up and our eyes meet again. This time I smile shyly and briefly before returning to my open Bible.

He must not think I admire him too well. I'll not become one of the silly lasses who cast longing glances at him in the hope he will dally with them. I have too much pride for such behaviour.

I cannot help one final glance, however, as we stand to end the service. He smiles. And my heart tells me it is too late. But I still do not realise that this man, Robert Burns, will have anything to do with my destiny.

Chapter Seven

"Yon wild mossy mountains sae lofty and wide,
That nurse in their bosom the youth o' the Clyde."
(R. Burns: *Yon Wild Mossy Mountains*)

Eilidh decided to go to Dunoon by herself this time. From reading the book on the American Years, she'd learned that when the US Navy sailed into the Holy Loch, depositing its sailors and families in the surrounding villages, it had transformed the quiet town and left a legacy of mixed marriages and GI brides that had repercussions beyond anything imagined. The Scottish and American children had all seemed to enjoy learning from each other's culture.

With her mother's photograph tucked safely in her bag, a surge of excitement quickened her pulse as the boat neared the quay. She tried to picture the bustling 1960s and 70s, now that Dunoon was an unassuming little seaside town again.

Many young girls had made the trip across the river on a Friday and Saturday night for their weekly fantasy fix. And her mother had been one of those enjoying the Navy's presence. Eilidh still found it difficult to identify the slightly prudish mother she'd known with the carefree young girl in the photograph with the naval officer. Yet she couldn't have been so prudish then, with a baby born out of wedlock. Eilidh wished she had known that younger version of her mother; she had never shown such joy to her, always keeping a reserve about her and sadness in her eyes, much as she tried to hide it.

A misty drizzle in the air met Eilidh as she turned right from the quay and walked towards the long promenade. She had come prepared, in her light waterproof jacket that she could take off or put on as the weather dictated. With no wind, it wasn't as cold as it could be at the side of the darkened river. She strode out, breathing in the salty sea air, revelling in the freedom. She had always loved walking in the countryside, but now the sea calmed her spirit and invigorated her senses. She even loved the hint of mist over the hills.

It was quieter away from the town and Eilidh admired the elegant houses on the other side of the road. It wasn't that different from the Esplanade at Greenock, except this promenade stretched far longer. After a while, she sat on one of the benches conveniently placed at intervals.

Taking out the photograph, she stared again at her mother with her officer. It had probably been taken along this very stretch of prom. The black and white snap was creased and faded but clearly showed a smiling couple, arm in arm as they strolled along, the woman in a long open coat with fur-trimmed collar and a mini skirt, long white boots and a scooped cap set at a jaunty angle over dark curls. The man was a head taller, broad shouldered, clean-shaven. He wore his light US navy uniform with assurance, his handsome face smiling with confidence and affection as he turned slightly towards his companion.

Eilidh traced their faded features with her finger. It was the only photograph she had ever seen of her mother and this man. Was this her father? That might explain why her mother had dragged her all the way to America, if he'd had to return there without her.

On the back of the photo was the single ball-point line: *Jack and me in Dunoon*. So he was not the 'R' who had written the impassioned letter to his Highland Lass.

"Who are you?" she whispered. It reminded her she hadn't done anything about finding her mother's old friend, Grace. That would be the next thing on her list.

A few drops of rain on her hand told Eilidh it was going to fall in earnest soon and she headed back towards the town. Sure enough, she'd hardly gone any distance when the sky darkened and the clouds shed their load. Hurrying now, she noticed a small coffee shop near the beginning of the promenade. Even better, it sold books and she turned in at its door.

It was small and cosy and Eilidh was glad to take off the wet jacket. A group of chatting people sat at one table, while an elderly woman sat by herself at another. The friendly buzz made Eilidh feel part of something. Sitting at a table for two, she had no sooner picked up the single sheet menu when a middle-aged woman approached her.

"Hello. You'll be glad to get out of that shower, no doubt. Welcome to our wee café. Are you ready to order, or would you like another minute?"

Eilidh smiled up at the friendly woman. "Thanks. I'll have a cappuccino, if you have one please."

"Aye, we do that. Would you like to try a bit of our shortbread with it? All home made."

"Why not?" The walk had given her an appetite.

As she glanced around the shop, Eilidh realised it was a Christian bookshop and tried to remember if it was attached to a church. She hadn't paid much attention to what was on either side of the door as she entered. She left her jacket over the chair and went over to browse through the books and pamphlets arranged on racks to one side of the room.

The group of people at the bigger table got up to pay their bill and left with much laughter and goodbyes to the woman and girl who served behind the counter. It was quieter as Eilidh browsed and the only other occupant drank her tea and read a magazine.

"Here's your coffee, dear," the woman who'd taken her order called to her, and Eilidh sat down to enjoy her drink and biscuit. She'd seen a little book of spiritual poems that she might buy for Sarah. She'd find something else for Kirsty, as she didn't think poetry would be her thing.

"Are you American, dear? Ah couldn't help noticing your accent." The voice broke into her thoughts and Eilidh turned to see the elderly woman at the other table turned towards her, her magazine closed.

Eilidh smiled, wondering if the old lady was lonely and came in here for a warm drink and a chat to anyone who would listen. It was probably better than being stuck at home with no-one to talk to.

"Sort of," she began. "I was born in Greenock but lived in America from the age of twelve. This is my first visit back to these parts since then, I'm ashamed to say."

"Ah, that explains the slight Scottish twang. Well we're no strangers to Americans coming and going here," the woman laughed. "Was your mother a GI bride then, if ye don't mind me asking? Or just tell me to mind my own business and I'll leave ye alone."

The woman who'd served Eilidh gave her a wink as she called across, "Maggie here knows everyone hereabouts, and she loved having the Americans in the town. Would you like some more coffee?"

"That's very kind of you. I would, thanks." Then Eilidh turned back to Maggie. As she suspected, the old woman was indeed a regular here.

"Would you care to join me? I'd love to hear more about the town when the Americans were here. I'm Eilidh, by the way." She didn't answer the woman's question about the GI bride; she didn't want to share those personal details. But she noticed the old woman's face light up at the invitation as she came across to Eilidh's table.

"More tea for you, Maggie?" The woman brought a teapot over, as though she knew the answer. She smiled warmly at Eilidh, clearly pleased that she'd asked Maggie to join her.

"I was married myself by then, of course," Maggie said. "But it didn't stop me appreciating all those lovely American sailors. They set this town on fire, I can tell ye." The woman paused as though seeing those days again.

"A big crowd of girls used to come over from the other side of the river, from Greenock and Gourock. And who could blame them when a wee bit of Hollywood glamour had arrived to this staid small town? Och, you can just imagine the excitement at the weekends. Then the Americans used to be invited across the river to dances there." Maggie's eyes glowed as though she too had been caught up in the fun. "Mind, as ye can imagine, the local boys weren't too pleased!" Maggie laughed.

Eilidh hadn't thought about that aspect of the American 'invasion' and could quite understand that many a young lad must have been put out at such competition.

"Was there much trouble between the local lads and Americans?" she asked.

"Surprisingly, it wasn't as bad as might have been. I suppose the young lads got caught up in the glamour too in some ways. Though there were one or two wee incidents now and then."

"And many of the local girls went off with an American sailor, you said?"

"Aye, and some o' them not for marriage in the end either. A few sailors hid the fact they had someone back home until it was too late for the lassie who'd lost her heart – and sometimes a bit more." She nodded knowingly at Eilidh.

Eilidh was silent for a moment, wondering if that had happened to her mother. Had she loved none too wisely?

"Anyway, dear, it's been nice talking to ye, but I'll have to be going now, for I've my lunch club soon." Maggie got slowly to her feet.

"It's been a real pleasure talking to you too, Maggie. And thanks for telling me about those days."

As the old woman put on her raincoat and lifted her umbrella, she turned again to Eilidh.

"You know dear, the most important thing is a mother's love for her child, no matter the circumstances of begetting." She left with a wave to the woman at the counter.

Eilidh wondered at the elderly woman's old-fashioned, biblical words. She had such wisdom in her eyes, and Eilidh had the feeling Maggie had sussed her at once. She had been right, too. No-one could have loved her more than her mother.

Afraid she might get tearful, Eilidh stood up and took out her wallet. "I'd like to buy this poetry book too, if I may," she said to the woman at the counter.

"I hope Maggie didn't bother you too much. She loves to talk to people who come in on their own, and she'd be even more overjoyed that you've come all the way from America."

"I enjoyed talking to her. She's a wise old woman, I think," Eilidh said.

"One of the best. She's a member of our church, and many a person in trouble or need has felt better after a chat with Maggie. Anyway, thanks for giving her the time and enjoy the rest of your stay here."

As she left, Eilidh decided she'd received far more than she'd given, as old Maggie had left her with something to think about. She hesitated about going back into the town and instead walked back to the quay. She'd return to Gourock and have lunch at the flat, then try to find out if Grace MacAulay still lived around the area. Her chat with Maggie had made her even more eager to find out the identity of the man in the photograph.

The first thing Eilidh saw when she entered the flat was the winking answerphone and she wondered if she should play the message. Kirsty and Sarah were both out all day. What if it was an urgent message for one of them? She could always listen and make sure she didn't delete.

Then she looked at it more closely. Two messages. Pressing the play button, she listened.

"This is Lewis Grant for Eilidh. Hi there. I have a couple of days free and thought we could start your research. Can you call me, please? I think you have my mobile number but I'll give you it again. Look forward to seeing you." And the number followed.

Eilidh had time only to register a tingle of pleasure at his voice when the next message played.

"Hi Sarah, it's Rory. Sorry I didn't make it last night. Call me. Please. I promise I won't let you down again. I've left a message on your mobile, too."

The automated number read out and the answerphone went silent. Eilidh stood in the hall hardly breathing. Rory? It wasn't a very common name in these parts. And it sounded like someone around her own age. Surely it couldn't be her Rory? The cousin she hadn't seen since a child, and hardly even then.

Then Eilidh knew that sense of inevitability she'd experienced before coming back to Scotland. And all thoughts of Lewis Grant fled as she wondered what this might mean.

Chapter Eight

1785

As we all stand for the closing Benediction, I glance across the pews and notice Robert Burns has already gone. Perhaps it is as well. He is handsome enough to make any lass blush when he looks her way, but I am mindful of the gossip about a certain young woman whose name is often coupled with his.

I think I have seen Jean Armour in the village. She is one of the Mauchline Belles, as they name them, and is slim and handsome and full bosomed. I can imagine any man being enamoured of her for there is an air of gaiety about her as she walks. Many of the lasses are jealous that she commands the attention of the poet, and even more so that he writes verses for her. Yet, there is rumour that her parents are far from pleased at his attention. His reputation makes them worried for her future, as she is not the only lass he is said to have dallied with.

As I pause to greet the minister, I sense there is someone watching me for it makes the hairs on my neck stir. Turning to walk down the path, I see him. He is speaking with another man but he smiles as he catches my eye. My face is warming but I do not want anyone else to see him single me out for attention. I walk on, all the time half hoping he might speak to me one day.

"Good day to you, pretty maid."

I gasp as he is suddenly here beside me, walking

along the path away from the church and curious eyes.

"I think you are part of my friend's household, are you not? A Mr Hamilton?"

His speech is not as rough as the other lads and I remember he is a man of some education as well as being a farmer. He is determined to have me answer him. I look up, into eyes that are mischievous with laughter, and possibly admiration. What maid could resist attention from such a man?

"Yes, sir, I am nursery maid to Mr Hamilton's son." I look away and continue to walk, for in truth he may be teasing me for his amusement.

"Please don't hurry away, for I believe we go in the same direction." He has stopped in front of me. "Forgive my lack of manners. I am Robert Burns, Esquire, of Mossgiel Farm." And he is sweeping me a fulsome bow.

Now I know he is teasing me but in a friendly way and I smile in response.

"I am Mary Campbell, sir, lately from Argyll." And I sink into my best curtsey.

He laughs appreciatively at this and continues to walk beside me, asking me about my family home.

And so, it begins…

Chapter Nine

"How wisdom and folly meet, and unite;
How virtue and vice blend their black and white."
(R. Burns: *Fragment*)

Eilidh waited in an agony of restlessness for the remainder of the day as she wondered if Sarah's Rory was her cousin. Since she'd have to content herself until evening before finding out more, she needed a distraction. First, she picked up the phone.

"Hi, Lewis, it's Eilidh." She was relieved when he answered.

"Hello there. How are you?"

She filled him in on her day so far, again finding it easy to talk to him, as though they'd known each other for a very long time.

"Are you free on Friday? I thought we could have a look at the Highland Mary information in the Watt Library."

"That'll be perfect. Thanks for suggesting it. See you then."

When she put the phone down, Eilidh remembered about her mother's friend, Grace. Rummaging through the pile of old magazines in the small hall cupboard, Eilidh finally found a hardly-used telephone directory.

The rain still drizzled outside, making the far-off hills mist-covered and hazy. Even the temperature had lowered and she was glad to stay in the cosy flat for a while. Autumn seemed to be arriving early and, although she didn't care about the rain, she looked forward to the kind of bracing, cool day that had once made it her favourite time of year.

After making a cup of tea and a sandwich, she settled down on the sofa, phone book on her lap, not expecting to get very far.

MacAulay. She traced her finger down each line, looking for those who lived around the Inverclyde area. Not quite as long a list as she'd expected and she noticed several different spellings of the name, which might make it easier. Fortunately, it wasn't something like McDonald.

Half a dozen or so lived in the right area. It was probably like hunting for the dodo, since Grace was most likely married or living elsewhere, but she could hope. And perhaps one of the people would be related or know where she might be found. Eilidh discarded the two numbers which had a man's full name listed, concentrating on those with an initial. Of those that were left, three were in Greenock, one in Gourock, and one in Port Glasgow.

It was a random shot, but she might as well try. Even if she did happen to find the woman, there was no guarantee Grace would remember much about her friend, Mary Campbell. But her innate sense of optimism gave Eilidh renewed hope that she'd find the answers she sought.

Conscious of Kirsty's phone bill, Eilidh made a note of how many calls she was making and how long each one lasted. She'd need to buy a mobile phone soon to save the landline cost. Kirsty had already told her not to worry as they had a good deal which covered television, computer broadband and phone. Even so, Eilidh wanted to make sure she paid her way while lodging with her friend. And she'd need to start looking for a flat and a job of her own, if she were planning to stay in Scotland.

Taking a deep breath, Eilidh tried the first number in the Greenock area. No reply, but a disembodied voice gave her the answer she needed.

"Susie and George are not here just now. Please leave a message after the tone."

She scored that one off and tried the next. A woman answered hello.

"Hi, may I speak to Grace MacAulay, please." She went for the direct approach, as though expecting the woman to be there.

"I'm sorry, I think you have the wrong number. There's no Grace here." The voice was quite snooty, so Eilidh quickly apologised and thanked her.

Two down, three to go. She dialled the final Greenock number and this time an elderly man answered. She asked the same question.

"Ay? Whit's that ye say? Speak up, lass, I cannae hear ye."

Eilidh tried again but wasn't getting anywhere fast.

"Sorry to trouble you, goodbye." She put the phone down, but didn't know whether or not to score that one off since she hadn't had an answer. She decided to leave it for now.

The next call was to the Port Glasgow number. No answer and no answerphone. The Gourock number rang out for a while, then an old lady's voice shouted, "Hello."

Heart quickening that this time she might be lucky, Eilidh asked her question.

"Grace, you say? Well I knew a Grace MacAulay, but she used to live in Greenock. Sorry I can't be more help."

Eilidh apologised for bothering her and rang off.

At least she'd been a pleasant lady, if not the one she wanted. Well, that was all she could do for now. There was still the possibility of the Port Glasgow number which she would try later.

The rain had cleared up and she was restless now that she'd done what she could with the phone calls. Her mind went back to that message from Rory. Kirsty and Sarah weren't due home until tea time, so she still had a couple of hours to fill. She hadn't walked right along Gourock yet, only passing through in the car with Kirsty, but it would be interesting to see what the small individual shops were like. Besides, she had to keep an eye out for a gift for Kirsty since she'd bought the poetry book for Sarah.

Now that the rain had stopped, the sun was trying to make a last-minute appearance. She threw on the anorak again and set out round by the pier, to cut out the busy road as far as possible. The boat was still plying its way back and forward to Dunoon.

Once in the main street, she was pleased to find Gourock still had the air of a small seaside town, with shops making a living from locals and passing trade. She stopped at an interesting craft shop filled with unusual pieces of jewellery. Maybe that particularly stunning ceramic bracelet in moss green and ivory might suit Kirsty. She'd leave it for the moment in case she came up with any other ideas. There was no hurry.

A little further on, she noticed an art gallery and went in to have a look. One room was on the main floor, filled with paintings of all mediums and sizes, with stairs leading down to a smaller gallery. One picture immediately caught her attention. A sunset over the Clyde that described the view she saw each day from Kirsty's window. She would definitely buy that one for herself, once she had a flat and a wall on which to hang it.

She couldn't resist the shoe shop next, though didn't succumb to anything for the moment, and even resisted the coffee shop. It was a good walk for window shopping. She eventually left the shops behind and walked briskly past the entrance to the open-air swimming pool, along by the crazy golf and putting green. She could remember all this being packed on childhood summer days. She walked as far as the Victorian yacht club building. She'd never tried sailing but could appreciate the sight of the yachts on the river. Maybe one day she'd give it a try.

When she eventually strolled back through the town, Eilidh saw him. She happened to glance in the coffee shop window and almost stopped, causing the person behind to bump her.

"Sorry," she said, and moved on quickly before she drew attention to herself.

Lewis Grant was sitting at an intimate table for two with an attractive woman. And they seemed to be enjoying each other's company; at least it looked sort of intense, from what she'd seen.

Eilidh hurried on, shocked at the shaft of jealousy piercing her. She hadn't realised quite how much she had started to care about this man after only two meetings and several phone calls. Although the first, on the plane, had been over many hours and close contact and she firmly believed in instant attraction, whether or not anything more lasting developed. But she'd just been talking to him on the phone not much more than half an hour ago.

Once back to the pier, Eilidh lengthened her stride. She didn't know what to think. Who was she? A friend, colleague, sister – wife? It was the last she'd immediately thought of but didn't want to believe. He had said they were divorced and had been angry that the woman at the hotel had mentioned her. Or was that for Eilidh's benefit? What did she really know about him, after all?

Out of breath from walking so fast, Eilidh slowed down as she reached the stretch of quiet road towards the flat. She stopped at the little swing park, not wanting to go inside yet. It was empty and she lightly sat on a swing, swaying backwards and forwards, looking out over the sea. She was suddenly homesick for the life she'd left behind in America and her few close friends like Cindy, with whom she'd shared the bookshop.

As the sun started hiding behind the darkening clouds, Eilidh walked along to the flat. She idly glanced at the other properties, some similar to the building Kirsty and Sarah occupied. Then she paused. A main door flat had a For Sale sign! That might be an option for her. She loved this part of town right beside the river and she had enough money to buy property, though she'd need to get a job to sustain her living expenses. Even if she didn't make her home in Scotland in the end, she could sell it again, or rent it out. Either way, it was an investment. She didn't think Kirsty would mind her being so close, since they'd been getting on so well.

In her excitement at such a possibility, Eilidh had pushed thoughts of Lewis to the back of her mind and had almost forgotten about the answerphone message until she saw both girls were home and that Sarah was upset.

"Hi, Eilidh, can you give us a minute, please? Man trouble." Kirsty made a face. "You couldn't make up a salad for us, could you? Everything's in the fridge."

"No problem." She was glad to make herself useful. It was a timely reminder that she didn't want to outstay her welcome here. They had been so kind, but she was in their way; the flat was meant for two people at the most. She'd bring up the subject of the other place for sale later.

As she rinsed the salad leaves and sliced the vegetables, Eilidh wondered how she was going to broach the subject of Rory, if he'd upset Sarah so much.

"Sorry about that," Kirsty opened the kitchen door. "Sarah's in a quandary over what to do about her boyfriend and she needed a wide shoulder to cry on. That seems to be my role in life," she added ruefully.

Eilidh smiled at her friend. She could imagine people wanting to confide in her, and she must be a marvellous nurse.

"Anyway, did you have a good day?"

"Yeah, it was interesting." She told Kirsty about the old woman in the café in Dunoon. She'd tell her about Lewis some other time. No doubt, her friend had heard enough trouble about men for one day. Eilidh would see what he had to say on Friday when they met.

"I saw a main door flat for sale along the road, and I wondered if that might be an option for me. If you wouldn't mind me living so close to you?"

"Don't be daft, what a great idea. But could you afford it? Sorry, I don't mean to pry but they are quite pricy." Kirsty frowned.

"Well, I have the money from the bookshop and my apartment, and mum's, so I should be fine. But I'd like to find some work." It wasn't only from the money point of view; she wanted something useful to do.

"Och, I really do think it's a great idea, and I know just the person to ask about it as he's a local lawyer. But I'd rather we didn't talk about it in front of Sarah just now, if you don't mind. She won't want to hear his name again for a day or two until she sorts things out."

And Eilidh knew at once who she was going to ask. It seemed she might meet this Rory sooner than she'd imagined.

Chapter Ten

1785

I dream of him at night, against my will. Meggie warns me against him, for his dalliance with the lasses is as natural as breathing to him and it's folly to take him seriously. But it is not his obvious charms of face and figure that capture me; it is his way of looking into my eyes and heart as no other man has ever done before. He speaks to me and I answer.

We meet oft times at the ceilidh in town. All the young lads and lasses are freer there to talk and flirt. He has already claimed me for the reel, in front of everyone. Forgetting all curious eyes upon us and the restless tongues of doubt, my feet dance and twirl in time to the music as our hands touch and part. It is impossible to tell which makes my heart beat faster: the skirl of the pipes or the nearness of him.

Now he visits me in my dreams, promising such things as I can but imagine, and my body heats in its virginal bed. In reality, we steal glances at each other across the Kirk as the minister preaches on God's love and man's sin in the same breath. Forgiveness and punishment. And I resolve to remain pure – in body, if not in mind.

The other lasses talk of those he has flirted with, and I hear the warning mingled with their longing. There is rumour, too, that he is to wed Jean Armour but he does not appear to be a man about to commit himself to another.

He reads his verses aloud sometimes and all who

hear them marvel at how he speaks of ordinary things with such passion, yet in simple words that all can understand. I long for him to write a verse to me, something that no-one else will share. But we are not that close… yet.

Chapter Eleven

"Humid seal of soft affections,
Tend'rest pledge of future bliss."
(R. Burns: *To a Kiss*)

By Friday, Eilidh had decided to wait and see if Lewis mentioned his wife, or any other woman. They were hardly in a relationship, after all, and he could see whoever he liked, which gave her little comfort.

They were meeting at the Watt Library so she took a bus along to Union Street. She admired the impressive building, almost Gothic in slate grey, with turrets and tiny leaded windows. A perfect kind of place for seeking out the past. She noticed the museum next to it and resolved to go back there herself another day.

As she was about to approach the huge wooden front door, she heard her name called and Lewis strode towards her.

"Eilidh. Good morning to you." He pulled her into a big hug then looked at her appreciatively.

"Hi, Lewis. This is some building, isn't it?" She softened the impersonal words with a smile, but her quickened pulse betrayed how much she had wanted to see him.

"It's a little gem right here in town. You'll know it's named after James Watt, of course, he of steam engine fame."

She nodded as he held the door open for her. He led the way through to a large room where a young woman sat behind a desk. Huge tables took up the centre space, with bookshelves all around the walls. Only one other person sat at a table, absorbed in going through sheets of paper, marking down anything of interest.

"Can I help you? Or are you just wanting to browse?" The girl asked. She had a pleasant, cultured local accent.

"We'd like to look at some books, but perhaps you can tell us if you have anything on Highland Mary?" Eilidh asked, hopeful of gleaning new information.

"You know she's buried in Greenock cemetery, I suppose? Here's a leaflet that tells you a bit about her. If you want to browse through the shelves, I'll see what we've got on our index. Most old information is on microfilm now, but I can tell you what to look for."

"Thanks a lot." Eilidh smiled at the girl and they followed her to the shelves where the relevant books might be.

"The Mitchell Library in Glasgow has the biggest collection of Burns' material and you'll find more there. But we have a couple of books of that period that might be useful, and the Greenock Burns' Club has archive material on Burns. I'm sure they'd be happy to let you have a look through what they have."

"That would be wonderful, thanks. I'll do that another day," Eilidh suggested.

As they searched along the row of shelves, Eilidh found a book on Lord Byron. Not what she was supposed to be reading, but she had always loved the "mad, bad and dangerous" poet, as Lady Caroline Lamb had named him. She was flicking through the pages when the girl returned with a list.

"These are all the references to Highland Mary from the old *Greenock Advertiser*, and older copies of the *Greenock Telegraph*. You'll be able to access the articles on the microfilm if you tell me what year you want."

"That's brilliant! Thanks a lot," Eilidh said. She'd never used the machine before but surely it wouldn't be that difficult?

"I can help with that." Lewis was at her elbow. "We use it at the college library sometimes."

Once the girl had loaded a year from her list, it was fun going through the pages of old newspapers and Eilidh was delighted to find references to Mary Campbell printed in 1823. She made notes as they went. She'd still need to visit Ayrshire, as that was where Mary had spent much of her short life and, more importantly, it was where she met Robert Burns. Eilidh wanted to stand in some of the very streets Mary had walked, to get a feel for the area where she had fallen in love.

When they had finally exhausted the microfilm, Eilidh was pleased at the morning's work. It would be a great place to come back to when she needed more information, and she thanked the girl again as they left.

"If we jump in the car, I'll take you down to the Custom House area," Lewis suggested. "You might find that interesting, and there's a place to eat nearby."

Eilidh nodded her agreement. She wouldn't mind playing the tourist for a while and might learn more about her companion. The spacious open area down by the harbour had retained its cobbled streets, but she was surprised to see lovely modern apartments in this prime position.

"Those flats belong to the college for students who need accommodation. Great view, eh? And the newer college building is further along. We've still got the one on Finnart Street, too."

They walked down to the river and Eilidh noticed a path stretching in both directions. She stood at the rail and stared at the deep water as the gulls cried out all around them.

"You know, the old Waverley paddle steamer still plies these waters on pleasure trips to some of the islands. We should have a day out on it next year when it begins the season again."

Eilidh glanced up as she realised the implication of his words. He assumed she would still be in Scotland – and would still be seeing him. She met his teasing blue eyes and decided to play along; she had no idea where she'd be next year.

"Mm, sounds interesting. It might be worth staying around here for that." She deliberately left it ambiguous and was rewarded by his appreciative grin. "So that's the grand old Custom House still looking out to sea, wondering where all the ships have gone," she said, turning to stare at the gracious Georgian building.

"The cruise ships call at Greenock now, of course, though they come in further down the river at the container terminal. This building recently closed, unfortunately, but it's being completely refurbished inside for offices or such like. It used to house the offices for gaming taxes, as well as a great display of an illicit highland whisky still. Anyway, what about lunch? Don't know about you, but I'm nearly fainting with hunger."

Eilidh glanced at his tall frame and broad chest and decided fainting was the last word she'd associate with him no matter how hungry he became. She laughed and took his offered hand. It was large and comfortably warm and the fact that her own small hand disappeared completely inside his made her spine tingle with pleasure.

They walked the short distance to a large modern glass-fronted building. "We can get lunch here," he said. "This is the new arts centre I was telling you about, The Beacon. The cafe's a good addition to the area and we could have a look at the programme for winter. See if there's anything that takes your fancy."

That assumption again that she'd be staying in the area, although she'd love to attend a concert or show with this man.

As they ate a snack lunch overlooking the hill-framed river, the brightness of her day dulled when Eilidh remembered the last time she had seen Lewis Grant sitting at a table – with an attractive woman across from him. She'd pushed the memory away, but knew it would always be there, gaining importance by not being mentioned.

She waited until they had ordered, then was silent for a minute.

"Is something wrong, Eilidh? You seem a bit distant suddenly. Or is there someone you're thinking about, maybe?" His words were light but he didn't sound quite so confident.

"Well, there is, but not in the way you probably mean." She didn't know how to ask him, yet she preferred to have things out in the open even to the point of bluntness, whatever it cost.

"What is it, pet? You're starting to worry me."

It was the endearment that did it. "Pet" sounded so reassuring, comforting.

"I didn't know how to bring this up, so I'll be

honest. I saw you the other day, in the café in Gourock. I was out for a walk and happened to glance in as I passed." She looked into his eyes, watching his expression.

He appeared more resigned than anxious. "And you saw me with Jan."

Eilidh remembered the easy way the couple had been talking together and had that sinking feeling again. They didn't look like a divorced couple. She didn't say anything but waited.

"I know how it must have looked, Eilidh. But I promise you there is nothing between us. Jan is… she's having a few problems just now. She wanted to discuss something with me and I only agreed to meet her if it was in a café or such like. I had no wish to be in private with her."

Although not exactly reassured, she had to remind herself she had no claim on this man and that he could see whoever he wished.

He reached across and touched her hand. "Surely you know I wouldn't keep anything from you?"

She didn't exactly know him well enough for that, but smiled. "Of course, you must have things to talk about now and then. I have no right to ask, but I'd hate to be taking you away from a girlfriend when you're giving up so much time for me."

He put his hand on his heart and kept his eyes on her as he said, "I categorically declare that I have no girlfriend, or anyone else who has a better claim to my time than you do right now. And I need to eat."

She laughed and the serious moment passed, leaving them to reminisce on their childhood days during the remainder of lunch.

After another short walk along by the riverside, Lewis took her hand. "Do you mind if I drop you back at your friend's, Eilidh?"

"Of course not. I've a lot to think about and you've given up enough time today. Oh, I meant to ask you again, can you make it to the charity dance I told you about? It's the last Saturday in August. Kirsty wants to know the numbers."

"That Saturday is fine. Yes, I'd love to go."

"Great. I'll give you the exact details later. I need to check them again myself."

Eilidh was keen to sort out her notes from the library. It had been a successful day and, again, she felt as if she'd known Lewis for a long time. Yet they had done no more than lightly hold hands and hug. Even that seemed right, as though there was no need to hurry things along, or to worry about the long-term.

She wouldn't even mention the possibility of her buying a flat yet, as she didn't know where he figured in her future if she stayed. While she was concerned with finding out about her mother's past, she was happy to have his company without any strings attached. Besides, he was a good companion to have while researching Highland Mary, since he was a Burns' fan.

They chatted as Lewis drove towards Cardwell Bay and Eilidh wondered if they might ever have a proper date. She could hardly ask what he did with his evenings.

As they drew up before the flat, Eilidh hesitated. Should she ask him up for a drink? It was Kirsty and Sarah's flat after all, and they'd never covered the etiquette of inviting people up.

"It was a pleasure to see you again, as always, Eilidh. I'll give you a call in a day or two and we can arrange something else. It's not that long until I go back to college and I've preparation to do before the dreaded day."

Was that his way of telling her he couldn't spend much more time with her? Well, she had things to do, too. "Thanks for your company, Lewis. I'll let you know about the dance. Oh, and I'm thinking of going down to Ayrshire for a couple of days. I want to see where Highland Mary and Burns spent their days."

He was silent for a moment. Then he took her by surprise.

"I could go down with you, if you wouldn't mind the company?" He must have seen her startled expression, as he added, "But if you'd rather go alone, that's fine."

"No. I just hadn't thought about that possibility…" And now that she had, she would very much like his company. "I think that might be a very pleasant idea," she teased.

"Let me know when you plan to go and I shall bring the carriage, m'lady."

They laughed, then both became silent at the same moment. Eilidh knew something had changed, as though they had tentatively committed themselves to a deeper understanding. Without another word, he reached across the narrow gap between them. It was an awkward and uncomfortable angle, but when their lips gently met for the first time, it was as though she had waited on this moment for ever. It was over in moments, but it promised so much more.

As he got out of the car and came round to open her door, Eilidh made sure she had her bag and notes. They were standing on the side of the river, away from the flats and she briefly kissed his cheek.

"Thanks for a lovely day, Lewis. I'll speak to you soon."

She walked across the road, aware he still watched, and she turned and waved before going through the gate towards the back courtyard. Thankfully the flat was empty, as she had even more to think about now. They were going to Ayrshire together. She wondered about the implications of a few days together. If that kiss was anything to go by, it would be an interesting time.

The answerphone was blinking again and Eilidh pressed the button. Kirsty had told her to take any messages for her and Sarah.

A hesitant female voice spoke softly. "Somebody called my brother when I wasn't in. This is Grace MacAulay. Can you please telephone me?"

Eilidh was astonished. Grace? Then that must have been her brother who had answered, and someone had dialled 1471 to get Eilidh's number. What were the chances of that happening?

She put all thoughts of Lewis Grant into another compartment to think about later. It looked as though she might have found her mother's old friend.

Chapter Twelve

1785

We have met for the first time alone. One day, I was in need of a long walk such as I was used to at home. My work was over and the sun still dallied with a few scattered clouds. There is a path above an embankment where few but the sheep and cattle enjoy the pasture. Kilting up my dress at the bottom, I set off with only my thoughts for company, wondering how my family fare so far away. There is little time to miss them for there is plenty to do here in service, but I remember them often.

The ground is firm and dry and I sing softly as I walk, for there is much to content me. Some time passes then I see a figure in the distance, coming towards me. I notice a familiar set to his height and shoulders and wonder if it's possible that it is he; that we should meet in such a quiet place.

As he nears, he raises his hand in a greeting. He knows me!

"Good day, my pretty maid. You are wandered far from your friends."

For a moment, I pause, remembering his reputation with the lasses. Then I look into his smiling eyes and naught else matters.

"Good day, sir. I had need of the countryside for company as a change."

He nods as though in understanding. He is used to the land.

"Do you go much further or might I persuade you

to walk back with me, for I go to the village to seek my friends? We can converse together if you allow me to intrude on your thoughts."

"It's time I return, and you make no intrusion." It is true, for how could my thoughts be anything other than of him now?

There is space enough to walk side by side along the path, but only if we are close. My heart beats faster at his nearness but I determine that he will not know it.

"How do you like our country ways these past months?" He sounds genuinely interested.

"It is different here but, in many ways, familiar with the same sheep and cattle. But there's more liveliness in the village of an evening."

"And you like to dance, of course."

Now I blush at his observation. It is true that music makes my feet dance and my spirits rise, as he well remembers.

"To hear such lively tunes, it would be difficult to sit still, I think."

We walk some more, then I dare to ask about his writing.

"Do you still compose your verse, sir? For I hear tell it is very fine work."

"You are kind, my pretty maid. But, yes, it's as natural to me as breathing the air around me. I grew up to the sound of my cousin's songs and stories and they have seeped into my blood. This world gives me so many things to think about, and to express those thoughts in verse keeps me sane in mind."

I nod in reply. Though some of his words pass me by, I understand his sentiments, for does not the very air keep me happy?

"Shall I recite something to you? If you are truly

interested in such nonsense."

"I would be honoured, sir, for I love the rhythm of song and verse."

He seems surprised at such words, then he smiles into my eyes and speaks softly, each word for my ears alone.

"Humid seal of soft affections,
Tend'rest pledge of future bliss,
Dearest tie of young connections,
Love's first snow-drop, virgin kiss."

Now I feel a warmth creep up my neck and face and down my arms, right to my fingertips, for he speaks the words while still looking into my eyes. Then I try to be annoyed. How dare he suggest these sentiments are for my ears when he'd most likely said them a hundred times before.

"They are very fine words, sir." It is all I will say, while I remember every sentiment.

"Thank you. But please speak my given name, Robert, or Rob if you prefer, for I grow weary of being called 'sir'. I'm not your master. And I know we are already friends."

His words seem to promise more and I think on his verse. What must it be like to be kissed by such a man? Then I chide myself for such musings. He has the pick of any lass, many prettier than I am. Glancing ahead, I see we are almost at the village road. It is time to part.

"I think our way diverges, sweet maid, for now." He stops and faces me. "Thank you for your company; the road is less rough when a pretty lass walks by your side."

His words seem full of other meaning, but I smile and allow him to take my hand. He bends over it and presses his warm lips to my cool fingers. Then his eyes are alight with mischief and he murmurs, "Humid seal of soft affections."

I pull back my hand, not too quickly, and say my farewell. I look back once and he too has turned. We smile and continue our separate ways.

And as I remember every detail of that encounter, I know that again something has changed. Inside me, and in my hopes for the future, however fanciful they may seem.

Chapter Thirteen

*"Some sort all our qualities each to its tribe.
And think human nature they truly describe."*
(R. Burns: *Fragment*)

Eilidh dialled the number with shaking fingers, hardly daring to hope she had found her mother's old friend.

"Hello. Who's this, please?"

"Hi. This is Eilidh Campbell. I called a few days ago and your brother answered. Someone called me back."

"Och, yes, I remember. One of the wardens knew to dial 1471, as not many people phone us and we wondered who it could be."

Warden? Eilidh wondered for a moment if she meant a prison warden, then realised it would be some kind of housing warden.

"Anyway," the woman continued and Eilidh suspected she was the chatty type, "how can I help you?"

Eilidh took a deep breath. "I know this is a long shot, but would you happen to be the Grace MacAulay who was friends with my mother, Mary Campbell, a long time ago?"

Silence. Eilidh could almost hear the woman's thoughts turning.

"I remember that pretty Mary Campbell. And you say you're her daughter? Wee Eilidh? Och, you must come and see me, lassie. Come for a cup of tea and we'll have a chat about the old days. How is Mary, after all these years?"

Better and better. Eilidh couldn't believe her luck, but she had to break the sad news first. "I'm afraid my mother passed away recently. But that's very kind of you, I'd love to come and chat."

"I'm sorry to hear that, dear. Make it Tuesday, about half ten, when Ronnie's away to his dominoes group. I'm in thon houses on West Stewart Street. First floor."

Eilidh put down the phone, elated at having found someone willing to talk about the past that included her mother. Grace sounded bright enough and was certainly chatty. But would she be able to tell Eilidh what she wanted to know? That was the million-dollar question. At least it was a positive step in the right direction. Then she could start thinking about going to Ayrshire for a few days. With Lewis Grant.

In the meantime, she wanted to have a girly day out with Kirsty and Sarah, to thank them for putting her up, and putting up with her. Although she'd been contributing to the household expenses, she couldn't go on like this much longer. The girls needed their space back and she needed her own privacy, especially if things progressed with Lewis.

The flat along the road was still for sale and Eilidh had promised she would arrange a time to view it. She was putting it off because she hadn't told Kirsty and Sarah about Rory yet. She couldn't decide if she was more afraid it wouldn't be him, or that he did turn out to be her cousin. But she needed to know one way or the other. Then she would have to see her aunt and uncle.

The girls had chosen to go to Glasgow by train on the Saturday, so they could enjoy the day without worrying about parking. Besides, it meant they could have wine with lunch if they wanted to since no-one would have to drive.

They boarded an early train from Gourock station, a fast one so they wouldn't have to stop at every single small station on the way, and they passed the time chatting and admiring the scenery along the coast.

"It's lovely along here," Eilidh said, as they passed a particularly scenic part of the River Clyde.

"Yeah, but wait till we get nearer to Glasgow, it's not so pretty then!" Kirsty laughed.

She was right, but there was still some lovely countryside on the way, until they reached the large town of Paisley. After that they raced past housing schemes and industrial areas, with the odd patch of green.

Soon they were drawing to a halt in Glasgow Central. Eilidh hadn't been there since a child and couldn't believe the difference. This was one stylish station, she decided. Busy of course, like any other mainline station, but it was friendly and welcoming with plenty of little shops and a couple of cafés from the concourse to the main exit.

As they headed for the town, light-hearted and chatty, Eilidh felt like one of the foursome from *Sex and the City;* they just needed someone else to complete the illusion. She'd probably be Carrie, since she liked to write and observe, although she lacked her wacky but stylish dress sense. Sarah would be Charlotte perhaps, optimistic and slightly prudish; Kirsty would be Miranda, down-to-earth and reliable. None of them had Samantha's predilection for casual sex and fear of commitment, as far as she could tell. Eilidh smiled at her thoughts and wondered how many other groups of females compared themselves to those four fictional women who had changed women's perceptions for ever.

As she glanced at her two companions, Eilidh realised she'd become fairly Americanised with growing up through her teens and twenties across the pond, but her early, formative years had been in Scotland and she had never quite lost that inheritance of personality and outlook. What was it the Jesuits said? "Give me a child until he is seven and I will show you the man." Or woman, in her case.

"Right, caffeine fix first." Kirsty broke into her musings.

"I know a good coffee place: the Christian bookshop up on Bothwell Street," Sarah said at once.

"You sure we'd like that?" asked Kirsty.

"Course you would. It does great coffee and it's Fairtrade. They also do a great selection of cards and things, as well as books."

"I'd like to try it," Eilidh offered. She'd enjoyed the small coffee/bookshop in Dunoon.

"Well, that's settled. Bothwell Street is this way." Kirsty turned left at the station exit.

It wasn't far to the bookshop and Eilidh liked it at once, happy to see it well stocked, with more books and gifts downstairs. The coffee area towards the back was obviously popular, judging by the number of tables already occupied. Discreet music played in the background, not interfering with the various conversations going on.

Once they had chosen iced gingerbread to go with the coffee, they managed to get one of the tables partly screened on a raised platform. Ideal for confidences, Eilidh decided.

She realised how little she'd spoken to Sarah

considering she was staying in the same house, but with the girl being a busy nurse their paths seldom crossed. It would be the same with Kirsty when she got back to work properly again, which made Eilidh even more determined to get her own place. Either she would disturb them or they'd disturb her and that wasn't fair to them when the girls worked odd shifts.

At first the chat was light-hearted and general, then Kirsty mentioned Jamie. "He's going to the charity dance with me."

There was silence for a moment then Sarah laughed. "Well! That was some announcement. So, what's the story there? Is he back in town already?"

"He got back a few days ago. I was going to tell you. Oh, and he wants to see you, Eilidh," Kirsty said.

"Well, I'd really love to see him, too. It's been so long, I guess I'll hardly recognise him."

"Oh, you will. He's still got hair!" Kirsty grinned.

Their laughter broke the slight tension Eilidh had sensed.

"Anyway, thought I'd better warn you both. He's just coming as my buddy since I don't have a partner. Nothing to get excited about."

Eilidh knew Kirsty well enough to suspect that wasn't completely true, but it was none of her business unless her friend wanted to tell her more.

"But what about this Lewis Grant then, Eilidh?" Kirsty asked, changing the focus away from herself.

Eilidh shrugged. No doubt her friend had been longing to ask her for a while, and she owed Kirsty since she'd got them together.

"Hmm. Well, he's kind and funny and interesting…"

"And just a bit gorgeous, in a manly way!" Kirsty

interrupted.

"That, too, of course. I honestly don't know where it's going. But I do know we're going off to Ayrshire for a couple of days. He's helping me with research," Eilidh added quickly, as both girls looked at her in astonishment.

"That sounds promising," Sarah said seriously.

"Well, it promises something," Kirsty laughed, and made a face at Sarah's admonishing look.

"Oh, you know, I'm not rushing into anything. I'm not desperate for a relationship – or not yet. But there's a real connection between us, as if I've known him for ever."

She decided not to mention her unease about his personal life, as she might be seeing problems where none existed.

"As long as you know what you're doing," Sarah said in her gentle voice.

"Och, I think she's old enough to know all the right moves." Kirsty laughed again at Sarah's face.

"Dare I ask how you and Rory are getting along now?" Kirsty ventured at last, turning to her flatmate.

Eilidh tensed as that name was mentioned. She didn't want to spoil their confidences by bringing up the subject of her aunt, uncle and cousin. Not yet.

Sarah shrugged, sadness clouding her face for a moment. "We'll sort it out eventually. He's going to come over one evening and we'll have an honest chat about everything."

"I've told Eilidh he might be able to advise her about buying property here, so maybe you could introduce him and they could arrange an appointment," Kirsty said. "We won't hang around, of course. You'll need space to talk."

"That's fine." Sarah turned to Eilidh. "Good to

know you're staying in Scotland, Eilidh. I'll let you know when Rory's coming over."

She hesitated before sharing her confidences. "We've been having some family conflict but are hoping to get married next year. He was brought up as a Roman Catholic. I'm a Protestant – well, a Christian – and we want to get married in my evangelical church. His mother is not very pleased. Would you believe that still goes on sometimes, in this so-called Godless age? No wonder many people couldn't care less about church."

Eilidh remembered that religious bigotry had plagued the west coast of Scotland at one time and she'd come across it herself when very young. But that was an interesting fact about Rory. If he was her cousin, had her aunt converted at some time? Her mother and gran hadn't been Catholic, as far as she knew, and she'd gone to a protestant school. Then she realised she hadn't replied.

"It's wonderful that you're getting married, Sarah. I hope you manage to sort things out."

At the back of Eilidh's distant memory lay that image of a self-righteous type of woman who had upset her mother. And this woman who was Rory's mother might well be that aunt.

Their chat became light-hearted again as they finished the coffee.

"Shops next," Kirsty suggested. "Let's walk across to Buchanan Street. You'll love what they've done with it, Eilidh."

They passed the station again then carried on until they were on the long pedestrianised street that ran down to Argyll Street and up to Sauchiehall Street.

"Wow, what a difference." Eilidh was suitably impressed. She vaguely remembered Glasgow when a child; they hadn't come to the city very often, and it was always a grand day out when they did. Now, it could take its place beside any stylish, cosmopolitan city in the world. At the top of the street stood the Royal Concert Hall, reached by a wide semi-circle of steps.

"There's a good mall up there beside the Concert Hall," Kirsty said, "and another one down at St Enoch's. Or if you want designer clothes, we can take you along to the Merchant City area."

"Whoa, slow down. I don't need that much, though it sounds as though there's plenty of choice. But I didn't know about the Merchant City."

"That's the trendy part of town now," Sarah offered.

"And of course, you must see Princes Square. We'll be able to get lunch there later."

Eilidh felt like a tourist again. Glasgow had changed so much that she hardly remembered any of this, apart from the architecture. She had noticed many high, modern, glass buildings from the train, but was pleased to see the old buildings still in place.

When she mentioned it, Sarah told her, "My mother always said you have to look up as you walk round Glasgow for that's where you'll see amazing detail. Do you like art, Eilidh?" Sarah asked.

"Yes, I do. I love all types of culture."

"We must show her GOMA, Kirsty. Eilidh can come back herself another day to spend more time there, but we must have a quick look."

Eilidh grinned at Kirsty's resigned expression, though her friend shrugged in gracious defeat.

"What's GOMA?" Eilidh asked.

"The Gallery of Modern Art, and some of the weird exhibits will blow your mind," Sarah said.

The nineteenth century building stood on the other side of the archway from Buchanan Street. Although huge and impressive, Eilidh saw that was nothing to the feeling of space within. Even though some of the exhibits took up a lot of floor space, there was a real airiness about it, enhanced by the very high roof. They wandered round the main floor to give Eilidh an impression of what was on offer, and she was determined to return on her own another day.

"There's an upstairs, and a basement which is partly a library again, with a coffee shop."

"Thanks for showing it to me. I'll be coming back here again."

"Right, the shops now," Kirsty said. "I've been patient long enough."

Kirsty was obviously the one most into clothes, Eilidh realised, after she'd been dragged around every floor of a huge department store. They'd tried on shoes and various items of fashion but only Kirsty bought a bag in the end. In another store, Sarah found a skirt and Eilidh bought a couple of sweatshirts since the weather was gradually getting cooler. After investigating a few smaller shops, all three decided it was time for lunch.

They'd promised to take her to Princes Square, and Eilidh was glad they did. The first thing she noticed was the metal peacock above the entrance, full feathers eternally displayed. Inside, it took her breath away. About four open floors of elegance and expensive shops were joined by escalators, while at one end was the most graceful staircase Eilidh had seen outside of a country house on some elaborate film set.

"Brilliant, isn't it?" Kirsty asked as she saw Eilidh's face. "We'll need to come back nearer

Christmas because it's really gorgeous then with shimmery hanging things, and wee schoolchildren singing down there in the music area. You can sit at one of the cafés all round that floor and drink while you listen."

They took the escalator to the top floor where various types of restaurant vied for custom. Eilidh chose a modern restaurant that offered a good two-course meal at a reasonable price.

"Much cheaper to eat at lunchtime," Kirsty whispered. "The prices go way up in the evening."

They took a table that was private enough to chat but allowed them to watch the comings and goings of the centre. It was unlike any other mall Eilidh had ever seen; in fact, she couldn't really call it such, as this was elegance personified.

Eilidh made one thing clear right away. "This is my treat today, because you've both been absolutely wonderful at allowing me to mess up your living arrangements for so long. And I'm not arguing, so accept graciously, or gratefully if you like!"

After a token protest, Kirsty and Sarah did as they were told and were happy to have lunch on Eilidh. They were idly chatting when Sarah unexpectedly asked a question.

"Do you miss the States, Eilidh, or anyone special there?"

She supposed it was a reasonable question since Sarah didn't know that much about her.

"Well, I do miss the sun sometimes, though I love the constant change of weather here."

She laughed at their rueful expression. Clearly most Scottish people wouldn't mind the guarantee of sunshine and warmth, instead of having all the seasons often rolled into one week.

"I've wanted to come here for so long that when Mum died, I didn't seem to belong there anymore. That's completely my fault as I had some good friends and colleagues. The way of life was more easy going and certainly more outdoors, though we had to drive everywhere. I love not having to do that here, for the moment anyway."

"Now you've met a Scottish hunk, hopefully you'll never leave again," Kirsty said sincerely. On a lighter note, she added, "Mind you, these transatlantic flights have a lot to answer for, so maybe that's what I should do. Why did I never get out to see you when you were still in America? You know, I read that a woman was travelling with her husband and when he slept most of the way, she got very friendly with the guy on her other side. I suppose it must be the enforced intimacy for such a length of journey, though I suppose it depends who you end up with."

Eilidh told them the similar story she had read, and they joined in bemused laughter at the things people got up to. But she knew it was something more with Lewis, a connection that went beyond the casual meeting of two strangers on a plane.

The conversation stayed light-hearted, aided by a bottle of dry white wine, although she noticed Sarah would only accept half a glass which left the rest for her and Kirsty.

They were on the way for their train when Eilidh stopped outside a shop she'd never seen before. She loved the style of clothes in the window, and next minute they were all inside persuading her to try on some of the gorgeous, jewel-coloured dresses.

"Och, you need one for the dance," Kirsty insisted.

When she tried on a swirling green and blue long

dress that showed off her neck and shoulders, Eilidh was hooked.

"That's definitely the one for you," Sarah said.

Since she needed something to wear and the flowing skirt part of the dress would give her freedom of movement, it didn't take long to persuade her to buy. She could imagine twirling round a Scottish dance floor in it.

They were in merry mood when they finally got back to the station to join the afternoon buzz. Discovering a train almost ready to leave, they started to run, determined to be on it. The guardsman saw them skittering up the platform and hesitated raising the green flag until they'd jumped on board. Kirsty threw him a wide smile and playful kiss as the doors closed behind them.

"Phew, that's not good on a full stomach," she groaned, collapsing onto a seat.

"Especially after wine at lunchtime. I'm light-headed," Eilidh answered.

They suddenly became aware that Sarah hadn't uttered a single word and they glanced round. She was staring down the carriage, where a man was engrossed in reading a newspaper.

"It's Rory," she whispered. "Down there. I don't think he's seen us yet." There was desperation in her voice. "I don't want us to meet up like this after our argument."

"You sit at the window across from me," Kirsty urged, "and Eilidh can sit on the outside seat. He won't know her."

Eilidh gulped at that. She couldn't see the man clearly enough, but her heart started beating wildly and she didn't want to bring attention to them. But Kirsty had decided it was the best idea so she tried to change places with Sarah as discreetly as possible, while they all had a fit of wine-fuelled giggles.

Just as they'd arranged themselves again, they were aware of someone approaching.

"Mind if I join you lovely ladies?" The voice was pleasant and cultured and Eilidh risked a glance.

Then Kirsty piped in," Of course you can. Any handsome man is welcome at our table, but you'd better sit next to your fiancée." Kirsty swapped places with Sarah so Rory could sit beside her.

Eilidh didn't know where to look, since he was sitting directly opposite her. At the moment his attention was on Sarah, but she was going to be introduced any minute now.

"Rory, this is my long-lost friend back from America. Eilidh Campbell. Eilidh, this is Sarah's boyfriend and the person who might be able to help with your flat hunting."

Eilidh looked at Rory and he looked at her. Neither said anything for a whole minute. Then he stood up as the train shoogled along. "Eilidh? You're little Eilidh?"

Under the astonished gaze of her two open-mouthed friends, Eilidh also stood up and said, "Yes. Oh, it's good to see you Rory." And they hugged.

"You know each other?" Kirsty didn't know what else to say, and Sarah was speechless.

They sat down again and Eilidh turned to the two women. "Rory is my cousin and we haven't seen each other since we were children." But she knew at once there was a familiarity about this man that she couldn't deny.

Chapter Fourteen

1785

I relive those precious moments alone every night. For some reason he has singled me out for his attention, but I hesitate to say for his affection. It is foolish to forget his way with other more experienced females, for one or two have claimed their bairn is the proof. My knowledge of such things goes as far as the coupling the farm animals perform and I can only imagine the rest, though some of the lasses here are keen to tell me more.

Although I walk some days, we have not met that way again and I saw him only one Sunday in the Kirk. He smiled and nodded across to me but we did not speak. Mayhap he's forgotten our talking together already. I know he's a busy farmer and he will have much to do with the running of the farm.

Then one day I see him in the village. But he is not alone. A handsome, buxom lass is with him and I recognise Jean Armour. They stroll openly down the street together, she with her hand on his arm, and I take steps to make sure I don't have to walk past them. I could not stand to see him smile at me with another woman on his arm, for then I would know he is but teasing me.

I ask Meggie about them.

"They do say he's going to wed her, lass, but I'll believe that when it takes place. I'm thinking he's maybe no a man tae be tying himself to one woman for the rest of his life. And it seems her ma and da are of the same mind for they dinnae seem tae be keen on the idea."

I have to be content with that for now. But I cannot remove the feelings that have taken root within my heart unless I tear it from my body. How can time go back to the day before our walk? It is no more possible than going back to my childhood days. And I confess I have no wish to be rid of these new senses he has awakened. But, oh, the longing to see him again, to find his eyes focused only on mine, and his warm lips against my hand. I dare not imagine them going further or my work will suffer.

So, I go about my daily chores with my mind elsewhere. For I know, with some ancient knowledge, that my future is entwined with this man, though it seems so unlikely this day. Soon it will be the end of this year, and there is talk of me going to a new post since the Hamilton bairn has no need of me longer. It may be the new beginning I need to rid me of this foolish hope.

Chapter Fifteen

"I backward mus'd on wasted time,
How I had spent my youthful prime."
(R. Burns: *The Vision*)

By the time they reached Greenock, where Rory was getting off the train, Eilidh had told them as much as she knew about her childhood and their departure to America, which didn't amount to much at all. She still held off talking about the mystery of her father, as this was too public a place for such confidence. They kept their voices subdued as Rory told her a little from his side.

"I wondered now and then why we didn't ever see you. Mother only said you'd gone to America. I thought it a bit strange, but you know what it's like when you're twelve. I was too busy thinking about the long summer holidays and then going up to the big school, and we'd never seen you that much before."

Eilidh nodded, well remembering she had soon forgotten about Rory in the chaos of going halfway across the world.

"It's such a shame we couldn't write to each other to keep in touch," she said. She'd tried once but somehow her mother had never got around to giving her the full address, and her new life had intervened.

He nodded. "I did think about it one day, when we were talking about pen pals at school. But Mother said she never knew your address and I gave up. I'm sorry I didn't try harder."

"You and me both," Eilidh said. There was no point in telling him her mother had been as much at fault as his. But there must have been good reason for it.

"Aye, well, you've got me nearly in tears here, you two." Kirsty lightened the moment, to Eilidh's relief. This was much too heavy for a public train journey.

"You must come and see mother and father. Mother will be pleased to know you're back here. Poor father isn't very well, but he'll be glad of a pretty face."

Eilidh suddenly panicked. She wasn't ready for that.

"Could you do me a big favour, Rory? I don't want you to say anything yet. I'm going to Ayrshire for a few days and I'd rather wait until after that to see them."

"Of course, if you like. I don't see them that much, so I'll wait until you're free then I can take you along the first time. Sarah might have mentioned that we're not exactly the best of friends with mother at the moment anyway."

Eilidh relaxed a little. She was pleased to see Rory take Sarah's hand at the mention of their problems, remembering they had things to sort out.

"Oh, there is one thing, though. I'm hoping to buy an apartment in the area – sorry, I mean a flat – and I've seen one along from Kirsty and Sarah. Do you think perhaps you could give me some advice on that, please? I'd consult you professionally, of course," she quickly added, lest he think she was taking advantage of their connection.

"Of course I will. We can meet up to discuss it,

and catch up on some of our lost years."

When Rory got up at his stop, Sarah walked to the door with him and was all smiles again when she rejoined them.

"Well, that was a shock, though a nice one." Kirsty couldn't wait to talk about it. "Y'know I completely forgot you had a cousin here because you never mentioned him in all the time you were away. I don't even remember him when we were children." Kirsty sounded bemused.

"I know. It's complicated. I didn't know him that well when we were growing up. They lived in the posh end of town, and my mother and his mother fell out and never spoke to each other again. That's it really."

When Sarah didn't say anything, Kirsty couldn't contain herself. "Well, it's no bloody wonder your mother fell out with that woman. Honestly, Sarah, if Rory wasn't such a nice guy, I'd think you were mad to take her on as a mother-in-law."

Sarah glanced at the few passengers remaining on the train and put her finger to her lips. "Shush, Kirsty, you don't know who's listening. Anyway, she's not that bad, and his dad's friendly, though not very well. She just has a very strong faith and wants Rory to marry in her church."

"You're far too kind, Sarah. She's got a strong bloody bigotry, more like!" Kirsty said.

"Look, I'd rather not talk about it here. Anyway, we're supposed to be talking about Eilidh and Rory."

Since the train was now running along the track beside the pier and they were about to arrive at Gourock terminal, all conversation dwindled away. Eilidh was relieved; she didn't want to be asked any more awkward questions when she didn't have the answers herself.

As they walked cheerfully back to the flat, she remembered the woman she was going to see. Maybe Grace would be able to fill in some gaps.

Eilidh couldn't contain her excitement on the Tuesday morning. This might be the breakthrough she needed in finding out more about her mother's past, but she tried not to get too hopeful since so much time had gone by. Although Grace had known at once who Eilidh was, there might be gaps in the woman's memory about those days. But it meant she could put off meeting her aunt and uncle for a while longer.

Meeting Rory like that had opened the floodgates of questions from Kirsty and Sarah, once they'd got over their shock at him being Eilidh's cousin. They accepted her brief explanation but she noticed Kirsty's speculative glance. Her friend knew there was more to it. Trouble was, Eilidh didn't know much herself so couldn't enlighten them even if she wanted to.

As Eilidh knew where to find the flats where Grace lived, she decided to take the bus. It was a fairly quick journey and the bus seemed mostly filled with over 60s going up to town.

She got off in the centre and walked up to West Stewart Street, having a quick look in some of the small shops as she went. She'd left plenty of time but didn't want to be late. Eilidh pressed the buzzer and waited until the door opened, allowing her into the building. Grace was waiting at the door of her flat with a smile on her face.

"Hello, Eilidh. Och, you've a look of your lovely mother about you. I'm that sorry I never got to see her again. Come away in and make yourself comfy."

"It's very kind of you to see me like this, Grace. I think I remember you a little." Eilidh was relieved to find the older woman so friendly. It would make it easier to chat and ask questions, though her accent was a little broader than Kirsty's and Sarah's.

"I've got the kettle boiled. Would you like some tea, or do you prefer coffee?"

"I'd love some tea, please. I drink far too much coffee." She suspected that would be easier.

"That's good, hen, I love a good cup of tea in the morning. D'you take sugar and milk? I've none of thae sweeteners, I'm afraid."

"A little milk will be fine, thanks."

Eilidh noticed the furnishings in the room were comfortably shabby, but it was clean and tidy, with no magazines or books lying about. She did notice the old basket next to the armchair beside the fireplace contained knitting needles and wool, something she hadn't seen since her granny's days.

Grace brought a tray with two cups, saucers, a milk jug and a little plate of biscuits.

"It's got to be a china cup for tea, it tastes better. Would you be kind and bring the pot, hen? My wrists aren't as strong these days."

"Of course I will. It's good of you to go to all this trouble."

"Och, it's nae trouble, hen. I always love a chat. And to think you're wee Eilidh all grown up into a beautiful lassie." Grace poured the tea and sat back to get a better look at Eilidh. "Have a biscuit."

While she drank her tea and ate a cream biscuit, Eilidh let Grace chatter on about her brother, her friends, the outings they went on, and the state of her health. The woman obviously loved having someone new to talk to. But how to bring the subject round to her mother?

She needn't have worried. Once she'd exhausted a few more subjects, Grace suddenly stopped and peered at Eilidh again.

"You know, as I said, you have a right look of her – your mother. We were great friends, though she was younger than me and I missed her that much when she ran off like that."

So here it was at last.

"Did she run off? Had she not planned to go to America?"

"Far as I can remember, when your granny died, your ma just decided to move away. I always wondered why she did that. Why then? But she never really said." Grace looked genuinely puzzled.

Eilidh's hopes sank. Would Grace not be able to add much after all? She decided to try.

"Grace, do you know who my father was?" There, a direct question that couldn't be avoided.

She saw the other woman's shock and more than a little discomfort. It seemed to be the last thing she planned to talk about.

"Well now, hen, that's a strange question. Did you never know him?"

"No. Mum and granny never talked about him, so I was kind of hoping you'd maybe have some information about him."

Eilidh waited as Grace rubbed her forehead, not looking at Eilidh. Was she trying to decide how much to tell her? Then she finally looked at Eilidh, sadness in her eyes.

"I'm that sorry, so I am, because I can imagine how much you must want to know. But she never told me what happened. She was good at keeping secrets was your ma, and that was when we started to lose touch a bit."

The disappointment was overwhelming. Eilidh hadn't realised quite how much she'd hoped to hear the truth at last.

"Don't worry, Grace, it was just a thought." She tried to reassure the elderly woman.

"I can show you some photos, if you like." Grace suddenly brightened.

That reminded Eilidh. She'd brought the well gazed at snap with her. Taking it out of her bag, she showed it to Grace. "Do you happen to know who that man is with my mother? I used to think he might be my father."

Grace put her spectacles on and stared at the photo, as though trying to make out the features. "Oh, I remember him! That's, now let me think. Jack Hargreaves, that's it! We all fancied him but it was your mother he fell for."

She was quiet for a moment, thinking back to those days. Eilidh held her breath.

"But he's no' your father, as far as I know, Eilidh. Your mother was pretty keen on him. He was part of the US Navy, you know? At the Holy Loch. If I remember right, he was posted back home. That didnae stop some of them enjoying the company of the Scottish lassies while they had the chance. Some even ended up married to one." Something in Grace's expression suggested she had enjoyed such friendship herself.

Eilidh stared at the couple in the photograph which she knew by heart. He was a handsome man and she'd always half wished he was her father. Now she was disappointed. Yet how could Grace know, unless her mother had told her friend something. Maybe Grace didn't want to say too much.

"How can you be sure?" Eilidh asked. "Did mum tell you who my father was?" Could Grace know about the letter with the initial R?

"Och, dear, does it really matter after all this time?" She must have seen that it did, as she continued. "The timing wasn't right for him to be your dad. It was after he'd been away for a while that she fell pregnant. Though there were plenty of other lads who liked her as well."

Eilidh noticed she still hadn't answered the rest of the question. She was about to ask again when Grace stood up.

"I'll get some more pictures for you, hen. They were great weekends. Whole crowds of us girls used to go over to Dunoon for the dancing. All those American sailors. And some of the big companies on this side used to arrange dances just to bring the Americans over here. Mind, it didnae please the local lads, on either side of the river!"

Eilidh remembered old Maggie in Dunoon had said something similar.

Grace returned from another room with a big old-fashioned chocolate box filled with seemingly hundreds of photos; black and white, and colour.

"Never seem to get around to sorting these intae albums. But they aren't as mixed up as they look," she said with a laugh, after glancing at Eilidh's face. "Could you move that tray away for me, hen?"

When Eilidh had taken the tray into the kitchen, Grace pulled out a huge bundle of photos and set them down on the coffee table. After looking through those remaining in the box, she lifted another bundle.

"Here we are. One of the boys had a camera and liked to think he was a photographer. There's some of your ma here."

Eilidh was fascinated by the old photos and saw one of her mother right away. She was posing with three other girls, and Eilidh could see a young-looking Grace. Then she paused. One of the other two girls looked familiar and she realised it was her aunt. A younger, happier, and friendlier aunt. She looked a little older than the others and her skirt wasn't quite so short.

"Isn't that my aunt?" Eilidh asked. "I didn't know her and mum were that friendly."

"Och, aye. They were quite close at one time and your aunt loved going to the dancing as much as any of us, though she was older than me even. We lost touch after your mother went away. Oh, here's one of your uncle William. He used to hang around with us sometimes. He was more your aunt's age."

The next photo she showed Eilidh was of a crowd of lads posing for the camera, some with hair slicked back, others in a Beatles cut.

"They all thought they were God's gift to us girls. But the competition from American sailors soon put their gas on a peep!" She pointed to one of the others. "That's my brother, Ronnie. He was the oldest of them all and didnae come with us very often." She hesitated. "He was always a bit slow-witted, know what I mean? But he liked to be included sometimes."

Then she pointed to one of the thinner men. "This one married that other girl in the picture. Annie, that was her name."

Eilidh studied the laughing young men. She picked out her uncle at once, as there was a look of Rory about him, but she'd never heard of any of the others.

"Was Mum close to any of them?" she asked hopefully.

"Och, all the boys liked her, every one of them. She was a real looker, you know, and she had a sweet personality, though she wouldn't put up with any nonsense." She glanced at Eilidh almost slyly. "Mind, some of us were jealous of the attention she got." This was said matter-of-factly, as though it hadn't stopped them being friends with her mother.

They looked through a few more photos, and she realised again that Grace wasn't quite answering the questions as fully as Eilidh wanted. There was a vague feeling that the older woman knew or suspected something, but wasn't going to be the one to tell Eilidh.

The idea was confirmed when Grace looked at the clock and began putting the photographs back into the box.

"Well, I did enjoy meeting you again, Eilidh dear. You've brought all these memories back, too. But Ronnie will be home soon and I'll need to get him sorted for the rest of the day. Maybe we can talk again another time and you can tell me all about America."

Eilidh stood up. She got the message. Grace had said all she was going to reveal for the time being.

"Thanks so much, Grace. It was real kind of you to give me tea. It was lovely seeing your photos and hearing about the past. Maybe I could take you out for a cup of tea sometime."

"Aye, maybe, hen." As she saw Eilidh to the door, Grace paused with her hand on Eilidh's arm.

"Your mother loved you very much from the day you were born, Eilidh. I can promise you that."

Impulsively, Eilidh gave Grace a quick hug. Then she turned and waved from the entrance door.

As she wandered through the town, she decided to

carry on and walk back to the flat. It was a pleasant, dry day and she wanted to think. That was a strange thing for Grace to say; what mother didn't love her child? It was almost as though there was need for such reassurance. And she suspected again that Grace knew more than she'd said.

She was halfway home when she suddenly remembered that Grace's brother was called Ronnie. Could he be the R in the letter to her mother? Then she shook her head. No, that didn't make sense if he was as slow-witted as Grace had said. It was hardly likely, surely, that he would have penned such sentiments or quoted from Robert Burns. But there was definitely something that Grace wasn't telling her.

Chapter Sixteen

1786

I have moved to another post in this New Year. There is need for a dairymaid at Coilsfield and I now work for Mr Montgomery, as his wife is known to my family in Campbeltown. I am sorry to be away from Mr Hamilton in many ways, for I had settled into a routine and he is a good and fair man. Yet I look for adventure and this change might be good. I still see Meggie and I'm near enough to the village where the dances are held. Best of all, Rob goes there and is known to my new employer.

It is familiar being with the cattle again and reminds me of my old home and of Ma and Pa. They write to me sometimes and Meggie helps me to read their words. They tell me news of my brother, Robert, who now works in the shipyard at the busy town of Greenock. It sounds dirty and crowded, but exciting too, and I hope to see him again one day.

Mr Montgomery is a fair and handsome man, but he's not my Robbie, as I call him in my mind. My only concern is that my employer has become quite liberal in his dealings with me and I sometimes wonder if he thinks I am of loose morals, such as others I could name. One evening, while I am sitting in the parlour of the local inn, Mr Montgomery is in his cups and he seeks me out. He begins making advances to me of an intimate nature. I hold him off as much as I am able, but he is my employer and likely does not expect to be rebuffed, since he is of some standing here. I refuse to sit on his knee but it seems not to matter and, before I know what he intends, he is close beside me and is fumbling with my bodice.

I can hear laughter and talking from the next-door room but know not who is present. When I finally escape from the unwelcome embrace, which he takes with good humour, I walk through to the other room. Imagine my horror when my Robbie is there with his friends. The shameful warmth creeps up my neck and face until I must surely seem guilty of something. I dare not look at him, and flee as his friends make ribald remarks at my expense. To make matters worse, I know that Mr Montgomery will have come through soon after me and they will know we have been together, although not in the way they'll most likely assume.

Rob must surely be done with me now, or perhaps he will think of me as an easy conquest from now on. Either way, I will be ashamed if he should speak to me again. And I have done nothing wrong!

Oh, how I miss my family and my quiet life at home sometimes. The other lassies will laugh at my discomfort if I say anything, and call me stupid for turning away such an important man. But I'll not be used for any man's pleasure and then discarded for another. Meggie sometimes calls me proud. And if it's prideful to want to stay pure for a man who will inspire my lasting devotion, then I am happy to be proud. But I can scarcely think what will become of my blossoming friendship with Robert Burns, such as it was.

Chapter Seventeen

"Tho', by the bye, abroad why will you roam?
Good sense and taste are natives here at home."
(R. Burns: *Prologue*)

Her visit to Grace had left Eilidh more unsettled than ever. Surely her tentative suspicions about Ronnie couldn't be true, and why on earth would Grace hide such a thing if her brother had fathered Eilidh? That would make Grace her aunt, a fact she'd surely want to share. No, it must be coincidence that her brother's name began with the same initial as the signature on the letter, though she was still convinced Grace hadn't told her everything she knew. She'd leave the puzzle for the moment and get on with doing something about permanent accommodation.

Eilidh had arranged to view the flat along the road from Kirsty for an evening during the week, but there was no point in discussing finances with Rory until she made up her mind whether or not to buy. If she didn't get this particular flat, she could find out what else was on the market.

As soon as Kirsty heard about it, there was no stopping her. "Brilliant! I'll come and have a nosy round with you. Wouldn't that be perfect if you were just along the road?"

Eilidh gave in gracefully. She'd rather have had a look round herself but, if she was really interested, she could always go back another evening. She didn't like to remind Kirsty that one of them, or both, might get married eventually and move somewhere else. It would be good having her friend along the road, but the main consideration was that she'd fallen in love with the area and the view.

The young man who owned the flat had agreed to show them around himself. The asking price seemed a fairly large amount, but the agent told them the owner was keen on a quick sale. He turned out to be chatty and open about his reason for moving. He'd inherited the house from his parents but didn't want to settle in this area. Since he'd met someone from further north, he was selling up and moving to be nearer her.

"This is a great place to live, good for walking in either direction, two railway stations within easy distance, good schools, buses, cafés, even the boat to Dunoon." He was eager to point out the advantages.

"She knows. I live along the road!" Kirsty interrupted at one point.

"Oh, right. So that's another good reason to live here then," he said with a smile.

Eilidh had to admire his sales pitch, yet there was an openness about him that made her believe everything he said. Once he'd shown them everything, he left them to have a look by themselves.

The good-sized hall led through a door on the right into a large front room with views to the swing park and across to the pier. The left-hand door opened to a double bedroom with an uninterrupted view of the slipway into the water. Perfect, Eilidh agreed. Along the hall there was a slightly smaller bedroom, a long bathroom, a large airing cupboard, and finally a square kitchen which was large enough to dine in. The back door opened onto a small courtyard where she could imagine a wrought iron table and chairs on sunny days.

When they returned to the front room where the young man waited, Eilidh asked, "Any negatives about the place?" She wanted to see if he was as truthful as he appeared.

"Nope. Neighbours are good people, mostly older and keep to themselves. The attic flat has a younger couple. We all pay into a monthly fund to cover maintenance costs and window cleaning, things like that. There's the odd bit of noise on weekend evenings – people on the way home from local pubs, but you'd get that most places. As you see, you can keep your car in the drive."

"Sounds ideal. Could I think about it and let you know if I want to take it further?"

"Aye, of course. Let me know if you want to have another look. I've had a bit of interest, but with the way the financial world is going at the moment, it's a bit slower than usual. I'm really hoping to move out in the next two months."

They thanked him and walked back to Kirsty's flat, chatting about the pros and cons.

"It looks real promising," Eilidh said. She'd liked the flat at once, especially being able to look out over the river like that. It was bigger than she needed but a spare bedroom was always a good idea. The most attractive thing about it was the fact she could move sooner than expected which would give Kirsty and Sarah back their space.

"I think you'd better speak to Rory next. You need a solicitor to act for you in the sale, and at least you know he'll do the best deal for you," Kirsty suggested.

True. That was the next step. Then she'd go back and see the flat on her own.

When Lewis called, Eilidh told him she'd have to hold off going away for at least another week, if he could manage the dates. She heard his surprise at her news.

"Well, that was fast!"

Was it only surprise? But she didn't have to ask his permission to buy somewhere to live.

"You're staying in these parts then?" This time she understood.

"Looks like it. But I could always let the flat if things change." She didn't want him to think she was staying because of him. Well, not completely.

"Do you want me to see a solicitor with you? I know a few good ones."

Eilidh was silent for a moment, remembering she hadn't told him about Rory.

"It's okay, I have one actually. He's Sarah's boyfriend." She couldn't tell him over the phone that she had a cousin. It needed a bit more explanation than that. Before he could comment, she added, "I've a lot to tell you, but I'd prefer meeting up to chat."

Now she sensed his wariness. What did he think she was going to say?

"That's fine. Can you spare a day to go to Glasgow and we could visit the Mitchell. You'll find their Burns' collection interesting. We could finalise the Ayrshire visit at the same time," he added.

"Sure. I'll make the appointment to see my solicitor then call you back and see if you're free when I am. Look forward to it."

When Eilidh put the phone down, she smiled. It didn't do any harm to keep Lewis guessing. Something was happening between them but she had no intention of rushing into anything serious. She still hadn't forgotten her discomfort at his ex-wife being so prominent in his life. Besides, she wanted to go to the Mitchell and it would help to have someone who was interested. Then she would think about their few days in Ayrshire. For the moment she had a flat to buy.

She was put through to Rory right away.

"Eilidh! Lovely to hear from you." He listened while she explained. "I could see you this afternoon. A client has cancelled, as it happens."

He gave her directions to his office in town and Eilidh guessed things could happen very quickly from then on. She was keen to buy and the young man was desperate to sell.

To use up the time before their meeting, she had a walk along past the flat. Since it was still the school holidays, a few children played in the little park accompanied by a mum or dad. Everything else was still and peaceful, with the same small craft bobbing on the water. In the distance, the boat was getting ready to sail to Dunoon.

She wished she could see inside the flat again right this minute but had to be content with surreptitiously examining the building and garden. It looked in good condition, nothing standing out to make her wary. She'd arrange another viewing after she spoke to Rory.

She walked on round the pier and back. Then, as she was passing the building again on her return, she paused. A woman was coming around the side from the back, pushing a wheelie bin. There was something vaguely familiar about her. As she caught sight of Eilidh, the woman smiled and called good morning. Eilidh suddenly knew who she was. The woman who had sat across from Lewis in the café. His ex-wife.

Of course, she had no idea that Eilidh knew her husband, but it took Eilidh all her time to behave as if she'd never seen her before. Surely she didn't live in this building? Why wouldn't Lewis have mentioned it? Or was that why he'd sounded a bit flummoxed when she told him about the flat.

Aware she had a fixed grin on her face, Eilidh stopped. This was one time she was happy to be direct.

"Morning. I was admiring the garden. I came to see the flat for sale the other evening. My friend lives along the road. Hope you don't mind me asking, but do you live in one of the flats? Only, it would be good to know who the neighbours are, if I decide to go for it."

"Oh, that's good. Ken's hoping to move away soon. No, I don't live here, but my elderly mother does. I'm just putting the bin out for her as it's a little heavy to manoeuvre."

Despite herself, Eilidh warmed to the woman's friendliness. She was slim and blond and obviously took care of her appearance, but was dressed in jeans and a t-shirt, appropriate for the job she was doing.

"Well, good to speak to you. I won't keep you back." Eilidh moved off.

"Good luck with the flat," the woman called. "You'd like it here."

Eilidh didn't look back and, instead of going into Kirsty's building, she walked on towards the bay, thinking about such a coincidence. Kirsty hadn't been kidding when she said everyone seemed to know someone else in the area.

Her initial disquiet had gone, especially when it turned out to be the mother's flat. But why on earth hadn't Lewis mentioned it, when he knew Eilidh was staying just along the road? Or perhaps that was why. If he was hoping to develop his relationship with her, he wouldn't want his ex-wife complicating things any further.

As she walked back to Kirsty's, she wondered if the incident had coloured her enthusiasm for buying that particular flat, then decided she was going to put it out of her head. The only awkwardness would be if Lewis was visiting her and bumped into his ex, or the mother-in-law. She didn't even have the flat yet. Maybe she should find out more from Lewis about his relationship with his ex.

The lawyers' office was part of a modern building in the centre of town and Eilidh was surprised to see they incorporated their own estate agency. Useful.

Rory came to meet her as soon as the receptionist had taken her name. He was genuinely friendly, as though keen to talk to her again, and took her through to a small office near the back. Instead of sitting behind the desk that occupied most of the space, he pulled his chair round beside her.

"You know, I haven't stopped thinking about meeting you like that. Talk about surprise! It's been hard not to mention you to mother." He held up his hand at her expression. "Don't worry, I haven't said a word. But I can't wait until she sees you again."

Eilidh wished she shared his enthusiasm. It was best not to say anything lest she said too much. She smiled instead, as though in agreement.

"So, you're becoming a woman of property, then? It's a good time to buy with the market so slow, especially if you're not having to sell at the same time."

"That's what I guessed. I suppose it would be easy

enough to let it out if I wanted to go back to the States at any time?"

He raised an eyebrow. "Well, I suppose it would. Are you not sure about settling here? You could always rent, you know."

"Yeah, I thought of that but I've kind of fallen in love with Kirsty's area and it seems like a good investment." There was no need to mention Lewis Grant at this stage, when she didn't know yet if he would reckon in her future plans.

Rory nodded. "It's a good idea, if you have the money. Property is always a safe bet and I'm sure the prices will rise again once we're through this bad patch. So, you won't need a loan, or a mortgage?"

She heard his hesitation, as though he was embarrassed at asking. She laughed to put him at ease.

"Don't worry, I should be able to cover the costs. As well as an apartment, I had a share in a second-hand book store which I've sold. To tell you honestly, I'd really like to get the money out of the US bank, the way the economy is going."

"I take it you have a bank account here already?"

"It was one of the first things I did, and they've already transferred some money for me, though not enough yet for this. I have dual nationality so hopefully that won't be a problem."

Rory smiled. "That sounds straightforward enough then. You can check there's no hold-up with the amount you'll need. I assume you're hoping to go ahead with this flat you've seen?" At her nod, he continued, "Then the first step is to get it surveyed. I can organise that. If there are no problems and the seller is agreeable, you might be able to put in an offer for immediate acceptance. I'll take all your details and arrange the surveyor. I know a couple of good ones. You do realise it could all happen fairly quickly?"

"I'll be glad of that, because I'm taking up far too much of Kirsty and Sarah's space. Though they've both been wonderful. Sarah's a lovely girl." She couldn't resist mentioning his bride-to-be.

He looked away for a moment. "I'm a lucky man. I just wish mother would keep her nose out of it." Then he shrugged and looked at her. "But you don't want to hear about my problems. Tell me how you come to be back here."

She filled him in about her mother's death and the need to return to her roots. She didn't know how his mother would take the news of her sister's funeral. Did he know anything about her past? Maybe this wasn't the time or place to ask. Besides, he was around her age, so was hardly likely to know more than she did herself. It didn't sound as though his mother had mentioned them much after they left Scotland from what he'd said on the train.

"Well, I'd best not take up any more of your time, Rory. Thanks for seeing me."

"A pleasure, Eilidh. I'll be in touch once the flat's been surveyed, and I hope to see you again soon."

Kirsty was excited when she heard things had moved on with the flat.

"You know you're welcome here as long as you like, but I'm so glad you'll be just along the road."

"I haven't got it yet," Eilidh reminded her. But she planned to go back and view it herself if possible that evening.

When she phoned to ask, the reply was immediate. The young man sounded anxious and relieved at her interest, and she persuaded Kirsty she needed to look around by herself this time.

As soon as the owner opened the door to her, he left her to wander around. It felt like home already. He had fairly good taste in décor, though she'd gradually change it to suit her own. Her imagination ran ahead of her as she visualised how she could arrange each room. Then there was the view. For her, this was the biggest selling point. She had hoped to find somewhere with a view and this was better than anything, as she liked the whole area. She wasn't blinkered enough to think there might not be one or two minor problems she couldn't see; wasn't there always in old property? But the surveyor would check for any major flaws.

When she had finally seen enough, the owner said, "Oh, I've had a call from a surveyor, he's arranged to come tomorrow."

"That was quick." Eilidh smiled at him, then decided to take a chance on being direct again. "If you don't mind me asking, would you accept a quick offer? You know, without waiting for a closing date and that kind of thing?" Kirsty had told her that closing dates and people bidding anonymously against each other was the normal way of doing things in Scotland.

"If I get what the flat is worth, then I'll be happy to accept a decent offer."

She nodded, unwilling to make any kind of deal – even a verbal one – until she'd had the survey results and spoken to Rory again.

"Well, how'd it go? Are you buying it?" Kirsty was like a little girl who couldn't wait for Christmas.

"It looks positive. I need to wait for the survey result then take it from there."

"That's fantastic! Oh, Lewis phoned while you

were out. He asked if you can phone him back."

Eilidh wondered why he had called so soon, especially when she'd said she would call him. She dialled his number.

"Hi, Eilidh, just wanted to check if you might be free to go up to Glasgow tomorrow. I'm tied up the rest of the week. Don't worry if it's too short notice."

She had a moment's indecision about whether she should be that available, but was surprised at how much she looked forward to seeing him again. So much for keeping him guessing. Besides, it would give Rory time to look over the survey. And she was looking forward to getting more information about Highland Mary if possible. With meeting Rory and thinking about her past, she was even more interested in the possibility of some ancient connection with Mary Campbell.

"I think I can do that," she finally replied. "Are we going by train?"

"No, I'll take the car. Pick you up about 9.30am? The morning rush should be over by then."

"That's fine. I'll look out for you."

Eilidh wondered when Lewis would tell her that his mother-in-law lived along the road. Wait until she told him she was likely moving in to the same building. It would be very interesting to see his reaction.

Chapter Eighteen

1786

Jean Armour is being sent away! Meggie tells me she heard it in the village. It seems Jean's father is having none of her friendship with Robert Burns after all, and forbids her to see him. They say she protests that he loves her and they will be wed, but they won't believe it will happen. Or they don't think him good enough for their daughter and have no intention of letting it take place. Whatever the truth may be, she is going away to Paisley.

Rob is often seen around the village and no doubt there are many lasses keen to mend his broken heart, if such be the case. Some say he does truly love his Jean and has written many poems to her. Others say his love will easily transfer to another should she not return to him. Of course, I want to believe she is not the love of his whole life. If he is out and about with his friends then he cannot be pining at his farm. Or so I persuade myself.

Then, I see him one Sunday again in the Kirk. It is the first time since my terrible embarrassment in the inn and I cannot think he will notice me now. But he smiles across as soon as he spies me. I don't look down, or blush too much, but return his gaze. At the end of the service, we happen to reach the front door at the same time and he allows me to pass in front of him. Once outside, we shake hands with the minister in turn and I wonder if I should continue walking, or pause so he might catch me up. I have no wish to appear too forward for, truth to tell, I am blushing inside.

But before I need decide, he calls to me.

"Good day, Mistress Campbell. Do you mind if I walk a little of the way with you?"

"Not at all, sir." I try not to sound too eager in case he should find me too bold and think I make eyes at any young lad. Besides, I think that a man likes to have some challenge. Soon we are past the people still talking, and we turn in the direction of my place of work which is a little distance away.

"How are you? Well settled at Montgomery's place, I trust, Mary?" he asks, as though unsure what to talk of. I'd not thought him to be at a loss for words, and the use of my given name makes me answer truthfully.

"I like my work and home well enough, thank you," and I wonder how on earth to convey my meaning, "but… I have no great wish to be in my master's company otherwise."

"Ah, I know his liking for a pretty maid as I do myself, in all honesty." It is all he says, but he smiles as if to reassure me he understands. "We are easy prey for a lassie's charms, Mary. Though I'll not take what is not freely offered."

How can I mistake his meaning? I cannot look at him and I walk with my eyes to the ground as though to be careful of the path. Then I ask a question.

"And are you well, sir?" I cannot ask right out about Jean Armour but I hope he might give some sign of having put her from mind.

"Well enough, thank you, especially for having seen your lovely face again."

So, he is not pining after Jean too much, or he is

hiding it well. Or perhaps he cannot help being of a flirtatious nature, since he is so admired by many. I should think him vain except for the fact he writes such far-seeing words, if what I hear is true.

I smile at his flattery and do not reply. I'd rather find out more about his poetry.

"And you still write such good verse, I hope, sir?" I cannot bring myself to call him by his name.

He stops and looks at me strangely, as though surprised I should talk of it.

"All the time, when work allows, Mary. I have hopes of having a collection published one day. It's hard work keeping the farm going and it's something to dream of. And what are your dreams, if I may ask, Mary Campbell?"

I shrug, for truly I have not thought of many things. "To be happy and to be loved, I think."

He laughs. "The one does not necessarily go with the other." His words sound bitter. Or perhaps I imagine that he speaks of Jean Armour.

Then he looks me full in the eyes. "But I should not think you'll have trouble in being loved."

I do not realise we are so close as we walk, but now his nearness makes the fine hairs on my arms stand on end. And before I can answer or guess at his intentions, he reaches over and kisses my parted lips.

My reaction is swift. I step back in confusion.

"Forgive me, Mistress Campbell, but you look so sweet with your concerned blue eyes. I forget myself."

My heart has returned to its normal beat, but I cannot look at him. His kiss will linger in my mind far longer than the quick touch on my lips. But I don't want his teasing, or his dalliance with a willing maid, or even his attempts at banishing another from his mind. The only way I will allow myself to be his, is if he is ever fully mine. And that day has not yet come, if ever it might.

"I must go now, sir," I say, without looking at him. I walk away, my body on fire.

Chapter Nineteen

"For there, wi' my lassie, the lang day I rove,
While o'er us unheeded flee the swift hours o' love."
(R. Burns: *Yon Wild Mossy Mountains*)

It was a dull day, but with a muggy warmth, perfect for going to the city. Eilidh pulled on smart jeans, a long-sleeved shirt and comfortable shoes. Reference libraries didn't tend to be full of over-dressed people. She had no idea what they would be doing afterwards, if anything, so slung her waterproof jacket over her shoulder.

He was on time. Tardiness didn't bother her that much and she wasn't the best time-keeper in the world herself, but it was gratifying to see he hadn't kept her waiting.

When she reached the car, he held the door open as before.

"How are you?" he said, after greeting her with a perfunctory peck on the cheek then sliding behind the wheel.

"Great. I'm enjoying getting to know the area properly after all this time."

He didn't speak again until he'd manoeuvred onto the main road towards Greenock and she didn't disturb his concentration. She never chattered in cars, preferring to watch the scenery go by and let the driver set the level of conversation they were comfortable with. If she was driving, she preferred to listen to music or let the other person do the talking if they felt the need.

She wondered if he had read her mind when he suddenly broke the silence to compliment her on not talking too much.

"I'm not really the chattering type," she replied briefly.

"I remember, from the plane," he said, smiling as though at memory of their meeting. "Now that we're nearly on the motorway, feel free to talk if you want. If I don't answer, or suddenly keep quiet, you'll know I'm concentrating on the road. There are some idiots who pass for drivers these days."

"Here, there and everywhere," she said, raising another smile from him.

She had seen most of this scenery when arriving at Kirsty's but was interested again in the way the road had changed around Port Glasgow, especially now they could drive beside the coast. In no time, they were on the motorway heading towards Paisley and beyond.

"Oh, my goodness!" She slipped down her seat as a huge jet soared over their heads, taking off from the airport. "That was even worse than the last time, when Kirsty was driving me down the motorway."

Lewis laughed at her reaction. "It's a bit freaky, isn't it? You get used to it, though some still take me by surprise."

Eilidh sat up properly in her seat again, feeling foolish. Then she remembered he'd seen her clutching the arms of her air seat, scared of take-off. This was no worse and she relaxed when he didn't say any more about it.

"So, tell me a bit about the flat you're buying."

She told him as much as she knew and he nodded to show he heard. She wasn't going to mention his ex-wife. He didn't ask any questions and she tailed off eventually, letting him concentrate on the next bit of motorway as it went into four lanes before cutting back to three again.

"There's something I didn't tell you, Eilidh, partly because I didn't think it would ever matter." He drove into the middle lane so he could keep a steady speed. "You're not going to believe this, but that's where my ex mother-in-law lives." He risked a quick glance at her face.

Should she tell him she knew that already, or pretend this was news? Was she a good enough actress? Then she saw he was frowning at her lack of response.

"You're not going to believe *this*." She had to be honest. "I saw your ex-wife the other day when I was walking past the flat. I recognised her from the day I saw you in the café. I even spoke to her."

He was silent and she was worried she might have distracted him too much from driving. Maybe she should have waited.

"You're right, I don't believe it!" he said eventually. Then he laughed, taking her by surprise. "Well I'm glad I came clean or you'd suspect I was hiding her from you." Then he glanced briefly at her again. "You know what I love about you, Eilidh? You're the most honest, open woman I've come across in a very long time."

Now she was silent. What a thing to say, when they were both glued to their respective car seats, unable even to look into each other's eyes. She made light of it in an exaggerated accent.

"Well, shucks. Thank you, sir. You can remind me of that later when we're in no danger of bumping the car in front."

He laughed and kept his eyes on the road.

The traffic was steady all the way to the Kingston Bridge and Lewis turned off for Charing Cross. "Might be difficult to get parked, but we'll see."

In the end he managed to find a place a few streets away. "Even better, it's not on a meter so we don't need to feed it endless coins or worry about a time limit."

As they walked towards the Mitchell Library, Eilidh's first impression was mixed. Undeniably impressive, the huge bronze dome that distinguished it gave the structure a classical look and she was amazed at the size of the building.

"That's Minerva on top," Lewis saw her looking upwards. "Or Athena, if you prefer the Greek; goddess of wisdom and the arts. Appropriate, eh? The old part was built in the late eighteen hundreds, but you'll see there's a more modern addition that's used for most of the books. Did you know this is the largest reference library in Europe?"

Eilidh was suitably impressed. What a place for a book lover!

The door they entered didn't seem like a main entrance, being quite narrow and a bit gloomy. It led them upstairs to where a man leant at a desk as though waiting for someone to ask directions. He smiled pleasantly and Lewis led her round to the left, obviously knowing where to go. They walked through two long, silent corridors with black and white tiles on the floor, until they eventually went through a door and down some stairs.

"There we are. This is the hub of the place and, as you can see, it's a bit more modern!" He laughed as though guessing her thoughts. "The café is the newest addition."

As well as a large eating area with tables and chairs, this bright, open area had the feel of an Internet café with rows of computers in front of which people of various ages sought information. Just above the café area, several curved desks were manned by staff offering additional information. Huge windows allowed plenty of light and Eilidh couldn't believe this was part of the same old building they'd walked through.

"The Burns Room is upstairs. I've made an appointment to see it as they won't let us loose on our own."

As they walked up more stairs, Eilidh realised he must have made the appointment before she confirmed today was suitable. He'd obviously been hedging his bets. No doubt he could have cancelled it if she hadn't been able to manage.

She liked old buildings and could imagine spending many hours here exploring some of the thousands of reference books available. But today she was here for a specific purpose.

A middle-aged woman waited to greet them with genuine pleasure. She obviously enjoyed showing people around, or Lewis had charmed her at once, especially when he explained his friend had returned home from America. From her understanding nod, Eilidh presumed she was used to these kinds of enquiry.

When she showed them the impressive memorabilia connected to Burns, and the several translations of his work, Eilidh noticed the most recent was one in Polish – no doubt useful for the influx of immigrants to the city.

The sheer amount of information made it difficult to find any specific references to Highland Mary that she hadn't already read. Then the woman brought out an obviously old book and invited them to sit down at one of the tables. Eilidh read the gold print on the damaged spine: *The Life of Robert Burns* by James Currie, M.D. It wasn't in the best condition and Eilidh understood the need for supervision.

"You can have a look through this, if you like," the woman offered. "But you'll need to be gentle with the pages. We'll have to get it rebound eventually."

Eilidh carefully opened the hard green cover. She was used to dealing with all kinds of second-hand books and it still caused some excitement when opening an old edition. This one was published in 1838. Then she noticed the smaller print. It was originally published in 1800 in connection with the Works of Burns, only four years after the poet's death. The next few lines pleased her even more as she read: 'Considerably extended by additional particulars, many of which were never before made public.'

"Wow, this is really interesting," she said, smiling across at Lewis who returned her grin.

Carefully leafing through the old yellowing pages with the tiny writing, she was thankful for good eyesight. She paused at a section which mentioned Mary Campbell. It reiterated a brief account of the story she knew already about her meeting with Burns on the Banks of Ayr in the May of 1786. The first part of the book was taken up with all kinds of details about Burns, including excerpts of letters, from the poet and some of his contemporaries. Then she reached the next section, "The Poetical Works of Robert Burns", to find an interesting inscription:

"To which are now added, Notes, Illustrating Historical, Personal, and Local Allusions."

As Eilidh skimmed through it, she found a treasure trove of anecdotes about Burns, his poetry and the context in which many of them were written. She came across *The Highland Lassie* poem and, although disappointed not to find any notes attached, it did confirm it was supposedly written to Mary Campbell. Next, she found the song *Highland Mary*, which contained the same kind of information she already knew about Mary Campbell and Burns.

The words were full of pathos and romantic love for someone who was forever out of reach, and she could understand how the story of their brief love had touched people down through the ages. The remainder of the book was filled with General Correspondence and if she had time enough, and was allowed unlimited access to it, she could happily have spent weeks reading through every single item.

She eventually closed the book with a sigh. "That was so interesting. Thank you very much." She smiled at the woman who had discreetly allowed them space to read.

"You're very welcome. You can come back again, you know. Something I should point out is that some of these earlier biographies may well contain some inaccuracies. For example, the most recent scholarly biography 'corrects' much that was assumed before. It might be useful for you to consult a more up-to-date version."

"That's good to know, thanks. I'll do that."

As they walked downstairs, she turned to Lewis. "Thanks so much for bringing me here, and for your patience. It's an inspiring place. And that book! Even if we find more updated findings, or opinions, that was really special. Imagine first being written at the turn of the nineteenth century."

"I'm glad it was a success. You might not have got much new information, but at least it seems to confirm what you already know."

"It was a bit of a tragic story, the Burns and Highland Mary part, no wonder it has been romanticised," Eilidh mused. "Maybe I should check out a more up-to-date copy."

"And women like a good romance, don't they?" Lewis asked with a grin.

"Only women? How sad." She smiled as they looked at each other in mutual appreciation. Maybe this was the right time to tell him about her search for her father, but he suddenly threw her by his next words.

"Have you been to Loch Lomond yet?" he asked.

"No. I can't even remember being there as a child, though I suppose I must have seen it at some time."

"Why don't we go now, after we grab a sandwich?"

Eilidh stared at him. "What, now? This afternoon?"

"Why not? Unless you have to get back right away. Look, the sun's come out and it would be good to get away from the city."

Why not indeed? She hadn't realised he was so impulsive but it wasn't a bad thing, and it added a touch of spontaneity to their day together. Besides, she looked forward to seeing the romantic loch immortalised in Scottish song, especially with Lewis Grant by her side.

It didn't take long to get back down the motorway.

"I'm taking you the way you would go from the Greenock end. Over the Erskine Bridge; there are good views from there."

Eilidh craned to the left and right as they crossed the highest point of the bridge. To the right, a hotel sat almost beside the river, but she liked the view to her left best stretching all the way up the River Clyde. A pretty, small village and church nestled along a stretch of the shore. Ahead of her the bright green of the hills climbed towards the sky.

Soon they reached a dual carriageway that eventually took them to the main roundabout for Loch Lomond.

"We'll go along to Luss first. You've got to see our famous little village where a television soap was once set. Then we can come back to this part."

Eilidh was content to let him decide where to stop. Already she could see why people talked of Loch Lomond with such respect, noting the heights and depths all the way along the coast road. It was all the more tantalising because she only caught glimpses of the water now and then – but always the looming mountains of every shade of green, from pale to dark, with occasional flashes of soft purple from the heather.

"It's quite stunning, isn't it?" Eilidh whispered.

"Wait until you see it close up," Lewis said.

Several miles on, he drove into a large car park, already half full of vehicles. "It's a short walk to the village as they're strict about the cars allowed in. You'll soon see why!"

Intrigued, Eilidh walked beside him as they reached the village street, then she caught his meaning. The single main street was the prettiest she'd ever seen. Apart from a couple of tartan-decked tourist shops, cute small stone cottages lined each side. An abundance of flowers and plants from gardens and flower boxes spilled their fragrance and colours all around. The street gently sloped down a short walk to a harbour, from where she could see the loch in all its splendour. Another small tourist shop sat tucked around the corner beside the pier.

"Wow, this is gorgeous." Eilidh immediately wanted to live there, in one of those fairy-tale cottages, close to the loch.

"Knew you'd like it." Lewis laughed at her reaction. "Shall we walk along the pier?" He took her hand.

She was content to keep her hand in his. This was the kind of place where people should have someone to enjoy the scenery with. The sun had decided to hang around for a while and some adventurous children were testing the water temperature by splashing each other. Further along the shore several ducks paddled along, and even further off a couple of swans were making their way towards the pier.

"Fancy an ice-cream?" Lewis suddenly asked.

Eilidh realised the tiny hut-like shop on the pier was serving ices. "I'd love a 99. I haven't had one of those for years."

While Lewis bought the cones, Eilidh admired the length of the loch, surrounded by the kind of landscape of hills and mountains she wanted to capture on canvas.

"Here we are. Paper napkins, too, which I'm sure we'll need."

As Eilidh licked a huge dollop of ice cream from the cone, she agreed; it was already beginning to melt. The chocolate flake sticking out the top suddenly reminded her of a day far off in another time when she had last enjoyed such a treat.

They stopped to watch the ducks and Eilidh tried to catch the memory. She had been with her mother, and a small boy had stood beside her. Rory? A man too, she was almost sure, but she couldn't see him properly. He seemed to be standing further away with her mother, and they were talking quietly together. But she knew they weren't happy.

Then the memory escaped as ice cream started dripping onto her hand.

"Whoops. I was miles away there." She looked up to see that Lewis had been watching her, and she quickly licked up some of the mess and finished the flake and cone.

Her hands felt sticky and the paper napkin hardly made a difference. She licked her fingers like a child and Lewis laughed.

"You've missed a bit," he said, leaning towards her, gently wiping a spot of ice cream from the side of her mouth.

For a heartbeat moment, she had thought he was going to lick it off. Embarrassed at her thoughts, and even more at her feelings, she turned to look back up the street of dinky houses.

They wandered over to the tiny shop at the corner and a blast of tartan tourism hit them as they entered. A man stood with a welcoming plate of shortbread, broken into bite-size pieces. Songs like *Loch Lomond* and *Ye Banks and Braes* accompanied them on their browse through shelves of woollen kilts, tartan rugs, tablet, and woven shawls, while displays of fridge magnets, tartan cardboard bags of Edinburgh rock and "Find your clan" posters vied for purchase.

Eilidh succumbed to a small slab of tablet, as she hadn't tasted the sweet, teeth-rotting confection for such a long time. She would eke it out and make it last for a few days, if she could resist the sugar-rush temptation. They both laughed in appreciation at the

Scottishness of it all, aware it was just the kind of treasure many tourists hoped to find.

Wandering back to the car, happy in the late afternoon sun, Eilidh was so glad they had made this impromptu visit to the fairy-tale village on the shores of the loch.

"We could have dinner at Duck Bay," Lewis suggested as they reached the car.

"Well, who could resist such a great sounding place? But only if we share the cost. I mean it," she added, as he was about to protest. It wasn't exactly a proper date and she hoped it wasn't too posh a place as she was only wearing her shirt and jeans, albeit her smart pair. Since Lewis didn't mention dress, she assumed it would be fine. After all, it was a holiday area, most likely full of tourists and walkers.

He shrugged in acquiescence as they got into the car. "Whatever you say, if it means the difference between getting dinner or not!"

She smiled at his reluctant acceptance of sharing costs. He obviously lived by old-fashioned rules. Relaxing into the passenger seat, she watched the mountains go by as they drove back the way they'd come. Some miles on, he pulled off the main road, onto a narrower one running beside the loch. A few yards along, she could see the low-level hotel set right beside the still water.

Although there was a distinct Scottish air about the place, it was low-key and tasteful and Eilidh was delighted with the art-deco lighting and fittings. Lewis asked for a table at the window and, since it was still fairly early for dinner, they were shown to the perfect spot overlooking the loch. As they scanned through the menu, Eilidh reflected on their ease with each other. She could get used to these outings with Lewis Grant.

She couldn't resist the haggis starter and he did the same.

"You do know we hunt the haggis in the hills, don't you?" Lewis said with a wink.

"Of course you do. And I bet you're wearing the kilt at the time. Don't forget, I was born in this country!"

They laughed and chose their main course.

"Wine?" Lewis asked. "I'd better not as I don't want to get stopped on the way home."

"I'd love a glass, if that's possible. Red, please, the house one will do. I know it probably breaks every rule with salmon, but I only drink red."

"Not a problem. Anything goes." He ordered a glass for her, and a lime and soda for himself.

"This is lovely," she said. "It's such a tranquil place, don't you think?"

For answer, he stretched over and lightly took her hand. "I'm really pleased you like it, as it's always been a favourite of mine and I haven't been for too long. Thanks for agreeing at such short notice."

She was going to answer him glibly but his expression held her back. There was such sincerity in his voice and his usual humorous teasing was missing for the moment.

"I wish I was a bit more smartly dressed for the occasion, but thank you for bringing me here."

The waiter interrupted them before things got too serious, and Lewis relaxed into his usual manner.

"So, tell me why you're really in Scotland." He took her aback with the question, and for a moment she wondered if Kirsty had said anything. But she'd hardly had a chance and her friend wouldn't do that. He probably only wanted to know more about her decision to leave the States, yet what better chance to tell him some more about her quest? A few more diners had arrived, but none sat so close to care what others were saying. The mood was right for confidences.

"Actually, I do have an ulterior motive, if you're really interested. I wasn't sure when I'd share it with you, but this seems as good a time as any." She noticed his slight wariness and smiled. "You know I mentioned Rory, the solicitor who's acting for me in buying the flat?" He nodded. "Well, turns out he's my cousin. How's that for coincidence? I'll bet loads of Americans dream of that happening when they visit the old country." She tried to keep it light, but she'd have to tell him the rest.

Before he had a chance to respond, the waiter brought their starters.

"Well, that's not what I expected to hear. I assume you knew you had a cousin here?"

"Ah, therein lies the story. I'll tell you when we finish the first course," she promised, between mouthfuls.

Once their plates were cleared, she told him about her quest for her father and the estrangement from her aunt and uncle. "It's not much to tell, but it is something I need to know one way or the other."

"I can imagine," Lewis said. "Our roots are part of who we are, although I think we become our own person in the end."

She smiled at his reassurance. As they ate their main course, she told him what she had heard and read about the Holy Loch. He was able to add some more detail since he'd learned a lot about it over the years.

"It was a fraught time when the US Navy was

154

foisted upon that small quiet town. The demonstrations and the protests are legendary. But the Americans integrated well in the end. And we weren't annihilated by a nuclear missile, as many had feared. Not yet anyway!"

By the time they reached coffee, it was nearly dusk and the restaurant was almost completely full. The subdued lights gave the room a romantic ambience, with the shimmering loch on the other side of the windows.

"I'll get the bill and you can settle up with me later, if you still insist. Or, even better, you can take me out next time."

"We'll see," she said, not wanting to spoil the moment by arguing about payment.

"I think we should have a walk after that, don't you?" he asked.

"Absolutely, but can I get my jacket from the car first, please. It's getting a bit chilly now." She shivered slightly, aware it wasn't only with cold.

He had a light jacket, too and once he locked the car he wrapped Eilidh's jacket around her shoulders while she put her arms inside, fastening it up. Then they turned towards the narrow path that allowed them to walk by the side of the loch while protected from the cars on the road. Just how narrow it was became obvious as soon as they'd gone beyond the hotel entrance; there was barely enough space for two abreast.

"We'll need to squeeze up," Lewis said softly and suited the action to his words by drawing her closer beside him.

"Good enough reason," she answered. "We don't want either of us to end up under a car." She snuggled into his side, relaxing against the strong arm that held her.

"Oh, I love that cottage. "Eilidh stopped suddenly as she saw the long, low building on the other side of the road. "It's a B&B, how delightful. Look, even in the dull light I can see how pretty the garden is. Doesn't it look quaint?"

"If you like it that much, we'll need to try it sometime," he whispered.

It was a subtle implication and Eilidh stopped to look up at him. He smiled into her eyes and even in the half-light she saw herself reflected back.

"The beautiful windows of the soul," he murmured. His kiss this time was long and lingering, and Eilidh responded as though they were cocooned in their own small world on a narrow path beside the silent loch. No traffic passed by, and anyone else in the area was obviously still in the restaurant, or had gone home. The only sound was the gentle hush of the water over shingle and the occasional quack of a far-off duck.

As she finally drew breath and turned in his arms to look out over the loch, she noticed the moon now completed the scene. It wasn't full, but even so it cast a silver glow over the outline of the now mist-covered mountains, finally spreading onto the still water.

Later, she would remember this as the moment when she knew this man was the person she had waited for all her life, and that one day he would complete her more fully than she'd ever known.

"I suppose we'd better be getting back," Lewis stirred, breaking her lovely fantasy.

Eilidh stood up straighter and took his offered hand as they walked back to the car. It wasn't quite the way she'd imagined the moment would end, but there was still something in his manner that suggested he didn't want to take things too fast, as though an inner distraction pulled him away from any deeper commitment.

She mentally shrugged. She had other things to sort out before questioning her burgeoning relationship with Lewis Grant.

They both sat deep in thought as he drove back to Gourock and Eilidh was happy to listen to the muted easy classics on the radio. She didn't feel like talking and Lewis had to concentrate in the darkening night.

"You know I really like you, Eilidh, don't you?" He finally broke the silence as they neared Kirsty's.

"I think I gathered that, thanks. And I really like you too. Is there a but?"

He laughed. "Not really a 'but'; it's just that I have some things to sort out."

"Me, too." She gave him a 'cop-out' card.

He didn't say anything for a moment and she had an awful feeling he was taking it.

"Why don't you get your flat purchase finalised and then we can have that trip to Ayrshire late next week? We'll have more time to talk there, especially if we stay a couple of nights." He glanced briefly at her before looking at the road again.

There seemed to be some kind of promise in his words and she nodded. "That sounds like a perfect idea."

Once she had the keys to the flat, she'd have little time to do anything but get it ready for moving into, though it hadn't needed much in the way of refitting. It made sense to have their few days away together first.

The street was silent when he drew up at Kirsty's.

"Thanks so much for today, Lewis. It was wonderful."

He leaned across and kissed her on the mouth, but briefly, then opened his door and went round to open hers.

"It was a pleasure," he said, as she stood beside him. "I'll phone you to see what's happening with the flat. Good luck with it." He kissed her cheek, as though indicating he took nothing for granted.

Eilidh was aware he watched as she walked down the path, then he got back into the car and drove away. She climbed slowly up the iron steps to the flat, trying not to make a sound, reflecting on the last couple of hours. Being completely honest with herself, she was a tiny bit disappointed that their closeness at the loch had seemed to dissipate by the time they'd got back here. But she looked forward to their Ayrshire trip. That would be the real test for any chance they had of a future together.

As she reached the door, she stopped. She could hear voices and laughter inside. Maybe Rory had come to see Sarah. Then, as she knocked the door and the sounds moved towards her, she heard another male voice, with a less Scottish accent.

The door opened and she knew at once who was visiting.

"Eilidh, my love, it's been a long, long time."

And she allowed herself to be engulfed in a strong, warm hug. Jamie had come home.

Chapter Twenty

1786

My lips still burn with his fleeting kiss since that day. I know I am foolish to have any hope of his complete adoration, for he is always in demand. I see him at a dance one evening, when the jigs are fast to the music that thrums through the barn. I do not lack for a partner myself but he is constantly in my view and makes me miss a step or two as I try to watch him.

Then, my heart beats wildly as he suddenly approaches me in between dances. A few of the other lasses smile coquettishly in his direction but he looks at me.

"Mistress Campbell, may I partner you in the next dance?"

And to the astonishment of some, I stand up and take his outstretched hand.

The music starts at once and we join the circle of other dancers for a reel. He knows how I love to dance, and my feet twirl and skip to the fiddle while my heart leaps in response to the touch of his fingers whenever we come together. The smile never leaves my face and his attention is all on me for this short time. As we spin together to the final notes, I wish we could spin away into the night, away from all these people.

At the end of the dance we stand for a moment facing each other, as though alone in the barn. Then the moment passes as the noisy chatter and jostling around us recalls him to his surroundings. As one of his friends claps him on the back and moves on, Rob breaks contact with me and bows.

"Thank you, Mary Campbell. You always dance very well." Then he leads me back to the side and leaves me with a smile.

"Well, ye're a dark one then, Mary Campbell, so ye are. I didnae think you knew the poet that well!" Meggie has a worried expression in her kind eyes. I notice a few of the other lassies beside us give me knowing looks, as though they suspect I am no better than I should be, to be so familiar with a man of his reputation.

"But I had only one dance with him," I protest to Meggie and all others who listen. "He has been a gentleman whenever we have met."

Meggie sniffs and one or two others snort like pigs. But I do not defend myself, or him, any further. Let them think what they may, or be jealous if they wish, they will not spoil this evening and they cannot take that dance away from me.

I hope he might ask me again during the remainder of the evening but he seems to avoid me, and I wonder if he's being careful of my good name. He does not single out anyone in particular, preferring to have a different partner for each dance.

It is another memory to lock away in my heart and examine when I become lonely for my family. As I walk back to my room with Meggie, I ignore her warning mutters about such a rapscallion and imagine instead I walk with him, his arm around my shoulder. I daringly wonder if I will ever feel the touch of his fingers on my body. The thought fills me with shame but also with such excitement as I have never experienced. I think this must be love, of a kind more intense than that for my family. But how will I live without being loved so well in return?

Chapter Twenty-One

"We darena weel say't, though we ken wha's to blame,
There'll never be peace till Jamie comes hame."
(R. Burns: *There'll never be Peace*)

After the furore and excitement of seeing each other after so many years, it was very late when Jamie finally left. Eilidh couldn't believe the difference in him. He'd always been a bit on the small side, with messy blond hair and a permanent grin on his face. Mischievous, the teachers had called him.

But the tall, good-looking man who opened the door to her was more than a grown-up version of the same. This person was confident and assured, with enough charm to make every woman feel special. Eilidh felt it immediately. And, although the cheeky grin was still there, the overall effect of greenish eyes, tousled dark blond hair and a reddish beard, gave him the air of a traveller or explorer, which he was in a way.

His welcome hug was genuine and Eilidh caught a speculative gleam in Kirsty's eye as she smilingly watched the reunion. Then she pushed the thought away, sure she had imagined it. Jamie was staying with his elderly father in Greenock and eventually left with a promise to see them all early the next evening.

As he was leaving, he took Eilidh's hand. "It really is so good to see you again." And he pulled her against him in another warm hug.

She watched him go down the steps and he turned

to wave at the bottom. Kirsty seemed a bit off-hand and Eilidh wondered if it was because her friend had a history with Jamie. Yet they had seemed comfortable enough in each other's company.

"Bet that was a surprise," Kirsty said.

"He's quite a character, isn't he?" Sarah said before Eilidh answered.

"Oh, he's that right enough. Very sure of himself." This time Kirsty's tone was slightly bitter.

"It was a lovely surprise to see him like that," Eilidh answered quickly. "He's changed a lot since school."

"He obviously remembers how much he liked you," Kirsty said sharply.

Eilidh ignored that. What on earth was wrong with her friend? She talked a bit about their school days, before remembering Sarah might feel left out since she wasn't from the area.

"How was your day, Eilidh?" Sarah eventually asked.

"We ended up at Loch Lomond." She laughed at their surprise.

"Very romantic," Kirsty said, looking a bit brighter.

"Mm, it was actually." Both pairs of eyes regarded her with raised eyebrows.

"Well, I'd better let you two get off to sleep," Eilidh yawned to show she was happy to go off to bed herself.

"We're both on late shift tomorrow so we can have a bit of a lie-in," Kirsty said, but Eilidh could see she didn't want to chat any longer.

Once they had all settled themselves for what was left of the night, Eilidh took out her mother's letter and read it again, wondering who had loved her so much. Then she opened the little book of Burns' poems and read a few verses, trying to understand the effect this eighteenth-century man must have had on that long-ago Mary Campbell. She had seemingly agreed to run off with him to Jamaica before their destiny went separate ways. Had her mother run away *from* loving someone?

The two Marys occupied her thoughts for a while. Then she switched off the light and pulled aside the curtains to look out over the river. The same almost-full moon that had shone on her and Lewis earlier in the evening now cast its glow across the water from Gourock to Dunoon. Was that where the answer lay as far as her mother's story was concerned? Back in the past, when giddy young girls became excited at the prospect of dancing with their American heroes? Hopes of having her questions finally answered was complicated by an aunt who may not want to see her.

As she closed the curtains and lay down, it was a while before sleep came. And it wasn't only Lewis who claimed her thoughts. She had a strong feeling that Jamie's arrival had upset the equilibrium.

Rory called the next day with some news.

"I have the surveyor's report, Eilidh, and everything's fine. No major problems with the property. Have you decided if you want to go for it?"

She paused a moment, but knew the decision had already been made.

"That's really good news, Rory, thank you. Yes, I definitely want to buy. Can you put in an offer for me, please?" She gave him the maximum amount she was prepared to offer.

"I'll make it a condition that it must be accepted or refused by five o'clock in two days' time, if you're agreeable. If he's as anxious to sell as you said, then I don't foresee any problems. I'll get in touch with you when I hear anything."

After a few more pleasantries, Eilidh put the phone down. She'd done it. No turning back now. She was going to be a woman of property: Scottish property. She had never done anything so impulsive in her life, yet it felt absolutely right. With Kirsty and Sarah along the road, she wouldn't be totally alone, and she'd get to know other people soon enough. That included Lewis's ex-wife and ex-mother-in-law, if necessary. Besides, she still needed to find some kind of work where she'd no doubt meet other people.

Since Kirsty and Sarah had gone on shift, Eilidh decided to try contacting Grace again, maybe take her out for tea. The phone rang out for a while and she was about to give up when a breathless voice answered.

"Hello? Who's calling, please?"

Eilidh knew at once that something had happened. The youngish female voice was distracted and anxious.

"I'm sorry to bother you. I was looking for Grace. I saw her last week and I promised to call her."

"Friend? Family?" The voice rapped out.

"Well, I suppose, friend. She was my mother's friend."

The voice softened. "I'm sorry, Grace was taken into hospital yesterday. She's in intensive care at the Royal, seems to be her heart. I'm trying to arrange care for her brother."

"Oh, I'm so sorry to hear that. I'll let you get on."

Eilidh sat with the phone in her hand for some time. Poor Grace. She had only just met her and now she might never get to speak to her again. She was glad to have found her. Then an awful thought struck her. What if it was anything to do with the memories she'd forced on the woman that day? How silly. The west coast was one of the worst areas in the country for heart disease, it had probably been threatening for years.

For some reason she was more distressed than she should have been at the thought of Grace lying in intensive care. Apart from her natural compassion for another human being, she supposed it was partly with coming so soon after her mother's death. Perhaps Kirsty or Sarah might be able to find out more about Grace's condition. She'd ask them later, see if there was any possibility that she might be allowed in to see her.

Meanwhile, she had to do something to take her mind off it, and what better way than to pay another visit to the Watt Library to read more about Highland Mary and Burns?

She took her notes with her, as it was a good place to sit and write them up. The idea of using all the research to write a novel set around the period of Mary Campbell's life was growing on her. She had never tried anything like that before, but with her passion for reading and love of all things literary, it might be a way forward. She could begin it at least, as she was already researching the period. And she wasn't tied down yet, a small voice insisted. She had no children and so far, no job. Once she had bought the flat and been to Ayrshire for more information, there would be nothing to stop her.

Or maybe she could set one around the time of the US Navy at the Holy Loch? No, she couldn't even think of that possibility until she found out about her mother's past. Highland Mary was the best option since she had become so hooked on her story.

It was the middle of the afternoon when Eilidh reached the library and she was pleased to find it empty apart from the librarian. Perfect for reading and writing. She hadn't written up the notes from last time so that was the first thing to do. The old *Greenock Advertiser* and then the oldest copies of the *Greenock Telegraph* had provided some insight into both Mary Campbell and Burns.

She had always known that Mary lived near Dunoon, of course, and that she was buried in Greenock. The in-between part was open to question, with scant information compared to that about Burns himself, but Eilidh could form some kind of picture from what she'd gleaned from the newspapers, biographies of Burns, and from all that had been written about the couple. It seemed obvious to some that his great love had been Jean Armour, his eventual wife and mother of his legitimate children. But many of the poems suggested it was Mary Campbell, his Highland Lassie, who had left the most lasting impression on his heart.

There was the supposed "marriage" on the Banks of Ayr when the couple had exchanged vows and Bibles over the running water. Were they married in law? Then their parting soon after. It was thought they had been going to sail away together to make a new life in Jamaica and, again, poems suggested the truth of it. Yet the tale had ended in tragedy, in this town of Greenock. And even that was open to speculation. Was it disease, or childbirth, or both that had caused Mary's death? Many sources said it was her innocence and purity that had captured Burns' love; others hinted that she'd borne his child at the end.

Eilidh could feel the mounting excitement at the prospect of trying to turn these bare facts – or not even that in some cases – into something resembling novel-length fiction.

First, she could start with what she had gleaned already. In the same way she had treated the bare facts of her own earlier life in her US apartment all those weeks ago, she started to make a list about Mary Campbell and Burns to get some idea of the timescale and basic events. Then she made it into a sort of précis of their story, or as much of it as she could glean from her reading.

Mary, possibly named Margaret originally, Campbell is born in Dunoon and her father pilots a boat up and down the River Clyde. Mary is sent to Ayrshire to work as a nursemaid, then a dairymaid, where she eventually comes across Robert Burns, the poet-farmer. Burns is going to marry Jean Armour, who bears his twins, but her parents move her away from the area, forbidding the marriage. Burns and Mary Campbell gradually fall in love. In 1786, they plight their troth over a brook on the Banks of Ayr, which he writes about in a poem. Burns asks Mary to go with him to Jamaica as his farm is failing and he hasn't made his name as a poet. Mary seemingly agrees, as Burns refers to it in another poem. They are due to set sail from Greenock, where they would meet up, and Mary travels to some relatives first.

Mary finally arrives in Greenock to find her brother very ill and she nurses him. Mary becomes ill herself. Meanwhile, Burns has his first book of poems accepted, and delays his journey to Greenock. They are destined never to meet again, and Burns immortalises his sorrow and his Highland Mary in verse and song.

Eilidh looked over what she'd written. Had Burns truly loved Mary Campbell? It wasn't much to go on, yet it had the air of a tragic love story, albeit with a hero as famous for his way with women as he was for his writing. At least it would be a good use of her time while trying to sort out her own life and finding out the truth about her mother and father.

Glancing at her watch, she was surprised to find it was almost closing time. Since the rain had stayed away, she walked back towards Gourock, along past the large Victorian houses of the West End. As a child, she used to wonder what it was like to live in one of those big houses. They still looked huge, though many were now separated into flats like those on the Esplanade.

It reminded her she hadn't been back to see her own childhood home yet. Kirsty had already told her the whole area had changed under new development, like much of Greenock, but at least she could still walk around the streets where she and her mother had once lived with her granny. She'd keep that for another day.

The phone was ringing when she got into the flat. It was Rory.

"Great news, Eilidh! The seller has accepted your offer right away. All you have to do now is to sign the relevant papers and organise insurance. If you come and see me tomorrow, late morning, we could have a quick lunch together and catch up a bit."

"Wow, so quickly! That's perfect. Thanks, Rory. I look forward to it."

Eilidh sat back after replacing the receiver, suddenly filled with all sorts of doubts. What had she done? Was it not all a bit quick, deciding to buy property here? Then she calmed down. It was a good investment, or it would be when the property market picked up again. Now she had somewhere of her own to stay, and it didn't necessarily tie her here forever. She still had friends in the US who would be only too happy to have a Scottish holiday flat to visit. Yes, all things considered, it was the best thing she could have done. Where Lewis figured in all this, she had no idea at the moment. But that would work itself out one way or the other.

Eilidh soon had the papers signed, relieved Rory could sort everything else out for her, including arranging transfer of the funds from her bank. It was more straightforward because she didn't have a mortgage, but insurance was essential, both for the building and the contents, once she had any.

"I thought we'd go round the corner for soup and a sandwich, if that's okay with you?"

"Sure, I'd like that. It's good of you to give up your time like this."

"Believe me, it's a pleasure to be out of the office and actually eating a civilised lunch!"

It was beginning to get busy in the café-restaurant, but they found a table at the side where they could talk.

"So, a woman of property, eh? Bet you didn't think that would happen so soon after arriving in the old country?"

"You know, I hadn't thought beyond the first few days, until Kirsty met me at the airport and took charge! And very grateful I was, too," she hastened to add.

They chatted about all the changes in the area for a while. Eilidh wanted to ask about the past but wasn't sure how to begin. Then Rory helped her out.

"It must have been a bit of an upheaval for you being taken all the way to America. Do you know why your mother went there?"

Did she imagine it, or was there an edge to his question?

"You know, I've tried to find an answer to that for years. I guessed it was because granny died and there was nothing to keep Mum here." She decided to be honest. "Then, as I grew up I wondered if a man had taken her all the way across the Atlantic. But I don't remember anyone in particular. There's a US Navy officer in a photo, taken at Dunoon when the ships were at the Holy Loch, and I thought he might be my father but now I don't think so." It was enough for now. This wasn't the time or place to tell him about the letter and inscription.

"I didn't realise you'd never known your father." He reached across and touched her hand. "But then, I don't know much about anything. Mother and father never talked about you or your mum, either before or after you'd gone, which is a bit strange since they were sisters. Mind you, mother is not the easiest person to get on with."

Eilidh asked after the wedding preparations and was pleased to hear they were back on track once Rory had put his foot down about the church. Sarah had the final say, he'd insisted.

As they were sipping their tea, Rory leaned across the table and lowered his voice. "Eilidh, before you meet my parents, there's something you should know. My father is in the early stages of Alzheimer's. That's partly why mother is a bit more frazzled than usual. He might not be very easy to speak to, and I didn't want you to think it was anything to do with you. He repeats himself a lot and is a bit confused."

"Oh, Rory, that's awful! Your poor father, and mother." The news had softened her a little towards her aunt. It must be one of the worst things to deal with, watching your husband gradually become a stranger and becoming a stranger to him in return.

"If it's still okay, I'll get in touch with you when I get back from Ayrshire and maybe I could see them, if it won't be too much of a shock," she suggested.

"Once you call me, I'll warn my mother in advance. Anyway, enough depressing talk. Why are you off to Ayrshire?"

Eilidh told him about her fascination for the story of Highland Mary and Robert Burns and how she wanted to see all the places where Mary had lived, since she was a Campbell, too. She also told him about Lewis, or as much as she could tell him.

"Good for you, he sounds quite suitable." Rory laughed, as though it mattered what he thought. "I can understand your interest in Mary Campbell since she's buried here in Greenock and shares your mother's name. I like Burns myself, and so does my father and many others. I'm not so sure about my mother, she's never shown much interest. And, of course, our town here is supposed to have the Burns' Mother Club, the first one in the world, although one or two other towns might dispute it!"

They ended lunch on a positive note and Eilidh was struck again by how well they got on, considering they'd hardly met throughout their lives. She hoped they'd remain firm friends from now on, if his mother didn't spoil things. He kissed her cheek as they parted and told her he'd keep her up-to-date with details about the flat. She promised to have a house warming party when she'd finally taken possession.

She was on her way along the town, glancing in

one or two shops, when she heard her name called. Thinking for a minute that Rory had caught her up because he'd forgotten something, she turned around to find Jamie instead.

"Well, this is lucky, Eilidh. Are you off somewhere in particular, or can I walk beside you?"

She laughed. Jamie had always made her feel light-hearted and he hadn't changed in that way.

"I'm actually on my way back to the flat. I thought I'd walk along the Esplanade."

"Good idea. Mind if I join you? I've just been buying a new card for the digital camera and I want to try it out."

If the camera slung around his neck was digital then it was a very good one; it looked a lot more professional than any she'd seen. She was already talked out and had wanted to walk by herself to think, but Jamie was hard to resist and she hadn't seen him for so long she could hardly refuse his company now.

They walked in companionable silence until they passed by all the shops and had to cross the busy road. Before she realised what he intended, Jamie grabbed her hand and rushed them both across the street before the next car came along. Eilidh was laughing like a child as they stopped on the other pavement. Obviously, time and age hadn't dampened his spirits.

As they reached the quiet of the Esplanade, they slowed their pace to talk and admire the scenery.

"So, how's life been treating you all these years?" Jamie stopped to gaze out over the rail towards the distant hills.

"Oh, you know, ups and downs. America was fun when I was in my teens and twenties but something was calling me back here, and when my mother died it seemed the right time to come."

"Or someone," Jamie said, turning to look at her, and she had a moment's panic he was coming on to her when they'd only just met again. Then he looked away to the sea again. "Anyone special left behind? I'm surprised you're not married."

"Well thanks. I could say the same about you. I did think I'd met someone special a while back, but we didn't survive my need to come here." She saw him nod. "But…" She let it hang between them and he turned to look at her again.

"But?"

"Don't laugh, but I think I may have met someone special on the plane coming over. We've been seeing each other since I got here. It's too early to tell where it's going, or if, but it feels right. Though I think there might be a few complications."

Jamie smiled ruefully. "I'm in no position to laugh. I've known Kirsty was the right one for me since high school, but I keep messing it up. He's a lucky guy, Eilidh, whoever attracted your attention. You're even more beautiful now." Then he stopped. "Stand right there, Eilidh, against the rail with the sweep of hills in the background. That's perfect." He brought his camera up to his eye and after a few moments of adjusting, he pressed the shutter.

So, he wasn't coming on to her, but was merely appreciating seeing her again. It was obvious that Kirsty filled his mind. "You're a bit of a flirt, Jamie Kilpatrick, but thank you for boosting my self-esteem! If it's any consolation, Kirsty hasn't forgotten you either. Sounds like you two need to have some serious time together."

They started walking again and Eilidh broke the silence by telling him about her long-lost cousin.

"I know Rory slightly," he said. "We belonged to the same gym for a while and, of course, he's engaged to Kirsty's friend, Sarah. You know, you do have a look of each other, but I never knew he was your cousin. Wonder why Kirsty didn't mention it."

"Because she didn't know either. Rory and I hardly saw each other when we were children. You can imagine our surprise when we met through Kirsty and Sarah. I'm going to go introduce myself to his parents in a week or two, as they'll most likely not even know me."

"Aren't families funny sometimes? I've been travelling the world so much I hardly ever see my young brother or his family. My fault, of course. They don't live here and it's a question of sending Christmas presents to their two kids, or dropping in if I'm in Scotland. It's only my father here now, but he's healthy enough and has loads of cronies to hang around with, including the odd woman friend to console him. My mother married again and lives in Spain, so I only see her when I'm over that way."

Eilidh wondered if Jamie was as nonchalant as he liked to appear. He had a faintly unsettled air about him and she had a suspicion his wandering days were beginning to pall. Maybe he had come back to try again with Kirsty.

They had almost reached the end of the promenade when Jamie spoke again. "Do me a favour, Eilidh. Can you pretend to fancy me a bit whenever we're around Kirsty? I don't know how else to get her attention again, and I'm sure she's the only person I'll ever want to be with."

Eilidh laughed at such a thought, then saw he was serious. "You do realise that could completely backfire on you and convince Kirsty you have no interest in her?"

"I'll tone it down, but if she thinks you're interested in me it might make her jealous enough to realise what she's missing."

"Or make her never speak to me again! And what about Lewis, the guy I was telling you about? I can't jeopardise anything we might have at this stage."

"I know, I know, it's the most stupid idea I've ever had. But you know Kirsty – she'll never believe I'm ready to settle down. And she might think she's over me. If she sees we're getting on too well, it might make her think again."

Eilidh was silent while she digested his theory. In one way, she could understand his warped reasoning. She had thought of something else she wouldn't mention to Jamie. She was already a little concerned about the exact relationship between Lewis Grant and his ex-wife. Maybe a little bit of flirting with another man might make him think, too. Though she'd have to make sure he met Jamie. But she couldn't do it to Kirsty, not even as a pretence, especially not after all her kindness.

She smiled at her old friend. "I can't stop you flirting with me, Jamie, but I'm not going to risk Kirsty thinking anything's really going on between us. I will not flirt with you or suggest I'm enjoying it!"

"Okay, Eilidh, my love. I'll pay you a bit more attention and you can pretend you don't like it." He gave her a smacker of a kiss on the cheek, making Eilidh wonder what on earth Kirsty would make of his behaviour. Hopefully not make her jump to the wrong conclusion.

Chapter Twenty-Two

1786

It seems all the warnings about my Robbie have some substance to them. I have heard murmurings that Jean Armour is with child; his child. I do not want to think of such a possibility. All my hopes of any future for us are shown for what they are; naught but the dreams of a foolish young maid.

Meggie tells me kindly, for she knows my feelings run deep. She also says that, in his defence, he wanted to marry the lass and, but for her father, they would be husband and wife already and the child not labelled a bastard.

Part of me knows he is an honourable man in his way, if a little too fond of a finely-turned ankle and sparkling eyes. I listen to him reciting another of his poems one evening, and his feelings for his fellow man are well known. Even his observations on the tiniest of God's creatures are immortalised in verse.

I would forget him, but wherever we go, he is amongst the young men. Besides, there is none else who can take his place in my affections. If I am not to know love with him, then I will die a maid still. My mother would tell me that love can come after the wedding of two people. But how can a maid get to that point if she has no love for her man? If what they say is true about the wedding night, I want my senses to be so on fire that I give myself freely and completely. These thoughts make me blush in my own company. It stands to reason that Jean Armour has already known this pleasure with my Robbie. Yet, she has been forced away from the union that would give them respectability in the eyes of the Kirk. I cannot understand why her parents would not rather have her wed to the father of her bairn.

I ask Meggie.

"Well, ye see, they were hoping for someone with prospects for their daughter. Robert Burns is a farmer, but the farm's nae sae good at the minute and he's mair interested in thae wee verses he writes. Ah suppose they're feart he might no' look after her, the way he flirts wi' the other lasses."

"But if he's the father of her bairn, surely he would be a good husband to her?"

"Aye, weel, that's what we'd all like tae think, lass."

I ponder on it for days and try to imagine myself in Jean Armour's position. Would Ma and Pa hurry me away in such a condition? Perhaps. But how can I know since we've never talked of such matters. Ma scarcely told me to expect my monthly bleeds before they happened one day. It's as well she mentioned them in time, else I would have thought my life was draining away through some disease. I know of course how the animals mate and birth, but can hardly imagine that it can compare.

It is foolish to continue thinking of such mysteries for there is but one man I want to teach me of them. Then, we meet by accident on the edge of the village while I carry my milk pails. He stops at once and sweeps me a bow as usual.

"Mary Campbell! The very maid I have been thinking of these past days. May I carry your burden for a while?"

How can I resist such attention? I allow him to don the contraption across his shoulders for a short time, and we laugh at the picture he makes. I confess all thoughts of Jean Armour and any bairn have fled, for his eyes are looking into mine and his smile is for me alone. He is practised in flattery and flirting, yet I know deep in my soul that he is sincere in his talks with me, especially when he speaks of the difficulties of farming and the condition of the land. I am flattered how he understands that I know something of farmland from my childhood home.

This is when my heart is fully captured, not by fine words of false love and promises, but by his speaking to me as an equal, as a young woman who understands his fears, and his hopes and dreams. This is when it truly begins.

Chapter Twenty-Three

"Cold, alter'd friendship's cruel part,
To poison fortune's ruthless dart."
(R. Burns: *Forlorn, My Love, No Comfort Near*)

Next day, Eilidh remembered to ask about the possibility of seeing Grace in the hospital. The nonsense with Jamie had put it out of her head, but she still felt a bit guilty that she had brought up so many memories for the woman, especially if there were some she'd rather forget.

"Mm, if she's still in the ITC unit they won't let you in if you're not family. But maybe Sarah or I can find out if she's been moved," Kirsty explained.

It would have to do. Now she had to tell Kirsty she was seeing Jamie later, as though it didn't matter that much.

"Oh, I hope you don't mind, Kirsty, but Jamie's offered to give me a guided tour of our old haunts today. I haven't seen where I used to live and all that kind of thing. He's picking me up in a couple of hours."

"Great. Why should I mind? He was your friend, too. Have you told him about Lewis? You know what Jamie's like, charm the wings off a butterfly."

Eilidh heard the surprise her friend tried to conceal, and smiled. Maybe Jamie wasn't so far off the mark after all.

"Of course, I mentioned him," Eilidh said, hoping that would reassure Kirsty. Then she changed the subject. "Oh, I forgot to tell you and Sarah – I've got the flat! I signed the papers yesterday."

"What! How could you forget something so important? I suppose you had too much distraction yesterday. That's brilliant news, Eilidh. Imagine, we'll be neighbours soon."

She must stop thinking Kirsty was less enthusiastic than previously. Surely she couldn't be jealous that Jamie was spending the day with her?

"I think I'll try and see it again. Think about what it needs. Rory's going to confirm the actual entry date. I trust him so much I didn't take it all in when I was signing."

"Well, you go and have a good day with Jamie. I'd better get ready for work. I'll find out about Grace if I can."

For some reason, Eilidh felt the lack of a job more keenly. She couldn't swan around indefinitely, having coffee and lunches. Starting to write would give her something to do but it wouldn't put money in the bank, at least not while it was being written, and no guarantees afterwards. No, she needed to find some kind of income now she had the expense of the flat, but had no idea what that might be yet. She'd give herself until after the Ayrshire trip and the move, then start looking seriously.

Jamie arrived just as Kirsty was leaving.

"Good day, my two lovelies," he said, giving them both a hug and a kiss on the cheek. "I see you're off to work, Kirsty, m'love, while we go out to play." He put his arm around Eilidh's shoulder as though to emphasise their togetherness.

"Someone's got to earn the money."

It was said lightly and with a brief smile, but Eilidh felt uncomfortable. She well knew that Kirsty had a sting in her tail at times, like the scorpion whose sign she was born under, and her remark seemed loaded with implied criticism. But she also knew her friend hadn't grudged having her there one single bit, so it must be the sight of Jamie with his arm round Eilidh's shoulders that prompted the jibe. She moved slightly away from him.

No more was said and they all left the flat at the same time – Kirsty going off towards the hospital, while Eilidh got in Jamie's old banger of a car.

"Dad gives it a home while I'm away," he said, as though getting his apologies about the car in first. "She's served me fine over the years and I've kind of grown attached, you know? Like with a comfortable old pair of slippers. Not that I wear any slippers, you understand."

She laughed at the idea of him wearing anything so ordinary and elderly. "At least you have some kind of wheels. That's what I'll need, and a job once I get the flat ready."

The easy camaraderie between them belied the twenty plus years between meetings, mainly due to Jamie's easy-going banter. He was used to travelling and probably made friends or acquaintances wherever he went.

"I thought we'd leave the car at the Well Park and have a walk about all the old places, as far as possible. Best way to see the changes, although it's still recognisable."

The park hadn't changed much except for the fewer number of mothers with prams and children playing than she remembered. Perhaps so many people had cars now that they bypassed the local park. She was pleased to see the wishing well still stood near the back gate, and imagined it was something modern children still enjoyed.

They wandered up towards the high street where the Co-operative and the chemist were her strongest memory. The big department store, where she used to get her school uniform and sensible shoes, had long gone. There was still a chemist shop but she doubted if it would be the same one. As they neared Trafalgar Street where she'd lived with her mother and granny, she couldn't believe the difference. The whole upper street had gone, to be replaced by modern flats, and it was difficult to see how it had once looked.

"Quite a change, eh?" Jamie seemed as sad as she did. "But that's the way things go, never the same when you return years later. There is one place you'll still like, though, but we'll need to go by car."

Intrigued, Eilidh tried to wheedle the destination from him, but he refused to say a word. Once back in the car, he drove up to where the old sugar factories used to provide one of the main sources of jobs and economy for the town, along with the shipbuilding. As he indicated left across from a primary school, she remembered.

"Loch Thom!" she said, as he manoeuvred the car up the winding road, past the golf course, and onto the narrower hillside road that wound through the countryside.

"Knew you'd guess as soon as we turned off. Remember we used to walk along the cut to the loch, when we were young and fit and stayed out all day during the summer?"

"How could I forget? I wanted to live out here, away from the busy town." She laughed at the idea, because much as she still loved the country, she now preferred the open spaces of the seaside as a place to live.

As Jamie drove, Eilidh felt again that long-ago sense of calm that the wild, empty moorland-like scenery used to give her; not a single person or car in sight, the only signs of life the sheep grazing peacefully on their own private hillside. They cruised past an elevated dam, then on beyond a solitary farmhouse where a few scratching hens ignored them. Jamie turned the car to the right and now they were driving along the side of the small loch itself, only inches from the shore. It provided a real shot of nostalgia and she was grateful to Jamie for bringing her here.

Eventually, they reached a nearly empty car park and Eilidh was surprised to see a large, custom-made building which seemed to be an information centre.

"That's new," she said. "I only vaguely remember a small hut before."

"At least this is a positive change, as lots of the school kids come here for projects and so on. There's a good display of some of the things you can see around the cut. We can have a look when we get back."

Eilidh nodded, then realised what he'd said. "Back from where?"

"The nature trail, of course. We have to walk round that."

She might have known he'd have something planned and, once again, she was relieved she'd put on her comfortable shoes. And she was keen to see the trail again. Once they'd gone through a small gate, they set off along a narrow path.

"We'll go this way round and come out at the top over there, "Jamie suggested.

The pleasant walk took them alongside the main flowing stream on their left and a large wall of foliage on their right, bordered by a thin, trickling brook along the bottom edge. Eilidh stopped now and then to look more closely at the wild flowers, delighted with the birdsong that provided a background accompaniment. Perfect. She had a sudden picture of this lovely walk with Lewis by her side, then felt a bit churlish when she had such a charming, entertaining companion in Jamie. Yet it was reassuring that she could appreciate her different feelings for these two men. Lewis Grant had not only invaded her heart, but had taken up residence.

"This is where it gets interesting," Jamie suddenly warned her as they got to the end of the flat, grassy path.

She saw what he meant as they climbed over a short stile then began to pick their way down an ever-descending, uneven pathway to the depths of the river bed. It was fun but tricky in parts, and they half walked, half ran at times. Then, at the bottom, they reached level ground again, where the running stream navigated over rocks and boulders. No wonder they had to keep on the narrow path to avoid ending up in the middle of the burn. A small bridge allowed them to cross to the other side and they stood and watched the rushing water beneath them. They might well have been in some fantasy world of their own.

"Beautiful, isn't it, kid?" Jamie broke their silence.

"Absolutely." She didn't want to ruin it with conversation, and was glad when he seemed to understand.

They moved off at the same time and gradually came to a flat grassy area where she could see hundreds of steps ahead.

"Sorry, this is where it gets tough." Jamie laughed

at her expression. "But you look fit enough." It was the only personal remark he'd made and Eilidh took it in its literal meaning. Fortunately, she was fit enough still, in a healthy outdoor kind of way.

"Well, here goes. Don't leave me behind too far," she joked, as she had no intention of lagging if she could avoid it. A light breeze saved the day from being too clammy or, worse, full of the notorious midges that reduced grown men and women to tears and covered in itchy bites.

The steps were wide apart and gradually inclined which wasn't quite as bad as walking up an ordinary flight of stairs, but Eilidh still felt the pull on muscles that had enjoyed a recent holiday. She was relieved when they reached the top, and the rest of the walk looked as flat as any promenade but with the added softness of grass underfoot. The ever-present stream now ran alongside them on their right and it brought back sudden memories of the three of them – Eilidh, Kirsty and Jamie – on endless summer days of freedom from adult supervision.

The path still twisted around the embankment where rebellious sheep had found fresh grazing, while their companions stuck to the hillside above them. Now they had resumed normal breathing, they chatted about their childhood for a while. It was a good place for confidences and soon Eilidh told Jamie about her search for a father.

"I never thought that bothered you at school, except when idiots like Billy Mac thought they were clever using swear words."

"It didn't really. Then I was told my father had died and I stopped wondering about him. It was a good excuse to invent one I would have liked, and eventually I assumed he was American, from the navy based at Dunoon." She hesitated at sharing too much, but this was Jamie, one of her oldest friends. She told him about the letter.

"Well, I can imagine your reaction. I'd want to know who this mystery man was, too. Let me know if I can help in any way."

"Thanks, Jamie. I've a feeling my aunt holds the answer but I've no idea if she'll want to tell me anything. I can but try."

When they reached the end of the path, Eilidh was happy to have a look inside the information centre. She was tired but invigorated, and marvelled that this was available so near to a busy town.

On the way back, Jamie chose the alternative route that took them through narrow hillside roads until they emerged just beyond the IBM plant. Rather than go straight back to Greenock, he headed towards the coast road by Lunderston Bay.

"Oh, I was here with Kirsty one day – this is another favourite place. You know lots of people would love to live in an area like this, with both the countryside and sea on their doorstep." She was even more pleased to think she'd soon be a resident herself.

"It's not a bad place to live at all," Jamie agreed. "There are problem areas like in any big town, but the area still has that great community spirit and there's a lot of regeneration going on, like at the waterfront. I'd not like to settle anywhere else."

Eilidh was even more convinced Jamie had come home to stay this time.

There was one place she still hadn't been: Greenock Cemetery, to see Highland Mary's grave. But she wanted to go there with Lewis, so that he might understand how she had felt when seeing it as a child. It was an odd thought but felt right that he should be with her when she finally returned to it. At thought of him, she realised how much she was looking forward to spending more time with him, especially away on their own for a couple of days.

"What would you like to do now?" Jamie asked, as he drove towards Kirsty's.

"Honestly? I'd love to go into town and have a browse. I could do with a couple of things, including a good notebook and some pens. But don't feel you have to amuse me all day, I'm happy to go on my own," she assured him.

"Aw, now you've hurt my feelings," Jamie pulled a sad face. Then he laughed. "Tell you what. Why don't I drive you there, we can have a quick sandwich, cause I'm starving even if you're not, then I'll leave you to enjoy your girly shopping."

"You do know you're a really nice guy, don't you?" Eilidh asked, making him smile. "That sounds perfect. I'll get the bus back to the flat later."

Coincidentally, they ended up in the same café-restaurant she'd been to with Rory. She fleetingly wondered what the waitress was thinking if she remembered her from the other day, now that she was accompanied by a different man, and one who didn't blend in with the surroundings quite as easily. Jamie was determined to give the young girl who served them the full blast of his charm. And she soaked it all up. Kirsty was a lucky woman, if they could overcome their problems and realise how right they were for each other.

They were still laughing together when they paid the bill. Eilidh was turned towards Jamie when they stepped outside into the street again. She didn't see Lewis Grant and his ex-wife until she nearly stood on his foot.

"Oops, excuse me…" she started to say, then she realised who it was. She had no idea how to behave.

"Hello, Eilidh, this is a surprise." He glanced briefly at Jamie. Then he turned to his companion. "Jan, meet Eilidh; Eilidh meet Jan." No formal introductions or explanations, and she had to admire his cool.

"Hello," both women said, and smiled at each other. Eilidh didn't notice any recognition from the other woman, and supposed she didn't equate her with the person she'd seen fleetingly on the road outside the flat. Again, she was struck by how pleasant the woman was and she couldn't help wondering why they had split up. Then she remembered Jamie.

"Sorry. This is my childhood friend, Jamie. Jamie, this is Lewis." That was enough. "Anyway, we'd better get on and let you go in for your lunch. Nice seeing you both." Eilidh put her arm through Jamie's and walked away without a backward glance. Let him puzzle that one out.

"Bravo, *ma petite*," Jamie whispered. "Pity Kirsty hadn't seen us, too!"

He'd summed the situation up at once and she was grateful he kept it light. She didn't know what to make of all these meetings between Lewis and his so-called ex-wife. Surely they didn't still have divorce issues to settle? How could she go away with someone who wasn't being completely open with her? Well, let him wonder how Jamie figured in her life.

Eilidh passed the rest of the afternoon wandering around the few clothes shops in town. There was nowhere near the choice of stores as in Glasgow, but a few of the well-known names were easier to browse through for being smaller. She eventually found a perfect, soft, heather-coloured cardigan that would serve as a jacket in the cooler evenings, and she couldn't resist some new undies in Marks and Spencer.

After she had said goodbye to Jamie, she half wondered if she might bump into Lewis and Jan again, but there was no sign of them. She noticed several charity shops and one in particular had a large book collection. Entering, she saw at once how popular this section was in comparison to the rest of the wares. It gave her an idea; she had part-owned a second-hand bookshop in the US, after all. Maybe that was a possibility here, although she couldn't compete with the ridiculously low prices these were going for. And there were several other low-cost ways of buying books on the Internet. Perhaps it wasn't such a good idea.

She had a browse through the titles on offer, scanning over an abundance of novels of every kind from cheap romance to crime and literary, and a few good non-fiction and reference books. One of the latter caught her eye: a large coffee table-type book on the Clyde steamers through the years, and she flicked through it to find several references to places like Rothesay and Dunoon. She bought it, along with a paperback of one of her favourite writers. The two women serving were friendly and it seemed a happy place to work.

When she was leaving, she saw a notice in the window asking for volunteers on various mornings and afternoons, and she paused. That might be a way into some kind of work, albeit voluntary, while she decided what to do with the rest of her life. But she'd wait until she moved and settled her problems a bit first.

When she finally got back to the flat, she was surprised to find Lewis sitting in his car across the road. What on earth was he doing there, since he had no idea when she'd be home? Was he spying on her, watching to see if she was still with Jamie? A myriad of thoughts flashed through her head in those few minutes.

He saw her at once and got out of the car.

"I was dropping Jan off at her mother's and thought I'd wait a while, to see if you happened to be home. Can I talk to you, Eilidh?"

Something was certainly bothering him. He seemed more serious than usual and she felt a huge surge of disappointment. So, this was it; she had read more into their whirlwind friendship than he had, and he was going back to his wife.

"Sure, come on up and I'll make us some coffee." She kept her voice even, hoping she wasn't showing any of her thoughts. Just get through this with dignity, she told herself.

When she closed the door behind them and offered him a seat in the living room, he stood looking at her.

"Eilidh, I want to explain something to you. I think I owe you that before we think of going away for a few days together… if you still want to go."

Not what she imagined he'd say. He obviously was hoping they could still go away together. They sat down on the sofa, coffee forgotten.

"I want to tell you about Jan. I realised today what you must be thinking, seeing us together like that, and I don't want any secrets or suspicion between us."

She waited, intrigued now.

"We've been divorced for a year, though we'd not

been getting on as a couple for ages before that. Married too young and paths diverging eventually; you know the kind of thing. Wanting different things out of life."

Eilidh nodded, as she didn't know what to say.

"Anyway, she met someone else and we were both relieved we could call it a day. Honestly, Eilidh, I've had no resentment, or jealousy, or wishing I had her back. Any love we had died a long time ago, but we were able to stay friends. That's why we've been meeting a few times recently, because she still regards me as a friend and she needed to share something with me."

"You don't have to explain anything to me, Lewis." She touched his hand.

"Yes, I do, Eilidh, because I need you to know there is nothing between my ex-wife and me." He took a deep breath. "Jan had to see a specialist recently. She thought she might have breast cancer and was meeting me to tell me the result. She's fine. It was just a very bad scare."

A sudden rush of memory caught Eilidh unawares, and she felt tears brush her eyelashes. Blinking quickly before he saw them, she squeezed his hand. "I'm sorry, Lewis, that's a hard thing to go through, waiting for results. Of course, she needed some support."

"Thanks, Eilidh, I knew you'd understand and I'm sorry, it must have reminded you of your mother. It was a shock, when it's someone you spent a large part of your life with, especially when it wasn't an acrimonious divorce. I know her fiancé; he's a nice guy and must be so relieved. As is her mother."

Eilidh could understand that. "This kind of thing affects everyone close, and some people don't know

192

how to handle it. I'm glad you were there for her." She pushed away the niggling little doubt about such a close friendship with his ex.

He moved closer on the sofa and pulled her into his arms. "Thanks for being you." It was all he said but it moved her deeply.

Before she threatened to blub all over him, she pulled back and stood up. "Right, some caffeine is called for."

"Definitely." By unspoken consent, they moved away from the subject and Lewis took the mugs through while she got the coffee.

"So, do you still want to go down to Ayrshire?" he asked. "We could head down on Monday, maybe stay until Wednesday, if that gives you enough time to do everything."

"That sounds great. I don't want to be away too long anyway, since I'm getting the flat soon. Oh, and I have something to explain to you."

He had seen her with Jamie earlier in the day and surely must be curious, even if he wasn't going to admit it.

"The guy I was with earlier, Jamie? Old school friend, world traveller, and hoping that one day soon Kirsty will realise they're meant to be together." She filled him in about her friend's previous disastrous engagement and his mad idea about trying to make Kirsty jealous.

"I'm glad I don't have competition. You were beginning to make me jealous, too." It was said with his lop-sided grin, and she felt a tingle in her spine that was completely new to her.

They were still talking and laughing together when the front door opened and Kirsty came in.

"Oh, sorry, I didn't mean to interrupt!"

"No, don't worry, we're just having a coffee. I'm sorry, Kirsty, you wouldn't be expecting us here. Anyway, I'm glad you've come in so I can introduce you two properly. Kirsty, meet Lewis. Lewis, this is my best friend in the world."

Eilidh watched as they summed each other up and shook hands.

"Well, she leaves with one handsome man and returns with another! Some people have all the luck." The edge was taken off the remark by Kirsty's laugh, but Eilidh wasn't deceived. Her outing with Jamie still rankled.

"It's a pleasure to finally meet you, Kirsty. And thanks for getting us together."

She saw Kirsty actually blush, as Lewis smiled right into her eyes.

"If you'll excuse me, I'll get going now." He turned towards Eilidh. "Shall I make the arrangements for Monday?"

"If you don't mind. You know the kind of information I want and you'll probably know the best locations."

"I'll give you a call before then and I'll pick you up on Monday morning. Bye, Kirsty, see you soon."

When Eilidh returned from closing the door, Kirsty didn't wait long.

"Wowee, he's even better looking when he's smiling at you with those blue eyes. You lucky girl. Maybe I should have kept him for myself."

Eilidh laughed, knowing full well that Kirsty had her heart set on Jamie, even if her friend didn't quite realise it herself. She told her about their proposed trip to Ayrshire the following week.

"And you're staying two nights?" The question was loaded and accompanied by a very knowing look.

"Better pack some nice undies."

"It's not like that," she protested.

Kirsty raised an eyebrow and didn't say another word. But it made Eilidh wonder what exactly was expected of her – and what did she expect in return? Then she remembered the effect Lewis had on her so far and allowed a delicious little shiver of anticipation to play on her back. She had a couple of days to prepare.

Sarah mentioned Grace the following day.

"She's still very unwell, but out of intensive care. I've checked with the ward sister that you can visit for a few moments." Sarah gave her the ward number and visiting times. "It's a hike to the hospital but you can get a bus that'll take you up the hill."

Since it was a Saturday afternoon, the car park and entrance were congested, with more children around than she had expected. A few people stood outside the main doors to have a cigarette, since smoking was banned from all indoor places. The building itself stood tall and dull against the sky but indoors it was bright and welcoming.

Taking the lift to the relevant floor, Eilidh wandered through the double doors of the ward until she found a nurse. She was waved in the direction of a pleasant room with four beds, each occupied by a female patient of various ages. Eilidh was surprised at the lack of visitors since visiting hour had already been going for fifteen minutes.

Grace was lying against the plumped-up pillows with her eyes half-closed. She watched for a while, wondering if she should leave, then the woman's eyes opened and she saw Eilidh standing there. Hoping she was doing the right thing, Eilidh took a step forward and proffered the magazine she had bought downstairs.

"Hi, Grace, I hope you don't mind that I've come to see you."

Several cards stood on the locker, as well as a jug of water, a bottle of juice, and some chocolates. Visitors obviously had called at some point.

"Hello, Eilidh, that's kind of you to visit, hen." The voice sounded weak and Grace hardly stirred. A monitor stood beside the bed, obviously attached to the patient somewhere.

"I'm not allowed to stay long, but I wanted to make sure you were okay."

"Och, I think it's just a wee scare. Ronnie took it worse than me. He's no' able to look after himself so well and they've had to put him in a respite home, so he's no' very happy. But I'll be out soon if I behave." Grace smiled.

Eilidh stroked the woman's hand for a moment. "I'm sorry Mum isn't here to see you instead of me."

Grace closed her eyes for a moment. "Aye, well, that would have been grand but I'm glad to see you anyway. You've picked the right day to visit, for my cronies are all away on a bus trip today." She was breathless after saying so much, and Eilidh was conscious of not tiring her out any more. There was a good reason for limited visiting time.

"Maybe I should let you sleep, Grace. I'll get into trouble if I tire you out."

"It's the lying here that's tiring, lass. I'm used to being out and about. I can't even be bothered to read at the moment."

"Is there anything I can get you from the shop before I go?"

"No, I'm fine, but thanks for asking. You've your

mother's kind heart, hen."

Eilidh smiled and stood up. The woman's voice was still slightly breathless and she was afraid she'd make her worse.

"Eilidh…" Grace lifted her hand and beckoned her closer. "Ask your Aunt Elizabeth about the night the Americans came over for the dance," she whispered, then closed her eyes.

"Grace?" Eilidh panicked for a moment, thinking the woman had passed out, but the monitor still flickered without any beeps and she saw the chest rising and falling slightly.

Then Grace opened her eyes again and she smiled at Eilidh. "Pretty like your mother, but I think you've maybe got your father's eyes."

This time, Eilidh was stunned into silence. So, Grace did know something, or thought she did. And it was her aunt who held the key, as she had guessed all along. She longed to question Grace more, but couldn't do it. She didn't want the woman's death on her conscience.

Bending over to kiss her cheek, Eilidh whispered, "Thanks, Grace. Get well soon."

There was faint response and Eilidh went quietly from the room. She took the lift then walked straight outside the hospital without looking right or left, deep in thought. The cool, dry air was perfect for walking, and since it was all downhill she ignored the bus and set off for the exit gates. When she had walked some way from the hospital, she ruminated on Grace's words. Eilidh had her father's eyes. But why was the old woman so reluctant to tell her anything else? Unless perhaps she had made a promise never to talk about it?

The revelation had unsettled Eilidh, and she

wished she'd gone to see her aunt in the first place instead of constantly putting other things before the visit. Surely, she must be able to tell her the real story of her conception? If she was willing.

But it would have to wait a short while longer. Although difficult to put this from her thoughts now, she must, until she returned from Ayrshire. She didn't want anything to spoil her time away with Lewis Grant. She had a strong feeling this trip would confirm their relationship one way or the other, and she wanted to give it every chance to go the right way.

Besides, she was looking forward to standing in the same streets Highland Mary had walked through, to see some of the places where she had perhaps met with her Robert Burns.

After all this time, the answers to her own questions could surely wait a few more days.

Chapter Twenty-Four

1786

We meet again by the Banks of Ayr. This time it is planned and he promises to bring some poems to read to me. Robbie enjoys my interest in his work, for I take it seriously. He tells me again of his hopes that some might soon be published. I notice his tired brow and his concern over the farm, then he mentions an idea that has been slowly forming in his head, though it's one he has not shared with anyone else.

"Have you heard of any countries far away across the sea, Mary?" he asks as we walk.

"Like Ireland, do you mean?" I am ignorant of the wider world and do not want him to laugh at me.

"Even further than Ireland," he says, and does not laugh. "I mean so far, far away that you would not believe it was possible to reach it. There is a country called Jamaica, in the West Indies, where a man might find work of a different kind."

He talks but knows not if I understand, as he seems to be in a dream thinking about this strange place. I listen but don't answer so as not to break his speech, for truth to tell I am caught up in this imagining of a country so hot and so far from these cool shores that the people are black-skinned to protect them from the sun's rays.

"Just think, Mary, of many, many days sailing across the great oceans. What an adventure that would be."

He seems to recollect my listening presence and he laughs so that the outer corners of his eyes crinkle with tiny lines. Then he stops on the path.

"Let's sit here a while and I can read to you, if that should please you, Mary."

It is a sheltered place on a grassy embankment, with only the sound of the brook below and the bird song in the trees beyond us. We might well have been the only two people in the land and strange, pleasant shivers run down my back when I think of how alone we are.

He has brought some paper with him and spreads out a sheet of closely-written sentences in black ink. "This is the first verse of a new poem, to a wee mountain daisy that got turned in the plough. You are the first to hear it, Mary, and you can tell me your thoughts.

"Wee, modest, crimson-tipped flow'r,
Thou's met me in an evil hour;
For I maun crush amang the stoure
Thy slender stem:
To spare thee now is past my pow'r,
Thou bonnie gem."

In truth, I am near in tears at the thought of the innocent flower's accidental demise, though it seems to be about more than a wild daisy. Or mayhap I'm listening with a different ear.

"I am no expert on poetry, sir, but it seems to me a very fine verse. And perhaps a powerful lesson on the uselessness of trying to rekindle something that has gone for ever."

He says nothing for some moments but regards me in something like wonder.

"Mary Campbell, I could not have had such praise

or insight from any other person. You understand more than you know, my Highland Lassie. There is some knowledge in you that goes beyond your years."

Again, I have little notion of what he means but his words please my heart. He gazes at me with such a glow in his eyes that I cannot look away.

"Mary…" He moves closer to me and before I can guess his intentions, he has clasped me to him with such passion that I can scarce breathe. He lets me go a little so he can look in my eyes but he keeps his arms around me and I want to stay there for ever.

Then he kisses my open lips and my senses whirl. So, this is what it means to be loved. His lips press harder and I half lie against his chest. My reason is slipping and my desire is rising, filling me with such longing as I have never imagined was possible.

But, just as my last sense of decency is in danger of disappearing, his hold slackens and he lifts his mouth from mine.

"Ah, Mary, my Mary. This is not the way I would use your sweet nature. Come, we must go now before I forget myself, for I would not have you hate me."

He stands up, leaving me bereft and foolish. I have to force the tears from falling on my lashes. He does not want me. It is all I can think about, and I cannot look at him for fear he sees my distress. I take a deep breath and pull back my shoulders.

"I could never hate you, sir." I look at him to see his frown.

"It's Robert or Rob, please, my Mary. And don't look so proud, else you'll scare me away from ever kissing you again. Say my name that I may remember it on your lips."

At that I smile and shyly repeat my words. "I could never hate you, Rob."

"And may I never give you cause, my Highland Lassie," he says in all seriousness.

He does not sound as though he wants nothing to do with me and I wonder if he truly is being careful of using me ill. The thought gives me cheer and a new respect for him, no matter what others have said.

As we walk back towards the village, I know without doubt that my heart is completely his for all time.

Chapter Twenty-Five

"Some hint the lover's harmless wile;
Some grace the maiden's artless smile."
(R. Burns: *The Vision*)

Eilidh was thankful for such a glorious late summer morning as she and Lewis set off down the A77 for Ayr. They'd decided to go to the town first to reacquaint her with the area.

She'd been quiet ever since getting back from visiting Grace, and it was only after discussing it with Kirsty and Sarah that she had finally put the elderly lady to the back of her mind for the moment.

Kirsty was practical as ever. "If you're not planning to go and confront that woman – your so-called aunt – right away, then what's the use of letting it spoil your time with Lewis?"

Surprisingly, Sarah had added her opinion. "You know, the secret has been kept all these years, whatever it is. Another week or so won't make a difference, really. It will give you time to think about what you're going to say." Then she'd added ruefully, "If you'll forgive me giving you one small tip, Eilidh. When you do see your aunt, don't let her talk you down."

Now, as she glanced over the vast moorland they passed at speed, Eilidh concentrated on the rich shades of green and the darkening heather that was now more brown than purple. So much space and not even that many sheep. She liked these wild areas, imagining what it must have been like hundreds of years ago before the industrial revolution had caused the building of so many towns and unsightly factories. Even stretches like this, without the mountain backdrop, had their own beauty.

"Are you okay about this, Eilidh? You seem a bit quiet today. Not having second thoughts about running away with me?"

She laughed as he broke into her thoughts. "Absolutely not." She meant it in any way he chose. "Sorry, I was admiring the emptiness around us. It's quite impressive, isn't it?"

"Well, some say it's extremely bleak, but I know what you mean. Since it's a fine day, d'you want to go straight to the seafront at Ayr and have a walk? Then we can decide the best places to visit."

"Sure. I'd love a walk by the sea."

The ensuing silence was comfortable and Lewis didn't disturb her thoughts again until they were nearly there, when they talked of general subjects. She hadn't told him about her visit to Grace, but would wait until an appropriate moment. She didn't want to go on about her concerns the whole time. She aimed to have some fun for a change, while learning more about Highland Mary. Her own family quest could wait until later.

Eilidh vaguely remembered the wide promenade and the glorious sandy beach that stretched as far as the eye could see, right to the Heads of Ayr. For some reason she remembered the small helter-skelter in the swing park across from the beach. She was amused to see footprints on a sign on the promenade, advising the number of miles walked at various stages.

They elected to go on the beach first, as there were only a few other people there since it wasn't exactly picnic or swimming weather. More like a good autumn day than late summer, and that suited her fine as it was better for walking.

They reached the firm sand that stopped them sinking with every step and set out along the beach away towards the Heads. They'd hardly gone any distance when Lewis took her hand and they synchronised their steps to match. It felt so right, her hand in his, and she turned her face up to the wakening sun to savour being alive and in this place with the man she… No, she stopped herself there, not wanting to analyse too deeply. Live in the moment, for the moment, whatever it might bring. She hadn't been this happy or carefree for too long and wasn't going to spoil it by too much reflection. It was an interlude, away from her troubles and his. As a bonus, she could visit some of the places where Mary Campbell had lived out her life.

"Happy?" Lewis smiled down at her.

"Very happy," she agreed, as he squeezed her hand. "You'd have to be a very sad or ungrateful person not to feel content in such a natural environment as this."

Gulls called to each other and swooped into the sea at intervals, the weak sun making an effort to warm them, while the beach closed them off from modern civilisation. The wide, ancient sea stretched to infinity, yet gently invited them to paddle in its shallows if they desired.

By the time they had walked a fair distance and returned, Eilidh was ready for a coffee. Finding a small café with tables and chairs outside, they sat and sipped their cappuccinos and watched the families pass by with hopeful children carrying buckets and spades. They both smiled, remembering their own childhood days building sandcastles and mud pies.

"I have a suggestion," Lewis finally said. "But feel free to disagree. As you probably know, Burns was born in Alloway, which is about three miles along the road. There's a great new Heritage Centre there and I want to see what you think of my idea of accommodation for the two nights. If we exhaust everything there for what's left of today, then tomorrow we could have a wander round the villages Mary Campbell knew."

He'd clearly done his homework and Eilidh was perfectly happy to let him organise their visit, since he was the one who knew the area and what it had to offer. If she wanted to do something in particular then she'd certainly say so, sure he'd be just as happy to fall in with her ideas. She liked a man who could take charge, so long as he treated her as his equal.

He waited for her response and she smiled. "I was considering whether or not to let you have your way." At his raised eyebrows and wicked grin, she wondered what she had said. Then she laughed. "I mean, of course, as far as your suggestion is concerned. Sounds great. I'm in your hands, good sir."

"Well, if I didn't know you better, I'd say that was two invitations which are hard to resist."

This time she felt a warm blush creep up her neck, yet it was a good feeling to flirt and one she'd not enjoyed for far too long. Jamie had been fun but she wasn't interested in him romantically so it didn't count. She took the outstretched hand waiting to pull her from her chair. This was different from anything that had gone before.

As Lewis promised, it wasn't that far to Alloway and he was soon drawing into a large car park beside some kind of centre and restaurant.

"Shall we have a walk around first then we could come back here to browse? There are lovely gardens as well as a few interesting sights from Burns' days."

"Lead on MacDuff," she said, and was rewarded with a bow. She had no idea what had got into her but it was hard to stop the banter, and he seemed to be afflicted with the same light-heartedness.

The plants and flowers were still impressive enough in late summer and it was a pleasure to wander among the well-laid paths. As they eventually reached a gate, Lewis led them through to a narrow road.

"Just across here," he said, and took her hand. "Look, that's the auld brig, or bridge, where Tam O'Shanter and his mare fled from the witch. You know, from the poem? Imagine it's been there from about the fifteenth century, although there's a new one in the distance there."

Eilidh wandered over until she could stand on the auld brig, trying to picture it when Robert Burns had seen it. The River Doon still flowed beneath and she could see away in the distance towards the new bridge and beyond.

"It's amazing to be able to stand here, isn't it?" She wanted to hush her voice as though they stood on sacred ground, yet it was just an old bridge, albeit one that had literary connotations.

"If we walk up the road a little, I'll show you where I've booked us in for the two nights. It's not cheap, but it's a lovely location and the food is excellent. I thought we could eat there this evening."

Intrigued, she followed him up a narrow pavement past a small teashop. At the top corner of the street, she saw the most beautiful hotel, clothed in ivy and adorned with flowers in the garden. She fell in love with it at once and knew he'd made the right choice. She would willingly blow some of her money on two nights here and she hadn't even seen inside.

"If we carry on along this other way, we can see the rest of the Heritage area and come back later in case they're not ready for us yet."

They walked round by the road for a while until he stopped at an old church. "That's the auld kirk where Tam saw the witches dance, and even came face-to-face with Auld Nick himself. I think this was from about the sixteenth century and it's where Burns' father is buried. It's a ruin now, of course."

She had to have a look, and sure enough there was the gravestone. It also mentioned Burns' mother, Agnes Brown, though she was seemingly buried in East Lothian. Eilidh was surprised to find it so accessible, yet you'd have to know it was there to bother coming over to look.

"Fancy some lunch, then we can have a browse? There's even an audio-visual Tam O'Shanter experience, if you want to have a look."

"Sounds good."

The centre was busy since the schools hadn't gone back yet, but they soon found a small table. Already she was gleaning a good idea of life in Burns' time and she still hadn't come across much reference to Mary Campbell.

When she mentioned it to Lewis he told her about the Burns' cottage and museum. After lunch, they had a browse around the very Scottish fair on offer at the shop, and she bought some postcards to send to a few friends back in the States. They opted to go and see the cottage and museum next, and leave the audio-visual for another time.

First, they took their small amount of luggage round to the hotel to check in. Eilidh hadn't asked, but was intrigued to see what kind of accommodation Lewis had booked for them; she wasn't sure what she expected or hoped. When they entered the reception area, she knew her first impression had been correct. She wasn't disappointed when she saw the thick tartan carpeting and dark wood panelling.

The girl at reception was friendly, welcoming them with a genuine smile. Lewis gave their names and Eilidh waited. Two separate rooms. She didn't know whether to be relieved or disappointed, but finally decided she was pleased that nothing had been taken for granted. She didn't look at Lewis but concentrated on the girl until they'd received their keys and been told where to locate the rooms.

The rooms were near each other on a narrow landing, and Eilidh opened her door first. It was a good sized, airy room with a Queen-sized bed, and she banished the first thought that came into her head – that two of them could lie on that. There was an en-suite bathroom and a hospitality tray with tea and coffee supplies.

"This is really lovely," she said, as Lewis watched from the door.

"Come and see mine, since I've seen yours," he said.

His had another Queen-sized bed and the room was much the same as hers, only facing a different direction and with different décor.

"Shall we take half an hour to unpack and freshen up?" She made the suggestion this time.

"Of course, take longer if you want. It's not far to the cottage and museum. Why don't you give me a knock when you're ready?"

Since he was busy setting his bag down on the edge of his bed, she left him to it. Eilidh closed her door and sat on the stool at the dressing table for a moment, looking at her reflection. If she was not mistaken, Lewis had seemed almost withdrawn suddenly, and it threw her. Had she misread their previous banter, or was he unsure about what she expected of him? She examined her teeth to make sure no bits of lettuce lurked there. Her hair wasn't any more of a wavy mess than usual. Maybe he was tired, since he'd driven the whole way. She'd find out soon enough one way or the other, even if she had to come right out and ask.

She hung her dressy skirt and two blouses in the wardrobe, and arranged her underwear and two clean t-shirts in the drawer. She'd brought one pair of heels to wear with the skirt and she put them on the floor of the wardrobe. Toiletries on the bathroom shelf, brush beside the mirror, then she shoved her meagre jewellery and make-up in the drawer of the dressing table. Book on the bedside table beside her notebook and pen; she was unpacked.

A quick brush of her teeth, a tidy-up, and she was ready. She looked out the window and was glad to find a view of the bridge, then tested the bed which was comfortable, and pushed her nightdress under the pillow. Checking her watch showed it hadn't taken long. She hesitated. Maybe she should give Lewis a while longer. Propping herself up against the pillows on the bed, she took up her notebook and started writing down an impression of what she'd seen and felt so far. It would be good for the novel, if ever it got written.

She was so engrossed in writing she'd forgotten the time until there was a soft knock at the door.

"Coming!" she called. He'd think she was still unpacking.

"Hi, I thought maybe you were waiting for me." He was still a bit hesitant, which she found quite endearing.

"Sorry, I got carried away writing. I'm ready if you are." She was relieved when that elicited his usual grin. She'd been worried he was moodier than she'd known. Maybe he'd just needed a rest. If he had seen all this before, then perhaps it wouldn't be as interesting to him.

They walked to the cottage and museum and, again, he took her hand right away. It felt as good as the first time. She was surprised and delighted to find the cottage was the authentic one of the poet's birth, with an audio-visual showing what life would have been like in his times. A small charge let them view both buildings, and it was worth every penny. She could imagine her eighteenth-century poet farmer in this low cottage, with a fire burning in the hearth on a cold winter's night. Now why did she think of that? she wondered.

The museum proved to be full of great artefacts from Burns' life, including several that mentioned Highland Mary. Eilidh was stunned to find the very Bible that Burns seemingly gave his Mary over the burn at Ayr. Even more amazing was the fair lock of hair supposedly taken from her head on her death and deposited inside the Bible. Besides that, she admired a few paintings of their meeting, of varying authenticity, but it gave Eilidh a renewed sense of their romantic and tragic story. She and Lewis even scanned the note Robert Burns had written about his song, *My Highland Lassie O*, describing his relationship with Mary Campbell until her departure to Greenock. Eilidh remembered reading an excerpt of this in the old book on Burns at the library, but this had even more impact. This was the actual note, written in the poet's hand.

"Wow, this is awesome stuff!" Eilidh said aloud, and Lewis smiled in response.

"Glad you find it useful. It's pretty amazing if you haven't seen it before. Your adopted countrymen are even more awed when they see how much has been preserved for us to look at in this century. It makes you appreciate history, don't you think?"

"I guess it does. No wonder they take schoolchildren to places like this. It makes everything come alive in a way words can't describe."

She didn't want to leave; it was all so interesting, but she didn't want to bore her companion too much. He made a good show of being every bit as interested as she was but he must have seen it all before.

"I think my head is stuffed full now. Maybe I should leave some space for tomorrow." She made the first move.

"Are you sure you've seen enough? I don't mind how long you take. Or if you're tired, we could come back the morning we're leaving."

"It's fine, honestly. I've had a great afternoon. Thanks for being so patient."

"I teach history, remember? I love old places like this. You can almost smell the past, can't you?"

Eilidh looked at him with new respect. He really meant it. She understood what he'd said, as she could just about smell that imagined log fire and hear the sound of the poet's voice.

They wandered back through the Heritage Park and stopped beside the tall nineteenth century monument that climbed towards the sky.

"You must come and see the statue house," Lewis said, and she followed him a short way down a path to a small building.

There, on a raised platform, were three life-sized sculptures: Tam O'Shanter, his friend Souter Johnnie, and Nanse, the proprietress of their favourite ale-house. It was quite eerie being confronted by such grinning figures. Tam and Johnnie had their drinks in hand, while Nanse coyly turned away from them. And on the wall between the two men was the well-known portrait of the poet himself.

Although Eilidh had never seen an actual framed painting of Burns until now, she had seen one on a website and in one of the books she'd consulted. This seemed to be the most famous one, depicting Burns almost in profile, with chin-length sideburns, and the sweep of dark hair to one side of his brow. She stared at it for a while, puzzled. There was something vaguely known about that portrait, a familiarity with the poet's face. Yet she had only seen this in passing, as had millions of others.

Then she happened to glance at Lewis who had come to stand beside her. And there it was. Not a likeness exactly, but a shadow of similarity in the shape of the head. She shivered at the thought. How absolutely fanciful, she chided herself. She was letting this place get to her in an uncharacteristic way.

"Quite a feat of workmanship, isn't it?" Lewis said, and the strange moment was gone.

She realised he referred to the statues. "Very creepy." She shivered again. Maybe it was the enclosed nature of the room, with these three lifelike inanimate figures enjoying themselves.

He noticed her shiver and put his arm around her as they walked to the exit. By unspoken consent, they turned towards the gardens again and wandered past the scented roses.

"I enjoyed all that, thanks again. I think I need a rest and a shower before dinner, though, if you don't mind." Dinner was booked for seven o'clock and she wasn't kidding about the shower. Rather than a rest, however, she suddenly needed some time on her own.

"Me, too," he agreed, and they headed back to the hotel.

She was quieter all the way up to the room and hoped he would put it down to weariness. He stopped at her door, but only briefly kissed her cheek.

"Enjoy your peace and quiet. Maybe we could go down for a drink before dinner? Give me a knock when you're ready."

Once she had closed her door, she did no more than kick off her shoes before lying down on the wide bed. What on earth had happened in the statue house? It had shaken her, that sudden deep awareness of continuity, that in some way her Lewis had the merest suggestion of the eighteenth century Burns about him. Two things struck her: he *was* her Lewis, and had been almost from the first, and she had absolutely no idea about his family origins. Maybe he didn't, either. Although stranger things happened in real life than in fiction, it really wasn't so far outside the bounds of possibility that he was connected in some far-off way to one strand of Burns' family.

The very thought should make her laugh, but the more she considered it the more she came around to believing it could be true. Not that she would suggest such a thing to Lewis; he thought her direct and matter-of-fact, not over-imaginative and fey. But being back in Scotland had changed her, it had seeped into her soul in small, undefined ways. Then she remembered even further back, after her mother's death, when she had felt someone calling her back to her own country.

Now she really was being fanciful and she swung her legs over the side of the bed. It was time to wash such thoughts away, along with the dust from all the old places she had seen.

The dining room was bright, spacious and had a slightly old-fashioned Scottish gracefulness, yet was discreetly modern at the same time. Impressive wooden beams and old paintings gave it a baronial feel, echoed in the large round table at the window. They were shown to a table for two, comfortably far enough apart from other tables to enjoy an intimate conversation. In the end, they had gone straight to dine as Eilidh had dozed off after her shower.

As they perused the extensive menu, which boasted good Scottish fare, Lewis ordered a bottle of red wine. A pleasantly busy ambience gave a homely feel to the restaurant and Eilidh noticed a young couple deep in conversation at a nearby table. As their respective soup and paté arrived, she gave her full attention to her companion. They'd hardly had a chance to speak about their afternoon and Eilidh pushed her fanciful thoughts about Lewis's ancestry to the back of her mind.

They were chatting in low voices, when Eilidh became aware of the young man at the other table standing up. She glanced idly over, then smiled. He was down on one knee and everyone else in the dining room was now staring at him with interest and admiration. There was no doubt he was in the midst of proposing, and had handed a single red rose to his girl. Eilidh saw her reddened cheeks and embarrassed smile and knew the poor girl would never forget this evening. Relieved sighs and hand claps sounded all around when it became obvious she'd said yes. One of the waiters brought a bottle of champagne to their table and everyone carried on with their own lives, leaving the happy couple to their romance.

"My love is like a red, red rose that's newly sprung in June," Lewis murmured, as he looked at Eilidh.

"I think that should be their song from now on. What a romantic place to propose, right in the heart of Burns country. She's a lucky girl." Eilidh hadn't meant to sound wistful, but young love always made her appreciate the romance that was possible if you found the right person to share it with.

"I wouldn't be surprised if they come back and have their wedding here; it's a popular venue," Lewis said, and he took hand. For a mad moment, she thought he was going to say something significant, too, then she calmed down at his next words.

"You sounded a bit sad. Have you never been in love, Eilidh?"

She waited until their first course had been cleared, surprised at his question.

"I don't think so, although I've thought so once or twice at the time." She didn't want to say "not until now" since she wasn't sure what this feeling promised.

"I imagine it's a rare thing to meet the right person first time round," he said.

It sounded more cynical than she expected, but his own experience wasn't exactly love's young dream in the end. Their main course prevented any more discussion for a while and they both tucked in hungrily. Their conversation was desultory and safe, with no more talk of love – young or otherwise.

When they finished, Eilidh sat back fully satisfied with her choice of salmon. She had noticed various desserts being brought to neighbouring tables and wished she had room for the sticky toffee pudding with butterscotch sauce and ice cream, but she'd be lucky if she could even manage a coffee.

Afterwards, they both had the same idea of taking a walk down to the auld brig. The evening was slightly balmy and Lewis took her hand as they wandered down the narrow pavement. Cars were parked all the way down, but no-one disturbed their peace. They strolled without talking for a while, and Eilidh was content to enjoy the evening air.

The bridge looked even more ancient in this half-light, its centuries-old clothing of ivy making it darker. It didn't take too much imagination to picture Tam O'Shanter fleeing across it with the witch behind him, grasping at the poor grey mare's tail. Eilidh wrapped her arms around her body, suddenly feeling a little chilly.

"I think there's more of a breeze now. Come and I'll keep you warm," Lewis said, and cosied her in against his broad chest. "That better?" And he bent down to lightly kiss her mouth.

"Much better," she smiled lazily. "Though I don't think I'll last out here much longer."

They turned back towards the hotel. It was enough of a walk to settle their meal and, if she was not imagining it, the sky was darkening by the minute. As they reached the hotel, Eilidh wondered what to do. Should she invite him back to her room for a nightcap? Would he expect more, and was she ready for such commitment? Thank goodness they had separate rooms as it made it slightly easier to stay in control.

In the end, Lewis saved her from any decisions when they reached her room.

"Well, if you feel the same, I think I'll turn in for the night. We've a busy day tomorrow and you'll most likely want some time to yourself now."

For a moment, Eilidh was taken aback that he didn't want to come in for a while and wondered again if she had misread their relationship. Then he pulled her against him and kissed her long and lingeringly as they stood on the quiet landing. She had no reason for any more doubts and was just getting really into the kiss when he released her gently.

"I don't want to take you for granted, Eilidh. You mean too much to me for that. Goodnight, sweet maid, sleep well. I'll see you at breakfast."

With difficulty, she adopted the same teasing tone. "Goodnight, good sir, and thank you."

He grinned, bowing slightly, and she watched him until he opened his own door.

Closing her bedroom door, Eilidh stood behind it without putting the light on, shaking slightly with the force of her desire. Not only because of his kisses, which certainly stirred her senses, but with a deeper longing that they might be part of each other, as though he was the only person who could ever complete her.

She smiled at her intensity but meant every tingling feeling. It wasn't as if she was a thirty-three-year-old virgin, although she had little experience. She certainly didn't give herself easily, even in this twenty-first century. But this was different, and she'd never been so convinced of anything in her life. It might not happen now, but they were meant to be together in every way.

She closed the curtains, switched on the light and got ready for bed. Then she sat against the pillows and wrote down some more ideas for her novel since she was in the very countryside that Burns and Highland Mary had known so well. Pouring her feelings into their ill-fated romance, she hoped her own would be more lasting.

As she finally put out her light and sleep claimed her, she was smiling at the thought of seeing Lewis tomorrow.

Chapter Twenty-Six

1786

Now my dreams are filled with visions of sailing across a wide ocean, on a ship bigger than the kind my father works on. And my Robbie is at my side, protecting me and loving me.

Then I awaken and know it is not real and I feel bereft, as though he is no longer in my life. Since that momentous day when he appeared to love me, I have waited to catch sight of him whenever I am about the village or on the pathways. But he does not come. I have told only Meggie about our meeting, and she is stern.

"I told ye what he was like, lass. Well ye've only yerself to blame if ye dinnae see him again. Be thankful to the guid Lord that ye didnae give him anything ye might regret."

I try to explain how tender of my feelings he was but she laughs at my foolishness.

"Aye and I'm right sure he'll no be sae tender o' them if he should have ye tae himself again."

No matter what she says, I am sure of him and his concern not to shame me in any way. And I know he has not forgotten me.

Then I hear news that makes my heart turn over with despair. Jean Armour has been brought to bed with his twins. Yet still she stays away in Paisley. Some even say they are secretly married, though I cannot believe that is true, else they would surely be together. But, how can I help but wonder if he goes to her? Other lasses in the village say he is still forbidden to see her and that she now stays away on purpose. Oh, what am I to believe? He seems so true in his words to me yet he does not speak to me these long days, to tell me what I need to know.

When will he come to me again? Mayhap he has already gone on his journey far, far away and I will never see him more. And my heart shall surely break in two.

Chapter Twenty-Seven

"Their titles a' are empty show,
Gie me my highland lassie, O."
(R. Burns: *The Highland Lassie*)

Eilidh was relieved to find they were relaxed and easy with each other over their full Scottish breakfast. Once she finished her tea and toast, she sat back replete.

"Well, I don't think we'll need much during the day after that, especially if we're having dinner here this evening again."

"I do like a girl who enjoys her food." Lewis smiled at her in appreciation. "Can't stand the stick insects who are always on a diet. Please don't ever change."

She wasn't quite as slim as she used to be, but his words gave her a warm glow. She liked her food and had no intention of dieting while she was fit and healthy.

"So, I thought you'd like to see the small villages of Mauchline and Tarbolton today. You'll recognise them from some of your research and it'll give you an idea of the surrounding countryside. I don't think it'll have changed that much since the eighteenth century."

"I can't wait," she said, glad to have such a knowledgeable guide.

A slight breeze made it a cooler day and Eilidh took a light sweater for over her t-shirt. She looked forward to visiting some of the villages where Burns and Mary Campbell met. Never had she been so caught up in past lives before and was amused at how much their story had gripped her imagination. The more she read, the more she felt sorry for poor, lovelorn Mary, whose romance hadn't had a happy ending.

She had mixed feelings towards the poet. She admired him and understood his need to express himself in verse and his frustration at earning a decent living. She even understood why such an intelligent, handsome, and witty man had wielded such a strong effect on so many women. She could feel the attraction herself, down through the centuries, through his poetry and letters and everything that others had written about him.

But one thing she found it hard to forgive him for: that he'd left it too late to find his Mary again, while she must have longed for his arrival every minute of every day. Eilidh was sure the tragedy of their separation had encouraged the legend around their story, for there was nothing more romantic than lovers who are forever parted. At least the poet had enjoyed a happy ending with Jean Armour, for a while at least, but Mary Campbell's story gripped her most.

Eilidh mused about her own mother and the fact that she had never married the man she loved, or who had loved her, and that their child hadn't known a father. She couldn't remember her mother pining, but neither had there been anyone special in her life in all the years Eilidh was growing up. That too was sad in its own way, though Eilidh still didn't know why it had happened.

"Are you okay, Eilidh? You've been so quiet, I

wasn't sure if you'd fallen asleep."

At the mixture of concern and amusement in his voice, she started. She'd been completely lost in her thoughts. "Oh, I'm real sorry, Lewis. I do that sometimes, get so inside my head I forget where I am."

"I remember that." He grinned. "As long as you aren't regretting my company. I don't think my ego would recover."

She laughed and left the past behind for the time being. "As if!" she said. "No, I really do appreciate you showing me around, and you're not bad company, you know."

They chatted until they arrived at the village of Tarbolton.

"I thought we'd start here as it's probably not quite so interesting to you. Mauchline is more the place where Mary would have met Burns. But it's still worth having a look here."

She was happy to get out of the car for a while to wander around the village. Burns had formed his famous club in this place, where he and his cronies could enjoy debate and fellowship, but that had been after Mary's time. Then she noticed an old whitewashed building with a sign proclaiming it to be the Bachelors' Club. She stopped to have a look.

"Now that's what I call a good idea," Lewis said. "A place for men to be safe from the women folk."

"I think in this case it might be a good place to keep Burns and his colleagues out of the way, so women would be safe from the men."

There wasn't much else to see, although it was a pleasant village with a quiet main street.

"If we drive a few miles on, you'll see the area Mary used to work in. And I know the perfect place to stop."

She was suitably intrigued. They hadn't driven very far through flatter, open countryside, when Lewis slowed down.

"The castle of Montgomery was around this area, where Mary worked as a dairymaid. Didn't she get to know Burns more during that time?" he asked.

"Yes, you're right. She seems to have worked as a nursemaid for Burns' friend, Gavin Hamilton, when she first arrived. I guess that's how they met in the first place. Burns seemed to have a predilection for servant girls. Or maybe they succumbed more easily to his charms. Though not Mary, I think."

"His farm at Mossgiel is just outside Mauchline and I believe there's a plaque showing the place, if you look out for it." Lewis kept his speed low so they didn't miss the spot.

"There, I see something," Eilidh said, and he slowed to a halt.

They got out to look, and sure enough, a stone-built cairn contained a plaque on the top giving details of Burns' birth and death and the fact that he farmed there from 1784 to 1786. Eilidh was amazed to find a working farm further up the field, and it wasn't difficult to imagine the poet and his brother ploughing the land.

Once back in the car, they headed to the village of Mauchline, the place Eilidh really wanted to see, as so much of Mary's life had been centred around there. She wasn't disappointed. Old buildings still predominated in the charming, small village and after parking on a side street, they wandered down the main road. Eilidh's attention was captured at once by an old, whitewashed building edged in black paint, seemingly some kind of inn. A large painting above the doorway reminded her of others she'd seen from Burns' time, and the name intrigued her at once.

"Poosie Nansie's? That's a strange name. Sounds like something from Burns' own poetry!"

"I knew you'd like this place. It is from Burns' time and it's even more interesting inside. Turn to the right when you go through the door."

Carefully ducking under the low lintel, Eilidh stepped inside a room that took her straight back to the eighteenth century. Robert Burns might well have left just before they arrived. Low, dark wooden beams, wooden table and chairs set before the fireplace, all combined to give the illusion of another time. Then she laughed, as she spotted the 'heads' of Tam O'Shanter and Johnnie Souter grinning at her from either side of the range.

"There's no getting away from those two," she said.

The dresser in the corner was still adorned with willow-patterned plates and a pitcher and ewer stood on its surface. An undeniable air of authenticity pervaded the room and, again, Eilidh could imagine Burns and his pals sitting at the table enjoying their ale.

Once she absorbed everything and reluctantly bade it farewell, they wandered on down the street until she caught sight of a statue. Jean Armour. The bronze figure was surprisingly slight, no more than a girl to Eilidh's eyes. One hand touched her hair where it flowed at her neck, while the other was held out in welcome – or in supplication? Eilidh had a strong feeling that all of Jean Armour's trials and worries were etched on this face, and she much preferred the statue of Mary Campbell at Dunoon.

Some distance away, she noticed a tall, red

sandstone tower, and as they neared a sign proclaimed it The National Burns Memorial. It was closed and she decided Mauchline deserved another visit some time.

As they strolled back along the main street, Lewis pointed to the church. "I think there's something of interest in the churchyard there, if I remember correctly."

There was indeed: Gavin Hamilton's gravestone, erected by Partick Burns Club in 1919. Eilidh remembered he'd figured a lot in the story of Burns and Mary Campbell. Apart from being his friend and well-respected lawyer, he'd rented Mossgiel Farm to Burns and seemingly had encouraged his poetry. And he had employed Mary as nursemaid to his child. It pleased her that he was so well-remembered as she read the two-line inscription beneath his details:

"The poor man's friend in need
The gentleman in word and deed."

"He must have been a wonderful friend to Burns," Eilidh said. "What an epitaph."

By the time they'd scrutinised everything around the church and walked down to Castle Street where Burns and Jean Armour had lived, Eilidh was happy to go back to Poosie Nansie's for a sandwich and cup of tea. The friendly waitress told them about the writing on the outside wall of the tavern. The Jolly Beggar's Howff was a reminder that Burns had written his *Jolly Beggars' Cantata* while sitting at a neighbouring inn watching the beggars and vagabonds coming and going.

"We could take our time and drive through some of the countryside. Give you a feel for the setting," Lewis suggested, when they'd finished.

She was in danger of Burns' overload but was

keen to see some of the surrounds. At another smaller village some miles away on the road back to Ayr, Eilidh had a sudden strong feeling the place was significant.

"Could you stop a minute, please?" she asked.

Eilidh was astonished to discover it was near to the place where Mary Campbell had worked at Coilsfield as a dairy maid, and very near the stream where she was said to have parted from Burns. A strange melancholy gripped her as she glanced around and she was happy to carry on to Ayr.

Quite suddenly, Eilidh had experienced enough of the past for today and wanted to enjoy the present, with this patient, exciting man by her side. The thought made her smile. Where on earth had that come from? She didn't care; it was true. They opted to stop for another walk along the beach at the coast and it was exactly what she needed after the slight claustrophobia of the small villages, with their celebration of the long-dead "ploughman poet" who still moved so many people in this day and age.

What a legacy, she acknowledged, and couldn't resist the sense of pride in this humble Scot who had gone on to mingle with, and affect, the very best in the land. Yet, still, that niggling feeling that he'd not been fair to Mary Campbell tore at her heart.

The light breeze was even more evident on the beach, but neither of them cared. To be out in the open air, striding out along the firm sands, was exactly what they needed and Eilidh lifted her face to the sky.

"Smell that sea air, Lewis. Aren't we the luckiest people to be able to enjoy all this?"

He smiled down at her. "Right now, I wouldn't want to be anywhere else in the world, or with any other person." He hugged her into his side. "You know, I've never been with anyone since Jan. I want you to know that, Eilidh."

She stopped and looked up at him, her laughter fading. He stared into her eyes, and neither said a word. Then he kissed her. Gentle yet possessive, and her response was uninhibited. She didn't know if anyone saw them, and didn't care if they did. This was their own small world on a long beach beside a vast sea and they were the only two who mattered.

Slowly, they pulled apart, eyes still locked on each other. She instinctively knew they were approaching a new level in their relationship, and was glad of it. She had no more doubts that this man was the only one she was meant to be with.

They strolled back along the beach, hands locked firmly together until they reached the car. Overhead, the gulls called their usual greeting, making Eilidh pause to observe them wheeling in the sky. About to walk on, she almost trod on something. Bending down, she found the most perfect little shell, almost as translucent as pearl. She wiped the tiny grains of sand from it and put it in her pocket. It would be a memento of this special day.

They remained silent as Lewis drove back to the hotel and Eilidh didn't want to break the powerful sense of connection she could still feel between them. When they reached her room, he didn't ask her permission but stepped inside behind her.

Closing the door, he held out his arms and she willingly went to him. All her longing was in their kiss. As he probed deeper, she wanted it to go on for ever, all the deep intensity of which she was capable flowing from every part of her.

Then he was kissing her face and her neck and she

strained closer against him. Their clothes proved too much of a barrier for such passion, and she pulled at his top. He helped it off then removed her t-shirt and they moved towards the bed, all the while kissing and touching each other as if afraid to stop the momentum.

She couldn't remember later who had removed what, though he'd been the one to think of protection. Her whole being was caught in the intensity of the moment, her skin electric as his fingers traced the shape of her naked body. She offered herself willingly, as though for the first time in her life. His strength was matched by her desire and their breath mingled as their bodies came together.

She had waited for this moment all her adult years, and it was worth every minute as their passion reached its peak. As they lay entwined and spent, Eilidh kissed his face and neck, feeling such depth of love for him that she wanted to hold him here beside her for ever. He put his arm round her shoulder and held her close against him, breathing the scent of her hair.

"I love you, Eilidh Campbell, with all my heart," he whispered, and she heard every precious word.

She moved away slightly so she could look at his eyes. "And I love you, Lewis Grant, with my heart, my soul, and my body."

As though pledging themselves to each other in that moment, they sealed it with a lingering kiss.

Some time later, Eilidh stirred and realised they had fallen asleep in each other's arms. She lay for a while watching his chest rise and fall as he dozed, feeling happier than she could ever remember. She glanced at the clock on the bedside table then slipped out of bed to take a shower.

By the time she was dried and in her bathrobe, Lewis was sitting on the edge of the bed in his underpants.

"Hi," she said, and went to sit beside him. "I didn't want to wake you but I'm hungry and I know we've booked dinner."

"Me, too," he said and pulled her to him again, kissing her deeply. Then he let her go. "But you're right, we'd better get dressed and eat. I need to renew my strength."

She loved those small lines at the corner of his eyes when he smiled, and she laughed at his teasing.

"I'll go and shower in my own room, since the towel is there," he said, throwing on the rest of his clothes.

When he finally left after a few more kisses, Eilidh dressed in her good skirt and the other pretty blouse. She dried her hair and did her make-up sparingly but carefully, wanting him to appreciate her in every way. Then she made up the bed and tidied her clothes away, removing all evidence of what had taken place. Remembering the little shell, she found it in the pocket of her jeans and washed it under the bathroom tap, then polished it on her soft sweater. She placed it on the dressing table beside her brush, musing on the possibility of having it threaded onto a chain she could wear round her neck. Something to investigate.

Only when finally ready, did she recall every detail of their lovemaking. And it was exactly that: making love, with love, in love. Not just clinical sex between two people who desired each other. Maybe she was being fanciful again, which seemed to be happening more frequently, but she finally knew what it meant to love someone completely, almost spiritually as well as physically. Then she laughed at herself and stood up to go and meet her love.

"Oh, what an absolute romantic ninny you're becoming," she told her mirror image.

Eilidh felt the subtle difference during dinner that evening, as though the slight reserve of the evening before was well and truly banished. They laughed freely and chatted more openly about everything they could think of. No romantic proposal from a neighbouring table interrupted, and the other diners seemed to be in good spirits. Everything had changed. No doubt through the rose-tinted spectacles of love, but welcome nonetheless.

Then, for one unexpected moment, the eighteenth and twentieth century Mary Campbells came to mind. Both presumably had loved as deeply as Eilidh did, yet neither had found lasting happiness with their loves. Eilidh shrugged the unwelcome thought away. This was her life and her love. This was very different.

They wandered down to the bridge again to walk off their dinner, and Eilidh's anticipation grew that this night would be unlike their previous one in every way. When they returned to their rooms, Lewis left her for a short time then knocked softly on her door and she welcomed him in.

Their lovemaking this time was gentle and lingering, and even more passionate for being so deliberate. As she began to fall asleep in his arms once more, Eilidh wished they could remain here for longer, and hold off returning to whatever awaited them. But reality beckoned and she wondered how they would adapt to being apart. She had a flat to move into, a job to find, and an estranged aunt to confront. Most important of all, she wanted to discover the identity of her father. She had a sinking feeling these two days would soon seem like a dream.

Chapter Twenty-Eight

1786

I am proved right in my faith and trust. He has sent word to me that we should meet beside our brook. He will tell me that those stories are untrue. I wash my hands and face and put on my best overdress and shawl. My hair is shining and half-braided away from my face. I slip out without being seen once my work is done, eager to see him again, to hear his voice, and to feel his lips on mine.

The air is bright with the warmth of spring. We have passed the first week of May and there is a promise of summer in the wild flowers and the blossom on the trees. My heart sings along with the birds as I walk along the embankment. I know it will be difficult to refuse whatever he asks of me, and I think of my mother and father, and of Meggie, to make me strong.

Then I remember the stories we hear at the Kirk and the way in which the minister talks about sin and punishment. I prefer when he talks of forgiveness and redemption. I know the story of King David and Bathsheba. How even God's favourite was tempted by a woman's flesh and caused murder to be committed in order to have his desire. And how God forgave him when David truly repented of those terrible sins.

That is the God I believe in; the one who knows

we are humanly tempted but who forgives us again and again when we are truly sorry. For what person never did a wrong thing? Even the ministers and priests must surely lie, or cheat, or gossip at times, if none is perfect save for God's own son. That is how I see it, but I have not the learning of some.

My musing has brought me to the place and there is no-one there. I sit down above the brook and wonder if he has led me here falsely, but I cannot accept he would do this. Then I hear a soft whistle and look up. He is coming towards me.

I stand to greet him and he clasps me close to his chest.

"You have come, my sweet Mary." Then he kisses me on my lips and I melt against him.

We sit on the green, grassy ground and he whispers such things in my ear. His lips touch my neck where my shawl has fallen away and I strain to be closer to him. He kisses my lips again and I part mine without conscious thought, that we might savour the touch more deeply. I hardly know his arm has moved across me until I feel the touch of his hand on my breast and I think my heart will jump through my gown. How can such feeling exist and not find release? His hand has moved and he fumbles at my skirts.

Did I moan without knowing it? For he has smoothed my skirt down and is breaking free from me. Why, oh why has he stopped? My breath still comes quickly and I long for his touch on my breast again. But his own breathing slows and he wipes his brow before he looks at me. I wonder if he is ashamed of how I have behaved. But he smiles and there is sadness in his eyes.

"My dear, sweet Highland lassie. I'm going away,

Mary, to that far off place I told you of. You remember I talked of Jamaica? There is nothing for me here any longer and I've decided to find a new life."

No, he cannot mean it. When I am here for him. I reach out my hand and take his. "I am here."

He holds my hand tightly. "Mary, would you be willing to leave everything you know here, to leave your family, and come with me to that land?"

My eyes widen at his words, for I had not expected to hear them. Then I know that it proves his love for me above all other people. And I remember Ruth, who goes wherever Naomi goes. Who says: "Your people will be my people."

"I will go with you to the other side of the world, if you ask it of me."

"Oh, Mary, my darling lass. But first we must betroth ourselves to each other, for I'll not shame you without promise of being wed."

"Oh, I would gladly do so today!" It is more than I dared to hope, and it will make my mother and father less worried for me if I travel with a husband. "Nothing will make me happier in the world," I assure him, although I now have some taste of what other pleasures might await me.

"We shall meet here again on the second Sunday of this month of May. Bring your Bible and we shall pledge our union in the eyes of God, over that brook. Then we can make preparation to sail. I'm sure you'll want to see your family before we go. We'll sail from Greenock, on the River Clyde, and I'll begin making enquiries as to which ship goes to the Indies."

We kiss once more before we part, for he goes in the other direction.

"Until the second Sunday, my love," he says, and

we take our leave of each other.

How much more my heart sings as I walk back along the path. I think I shall shout my joy to the trees for I do not know how I shall contain it. He loves me, he loves me! And if I feel a slight worry about going so far away, I soon forget it is there. If we leave from Greenock, then I will be able to visit my brother first. I have wanted adventure and I've wanted true love, and now I am to have both together.

Chapter Twenty-Nine

"All hail, ye tender feelings dear!
The smile of love, the friendly tear."
(R. Burns: *Epistle to David*)

When they arrived back in Gourock on the Wednesday afternoon, Lewis dropped her off with a promise to see her later.

"You know, I've just realised you haven't even seen my humble abode yet. We'll need to rectify that at once. You can stay over if you like and I'll make you breakfast in the morning."

He kissed her so that she couldn't think of anything else but seeing him again as soon as possible. The problems might arrive on the subsequent days when he was back at work and she was busy at the flat. But she said goodbye with joy at discovering how much she loved him, and sadness at their parting.

Sarah was at home by herself, and had obviously been crying.

"What's happened, Sarah? Are you okay?"

"Oh, I'm sorry, Eilidh, I didn't mean anyone to see me like this. It's all so difficult sometimes and I'm probably being over-sensitive…"

It wouldn't take much for the girl to cry again, and Eilidh went over to sit beside her. "I don't want to pry, but if it helps to talk, I'm listening. Is it the wedding?"

A nod then Sarah blew her nose. "I really love

Rory but his mother is making it so hard for us with all her interference. I thought she had accepted we were getting married in my church but she's still talking about me converting!"

"What does Rory say?"

"He's putting his foot down, but she's devious and manipulative sometimes."

This last was said with more anger than Eilidh thought the other girl capable of. She always seemed so sweet, yet if Sarah was a nurse she most likely had a tough side when necessary.

"What about your own pastor? Could he help?" Eilidh suggested.

"We've spoken to him and he's very supportive but can't interfere between mother and son in this situation."

She didn't even know if Sarah had parents, and asked her gently.

"My dad is married again and lives on the east coast. He doesn't care one way or the other. Mum died when I was at high school. But none of my family is religious anyway."

Eilidh remained silent as she put her arm around Sarah. This girl was going to be her cousin by marriage soon and she felt a sudden tenderness for her, sad that she was in this position. Then the anger against her aunt resurfaced and she knew the time had come to face her.

"Let your faith keep you strong, Sarah. You know Rory loves you and won't do anything to hurt you. This is his mother's problem. You are the bride, it's your big day, your future husband – and the bride always gets to choose where to be married."

Should she say any more? It might help. "You know something, Sarah? I might not have seen my aunt for many years but I know damn well she wasn't that religious when she and mum were younger."

She was glad Sarah seemed a little brighter, and Eilidh went to put the kettle on. A cup of tea was called for; the panacea for all upsets.

Once the tea and biscuits were on the table, they changed the conversation.

"How was your visit to Ayrshire? Did you get what you went for?"

Eilidh nearly laughed aloud at that and Kirsty would certainly have made some ribald comment. But she just smiled and nodded. "It was very successful, thanks, in every way." That was enough for now. She'd rather wait and include her friend in any more information, or as much as she was going to tell.

"I'm glad for you. And thanks, Eilidh, it helped talking to someone not directly involved. Kirsty was on an early today, by the way, so she'll be back soon."

"Is it okay if I use the washing machine just now?" Eilidh asked.

"Of course, it's empty anyway. I'm meeting Rory in town after his work so I'm away to get changed now then I'll be out of your way."

She thought again what a sweet girl Sarah was and what a lovely couple she and Rory would make. How dare his mother try and spoil things for them, when it was great they had such a strong faith of their own.

Surely there must be something more to it. Her aunt must have converted at some time. But why? One more thing to find out. And she was going to do that very soon. She would phone Rory tomorrow and arrange to see her aunt and uncle as soon as possible. It would give his mother something else to think about when she was confronted by her long-lost niece. Eilidh smiled at the thought. When did she get so nasty? Then she thought of Sarah's tears, Rory's anguish at trying to stay friends with his troublesome mother, and the scene from her childhood when that same woman had upset Eilidh's mother. It was time to meet this dragon.

Once Sarah had gone, Eilidh did her washing, hung it on the rail over the bath, and was tidying away her belongings as neatly as possible when the phone rang.

Lewis. His voice gave her a warm glow and she was smiling when his words burst her bubble of happiness.

"I'm really sorry, Eilidh. We're going to have to make it another evening for you to come down here. Something's happened. I'll fill you in when I see you. I'll call you again tomorrow. Love you."

She hardly had a chance to reply when he said goodbye. She stood holding the phone, wondering what on earth had just happened. More to the point, what had happened to their intimacy from the trip, when they had shared everything? Maybe she was being unreasonable. If it was an emergency then of course he had to cancel. But it was the kind of emergency that concerned her; she had the strongest suspicion it involved his ex-wife. Yet she was supposed to have a fiancé of her own.

The thought made her uneasy. She couldn't go into a committed relationship without being the most important person in a man's life. It wasn't jealousy exactly, more a deep need to know that their commitment would be to each other first. Not to exclude others, but to face the world and all its problems as a couple. But there was no sense in projecting to a future that hadn't even been mentioned. Lewis wasn't committed to her in that way yet, and she'd just have to wait until he shared whatever it was with her.

She was still mulling things over when Kirsty arrived, with Jamie behind her.

"Eilidh! How was your trip?" Kirsty got in first. "Successful in every way?"

She knew exactly what her friend was hinting at, and a couple of hours ago she would have been longing to share her joy with Kirsty. Now she was glad Jamie was there, too.

"Very successful. We had a great time." That was all she could tell her for the moment but it would satisfy the underlying question. Then she grinned at Jamie. "Hi Jamie, good to see you again."

"You too, Eilidh, my love." He kissed her cheek. This time Kirsty was all smiles and Eilidh knew these two had reached some new kind of understanding.

"Sorry, we're going out for dinner once I've changed. You don't mind eating on your own, do you? Or maybe you could ask Lewis round."

"Don't worry about me. You go and have fun." She didn't feel like telling her about Lewis and his emergency.

Then Kirsty paused. "Oh, I've some bad news, I'm afraid. Your friend, Grace – she had another massive heart attack. She didn't make it, Eilidh. I'm so sorry."

The news wasn't totally unexpected, but she wished it wasn't right now. How sad that she had only got to know the old woman so recently. And whatever Grace had known died with her.

"That is so sad, Kirsty. Thanks for telling me." She spared a fleeting thought for the poor brother she had never met, and who would now be looked after by strangers. At least he was being cared for by someone.

While Kirsty got ready, Eilidh sat on the chair across from Jamie. "So, you've patched things up then? I'm really pleased, Jamie."

"This far, this good. You'll find out soon enough if it's going as well as I hope." And that was all he would say. "Anyway, sounds like you had an interesting time yourself since last we met." His wicked grin suggested he knew exactly how interesting and she laughed at his unsubtle remark.

"Ah well, I don't tell tales, you know. But I learned a lot more about Burns and his Highland Mary." She grinned to show that was all the information he was getting.

She felt slightly more cheerful by the time they left for their dinner. Kirsty and Jamie were probably going to have a more volatile relationship than Rory and Sarah, if she discounted the problem with Rory's mother, but she had a feeling her feisty friend had need of Jamie's laid-back good humour. And she had a strong suspicion this was no ordinary dinner. Kirsty didn't usually put on a dress – even the kind of understated one she wore tonight – unless she was going to some big do.

Eilidh was happy for them, but as she switched the television on and ate her lonely meal, she couldn't help thinking back to the previous two evenings. This was not how she had hoped to spend tonight.

It was late when Kirsty and Jamie returned. Eilidh had gone for a short walk round by the shore during the evening, then settled down to watch an old film she had seen many times before. A comedy rather than a weepy, so it stopped her thinking too much about Lewis and whatever he was doing, and with whom.

She switched the TV off as soon as she saw Kirsty's face.

"We're official. Look!" Kirsty thrust her left hand at Eilidh so she could admire the solitaire sparkling on the third finger.

"Oh, Kirsty, I'm absolutely delighted for you." She hugged her tight. "You, too, Jamie. Well done for coming to your senses at last, before she got away for good." She hugged him, too.

"There's a bottle of wine in the fridge. Sorry it's not champagne," Kirsty said, fetching the wine opener.

She poured them each a glass and Eilidh toasted the happy couple.

"I phoned Sarah on her mobile," Kirsty said. "I couldn't leave her out of the news, although she had an inkling it might happen soon. She's staying at Rory's tonight. Oh, and I hope you won't mind, Eilidh, but Jamie's going to stay here tonight."

"It's your flat, Kirsty, and of course I don't mind."

She was glad Sarah and Rory seemed to be sorting things out again. And she genuinely didn't mind Jamie being at the flat, except that it reminded her of what she was missing by not being with Lewis. But she pushed that aside for now. She wasn't going to put a dampener on their happiness.

By the time Kirsty and Jamie went off to bed, the three of them had finished the bottle of wine between them. Eilidh was sleepy but couldn't get off to sleep. So many thoughts fought for precedence in her head, including the unknown secret Grace had kept for so many years. Then that was superimposed by the memory of Lewis and his shadowy resemblance to the portrait of Burns, which led her to wonder again if her mother had been right, and that she was distantly connected to Highland Mary's family line. Surely that was way too fanciful a thought, that they both had connections to this particular past?

As she tossed and turned, Eilidh made a decision. Apart from struggling with the kind of future there might be for herself and Lewis, she resolved to make that phone call to Rory first thing tomorrow. She had to see her aunt before wasting any more time.

Chapter Thirty

1786

I have told no-one but Meggie what we have planned. She is shocked, although whether it's because we are to leave or because he will marry me, I know not. Neither of us speaks of Jean Armour. He is over her, I am sure, else why would he ask me to go with him?

"Are ye sure ye know what you're doing, lass? It's a big step to go off across the world with a man your ma and pa haven't even met." I can see she wants to say more but is loath to spoil my joy. Truly she has been like an older sister to me and I shall miss her. I've given in notice to my employer that I am to go back home to see my family. It is true, although I do not say why I go to see them. I am so afraid I'll find I have been dreaming these last days.

I begin to gather my small belongings ready for the day I'm to leave. But first we must plight our troth, and I wait with such impatience for the Sunday we should meet. Surely the cattle must wonder what I do to them for my mind is not on anything but my love.

Soon the day arrives! On that Sunday morning in the Kirk, I listen carefully to the minister's preaching and am relieved to hear nothing that could seem like a warning. He talks of love for a change, of how that is more important than any other commandment, that without love for our neighbours, we sin against God's word. I scarce can stop from smiling and must keep looking at my Bible lest people think me soft in the head. No-one smiles during the service for we are meant to be learning how to be good Christian men and women. Inside, I am smiling and I cannot think that God would grudge us some joy in his presence.

I wear my best cotton gown, with my finest shawl across my shoulders. My small Bible is in the bag at my wrist, and kind Meggie has given me a delicate cotton handkerchief embroidered with M for Mary and C for Campbell. I shall treasure it always. I will return to my lodgings for one night before I set off to see my family, and will take my leave of Meggie then.

The sun has blessed us with its presence as I walk to the brook. My Robbie is there before me and my happiness is complete. I confess I oft imagined he had never said the words and that I would find myself alone. But he looks at me with love.

"You are still sure you will go with me, my Mary?"

"I have never been so sure of anything in all my life," I reply, and mean every word. For what would my life be worth without him by my side?

We stand, one on either side of the narrow running brook. We clasp our right hands together and hold a Bible in the left. Then we place our clasped hands under the running water. I know about these old ways that show we are promised only to each other, without need of a minister to say we are wed. We pledge to love and honour each other for all of our lifetime. Then he comes over beside me and we exchange our small Bibles. It is as binding as if it was written down for all to see.

We kiss and my happiness is complete. When he takes me into his arms and we lie down on the soft grassy bank, my love is so deep that I want to lie here forever in this place so that we might never be parted. His lips are warm and when they find the opening at my bodice, I feel I should die for the wanting of his hands on me.

There is no fumble at my skirts this time. His hand is sure as he caresses my trembling body, and I clasp him tightly to me. The trees and birds and sky are our only witness and even they cease to exist as my body cries out for this passion to be assuaged, and I think again that I shall die. Strange tingles are playing over my back and my belly as he grips me with such urgency, then I lose myself completely in this single moment that is unlike anything I ever knew. I now understand what is meant by love.

We whisper to each other and he promises to find us passage to Jamaica. He tells me we are now husband and wife as truly as if a minister has proclaimed it. I wish we could live together from this day, but I go from these parts on the morrow.

We stroll along the path, postponing the moment when we must part. Then we take our leave with much sorrow, and I endeavour not to weep aloud.

"I shall join you later in the summer, my love," he promises between kisses. "I will find you in Greenock and we will sail away together, for always. You have my heart and my hand, my Mary."

My tears almost blind my eyes as we part. How shall I wait so long until I see him again? We kiss for one last time and I do not look back as I leave him, else I should run and clasp myself to him and never let him go.

Chapter Thirty-One

"Is there a man, whose judgement clear,
Can others teach the course to steer."
(R. Burns: *A Bard's Epitaph*)

After a sleepless night, with dreams of a quiet embankment in Ayrshire mixed up with dragons and faceless men, Eilidh was relieved to get up in the morning. Kirsty and Jamie hadn't surfaced and she managed to take a shower and breakfast without disturbing them. Then she quietly left the flat. She felt a bit guilty but couldn't face their happiness this morning when she was feeling so rough, so she left Kirsty a note telling her she'd gone out and wishing them well again. She could look for an engagement card while out.

The breezy morning air soothed her at once and she walked along by the pier towards the station. The Dunoon boat was about to leave, and for a mad moment she thought of jumping on it. Another cop-out. She was going up to Greenock to see Rory. He might not be there, or be unable to see her, but she wanted to show him how necessary it was for her to see her aunt.

Checking her new mobile phone for the umpteenth time, there was still no message from Lewis and he hadn't phoned the flat. She refused to call him first. She had got up on a different side of the bed this morning, as it were; a more forceful side, determined to bring things to a head. That included not being messed about by Lewis, or being intimidated by memories and stories of her aunt.

Only yesterday she had wondered if she'd made a mistake buying a flat when things were moving on with Lewis. Now she was very grateful she had, as she was independent and could stay that way if she felt like it. She couldn't wait to have her own space, especially if Kirsty and Jamie were an item now; there was only so much she could take of the two together. And, with Sarah getting married soon, it would mean Kirsty and Jamie could have the flat to themselves.

She had been walking so fast Eilidh was surprised to find herself at the station, but felt better for the exercise and the sea air that made her cheeks tingle. The commuters had already gone and it was early enough for only serious shoppers to be on their way to town.

For all that it wasn't busy, a young mother with a toddler son sat in the seat at the window across the aisle from her. She smiled briefly when she caught Eilidh's glance then gave her full attention to the little boy beside her.

Eilidh hadn't brought her book, content instead to watch the scenery go by, but it wasn't long before the toddler started chattering to his mum, asking non-stop questions. Eilidh was amused at his persistence. He was cute, with blond wavy hair and seemed fairly well behaved for his age. It made her think of something she had fleetingly considered now and then. Did she want children of her own?

She was into her thirties now, her hormones might not behave for that much longer, and she liked children well enough, though she hadn't had much to do with them. She had no siblings, no cousins apart from Rory, no friends with young children, her own mother and her sister had hated each other, and there was no-one she'd positively wanted to have them with. *Until now*, a small voice whispered in her head. The realisation blew her away.

She let the mother and child sounds fade out as she contemplated a future that might involve children. If Kirsty and Sarah were getting married, there was a good chance their children could all grow up around the same age. Then she reined her thoughts in. There was one major problem: right now she didn't even know if she had a permanent man in her life, or if Lewis even wanted children. He had some years on her and might have given up any idea of being a father.

The train arrived at the station before she had any more time to think along that track. The small boy waved to her as she passed their seats and she waved back. Very cute, though she knew there were just as many little monsters who cried and kicked to get their own way. Putting all musing about children firmly out of her mind, she walked into town.

She wandered past the library then through the mall, browsing in shops as she went. As she reached the stretch of road where the lawyer's office was situated, she thought better of arriving unannounced and took out her mobile phone to find she had switched it off. No sooner had she pressed the 'on' button for it to power up, when it beeped to alert her to a message. She found a quiet spot and retrieved the voicemail.

"Eilidh, can you call me back? I'm so sorry about last night. I promise I won't let that happen again. Please ring me and I'll explain."

She listened again, gratified that Lewis sounded

sincere, and worried. Good, she'd let him suffer a while longer. But she smiled in relief that he'd got in touch. She dialled Rory's number and was put right through. When she explained she was in town, he agreed to see her right away, between appointments. Let him think it was about the flat.

They got the pleasantries over with first and she asked after Sarah.

"She's fine, we're fine. She told me how helpful you'd been yesterday. Thanks, Eilidh, she really appreciated a level voice."

"Glad I was there to help. I'm looking forward to having her as a cousin-in-law."

She didn't miss the awkward smile or the shadow of pain across his eyes, and guessed everything was not exactly sorted. That made her even more determined.

"Rory, I haven't come about the flat. I want to see my aunt and uncle as soon as possible, if you can warn them I'm here, please."

She noticed the apprehension in his expressive face. Just as well he was a conveyance lawyer and didn't appear in court, as he'd be hard pushed to hide his thoughts.

"Are you sure about this, Eilidh? What if you hear something you don't want to know? What if mother refuses to see you?"

"Rory, I did not come all the way back to Scotland to avoid seeing my aunt. She's the only person left who might be able to tell me what I need to know, at any cost. I'm afraid she won't get the chance to refuse to see me. I shall go and ring her doorbell until she answers, if she doesn't invite me over."

"Heavens, I didn't know you could be that determined. Maybe you have a bit of my mother in you after all, though you won't want to hear that!" He smiled to show he was teasing her, but it brought her up short. She hoped not, from what she'd heard about her aunt. But Eilidh did have enough determination when it mattered, or stubbornness even.

"Please, Rory, tell her I want to see her and your father. Apart from anything else, I want to tell her about my mother."

"I know, Eilidh. Leave it with me and I promise I'll tell her tonight. She'll be pleased to see me after the latest hassle."

"Thanks. It might divert her attention from you and Sarah for a while. Anyway, have you heard anything else about the flat, is the entry date still okay?"

"Everything's fine. It's all signed and sealed, and the original date still stands."

"Well, I won't take up any more of your time. Thanks for seeing me like this. And thanks for being such a nice cousin, Rory."

Her comment pleased him, as he stood up and saw her to the door. Maybe he was too nice for his own good, and surely must have got that from his father. She looked forward to meeting her uncle, then remembered he had the beginning of Alzheimer's. That must be a dreadful sentence for them both.

Eilidh finally called Lewis back in the afternoon.

"Eilidh! Thank goodness you've phoned. I'm at my wits' end here. Jan's fiancé has had an accident and she's in a right state. I did what I could last night but she's really upset. I hate to ask, but could you come down here for a while and help me out? She doesn't want to involve her mother too much and I've tried to persuade her to call her friends. But she's got into this habit of still turning to me whenever there's a problem, and I thought it might be a good idea if she meets you properly…" He trailed off to give her time to speak.

She didn't know how to respond. Sympathy for the woman, annoyance that she still used Lewis when it was convenient, anger that he allowed her to, and relief he had a real reason for cancelling their evening together. The ex-wife might not appreciate seeing the 'new woman' when she was so upset. But Eilidh didn't say any of that.

"It's fine, Lewis. I'll get the train and you can pick me up at the station. No, don't come away up here. In fact, it's probably easier to get a bus. I'll phone you when I'm nearly there. See you soon."

She hadn't even asked how the guy was and why Jan wasn't up at the hospital with him. Surely he hadn't died. The more she thought about the situation as she went to seek out a bus, the less sure she was how to handle it. The poor woman had just had a scare with her own health, and now this. And Lewis? Why were men such suckers when it came to the women in their life? Although a tiny part of her was pleased he was so caring.

He was waiting for her at the bus stop on Inverkip's main street. He hugged her tightly and she was reassured.

"Thanks a lot, Eilidh. I hate to put this on you, but I need a woman's touch."

"Is he going to be okay?"

"They're operating on him now. Jan's not going up until tonight. She's not handling it so well."

He drove her to a modern detached house at the top of the hill. It was slightly apart from the others on the estate and was near enough the countryside to be almost rural. Much as she was curious to see it, her priority was the woman in the living room.

She stood up as Eilidh entered and held out her hand. She'd been crying but had wiped the tears away and was trying to smile. "It's good to meet you properly, Eilidh. May I call you that? I'm sorry I spoiled your evening but I didn't know what else to do last night. It was all such a shock."

Eilidh shook her hand and they sat down. "I can imagine," she said. "I'm sorry you're having to cope with this."

"John's son is coming down to the hospital tonight, so he'll be a good support. Thankfully, we get on well. He's a student at Glasgow. John's some years older than me," she added, as though aware of Eilidh's surprise. "Lewis has been great, as always." She turned her large brown eyes on her ex-husband, and he shrugged.

Although Jan was friendly enough, it didn't take Eilidh long to sum her up as the type of fragile female who was used to having men at her beck and call, though sometimes they weren't quite as fragile as they appeared. Then she felt uncharitable, considering what the poor woman was going through.

"Tea for you both?" Lewis asked.

"That would be great, thanks," Eilidh answered, and Jan nodded. "Let me help," Eilidh said, and followed him through to the kitchen.

Making sure they couldn't be seen, he pulled her to him and kissed her mouth. "Thanks again, love. Please stay tonight."

She nodded, briefly returning his kiss, then took the proffered mugs through to the coffee table.

"Lewis tells me you've only recently come back to Scotland. It must be quite a culture shock for you,"

Jan said.

"In a way, but it also feels like home." Eilidh smiled up at Lewis, who was holding the teapot.

She didn't miss the speculative look Jan gave them and knew she suspected they were already more than friends. Women seemed to have inbuilt radar for that kind of thing, or super sensitive antennae that picked up on sexual tension.

Eilidh didn't care. All the better if she knew Lewis wasn't quite so available, unless it was a real life and death situation like this. Then she felt guilty for such thoughts.

The tension in the room increased as the time wore on until Jan suddenly stood up.

"I think I'll get back to the hospital now, if you don't mind. There should be some news of John by now, and Paul's going to meet me there. I'll let you know how things are, Lewis. But I won't disturb you tonight." This last was said with a glance at Eilidh. "Thanks again for being there. Nice to meet you again, Eilidh."

"Will you be okay to drive?" Lewis asked.

"I'm fine now, thanks." She smiled tremulously, as though on the verge of tears again. "Enjoy your stay," she said to Eilidh.

As Lewis saw Jan to the door, Eilidh felt like a guest who'd outstayed her welcome. Something about the way the last remark had been thrown at her. The treacherous thought ran through her mind that she hoped to God John survived so that Jan wouldn't be at her ex-husband's door all the time.

You horrible person, Eilidh told herself.

When they were alone at last, Lewis sat down on the sofa and drew her into his arms. "You were really kind, thanks. I know she's a bit needy sometimes, but we were married a long time and I guess old habits, and all that. But I'm learning." He kissed her deeply and longingly.

"I don't have anything with me to stay the night," she pointed out.

"No worries there. You can borrow anything you like of mine."

"Just as well I bought some undies in M & S, isn't it?" She teased him. She'd succumbed to another set of knickers after she'd seen the amazing choice. "I'd better phone Kirsty and tell her where I am. I left this morning before she was awake."

Although Kirsty was curious, she didn't ask too many questions. Eilidh guessed she was too caught up in her reunion with Jamie to worry much about anyone else.

Lewis was a good cook. She helped him cut up the vegetables and watched while he made them into a quick stir-fry with chicken, then served it on a bed of noodles.

Once they'd polished off the lot, along with red wine, she was happy to go for a stroll with him around the village. They walked down the hill to the single main street with its hotel and small shops, then crossed the busy dual carriageway to the marina, now a kind of village with new flats all the way round the tied-up yachts. A restaurant took prime position overlooking the inlet. The dull evening made it seem dark for early August and the lack of breeze gave it a still, silent feel. They wandered arm-in-arm without talking much, content to be together. Eilidh was glad of her fitness since the walk back up the hill was more strenuous, and she was uncomfortably hot and sticky by the time they got back to his house.

"You can have a shower first, if you like. I'll get

you a towel," Lewis offered, as she flopped down on the sofa exhausted.

"Thanks, I will." She stood up and they gazed at each other as though it had been more than one day since they'd been together. Then she was in his arms, all thoughts of a shower forgotten as their passion flared as though for the first time.

Later, during the night, Eilidh lay and wondered about the future. Their future. She was sensible enough to know they were in a kind of holiday mode at the moment. But soon, Lewis would be back at college with all its business and stress, and she would be looking for a job of her own, and writing as much as possible. Would their relationship work on those terms? How could they know without trying? Right now, she wanted to spend the rest of her life with this man. As she cuddled in beside him, her last thoughts were of the upcoming meeting with her aunt and uncle. The sooner the better.

Lewis dropped her at the flat next day. He was going to check how John was doing, and make sure Jan was okay. She appreciated his honesty and knew she had nothing to worry about, on his side at least.

Kirsty was getting ready to go on shift. Her comically raised eyebrows when she saw Eilidh were question enough to bring her up-to-date with what was happening with Lewis. As usual, she was more outspoken about the situation with Jan.

"She sounds a right clinger-on, or the type of female that wants every man to fall at her feet. I'm sorry for her problems, but don't let her use that to get away with spoiling things for you and Lewis. Mind, I wouldn't have thought he'd stand for any nonsense."

"He's a man! But, seriously, I think he summed

her up a long time ago. He's just being caring, which isn't a bad thing. Anyway, I think she got the message last night and at least he involved me as soon as he could."

"I'll try and find out what's happening at the hospital if I get a chance. There shouldn't have been that many accidents brought in two nights ago."

"So, what happened with you and Jamie?" she asked.

"Ah, well, I don't know exactly but we suddenly realised what we've been missing all these wasted years. We'll wait until after Sarah's wedding to get hitched ourselves. It'll be a low-key affair, unlike Sarah and Rory's. If they ever get there."

Eilidh told her about insisting to see her aunt. "Maybe I can find out what's going on with this church business."

After Kirsty had gone, Eilidh got out the limited notes she'd made on her own life and started reading through the meagre list in preparation for seeing her aunt and uncle. There wasn't much to go on. The fall-out between her mother and aunt when she was very young, and the fact she had never seen her uncle and cousin in all those years.

The day her aunt came to the house before they left for America. Her granny's upset at some kind of scandal. Eilidh's crescent-shaped birthmark that her mother hadn't shared; therefore, it might be from her father's side. Her mother's flight to America as soon as Granny had died. And the man in the photograph, who most likely hadn't written the letter to his Highland Lass.

Then the most terrible thought came to her and she realised it had been there subconsciously since that remark Rory had made about Eilidh's determined nature. What if her aunt was really her mother? Maybe for some reason she couldn't keep Eilidh so had let her be brought up by her sister. Plenty of stories told of that happening.

No, she refused to believe that was possible. It was just a bit too fantastic, and she couldn't think of one single reason why that would be necessary. Rory was around her age, so her aunt had obviously wanted a baby. Anyway, why had Grace told her to ask about the evening the Americans came over?

She put the notes away. Hopefully she'd learn the truth soon enough. She was still thinking about her aunt and uncle when the phone rang. It was Rory.

"Glad I caught you, Eilidh. Can you come to dinner with mother and father tonight? Mother said she wants to see you, once she'd got over the shock of you being here. 'Maybe it's time', she said, whatever that means. I didn't tell her about your mum, thought it better to come from you."

Thank the Lord, Eilidh thought, not appreciating until now how much she had imagined this happening.

Rory offered to pick her up. "I'm invited, too, but Sarah won't be there. Mother said it was family business. Honestly, Eilidh, you'd think she didn't like her future daughter-in-law, but she does. I think Sarah's the only kind of girl who'd even contemplate getting along with her."

Eilidh put down the phone with slightly trembling hands. Excitement, coupled with nerves. Maybe, finally, she was going to find out the truth at last. She only hoped she didn't regret it.

Chapter Thirty-Two

1786

My heart is so heavy when I leave my love behind and depart from this place. How can I bear to be so long apart until we should come together again? Yet I must go to visit my family and prepare for my long journey to that far country. That thought keeps me going and fills me with excitement.

Ma and Pa and the little ones greet me with such pleasure when finally I reach Campbeltown. It has been a long, weary road to travel but I can rest here a while. They look at me with wonder that I am grown and now a woman. I reassure them that I am well and in love with my Robbie. They cannot understand why I should wish to go so far but they see I am set on this course and nothing will dissuade me from it. I stay with them for some weeks, which helps them to accept my decision. We have distant family in Greenock and I long to see my dear brother there while I wait for my love to come for me.

Robbie has written a letter to me! I am overjoyed. He has not forgotten me. He talks of meeting me soon when I go to Greenock. Eventually, I pack my clothes and small possessions and get ready to make the journey across the river on Pa's ship again. My mother is sad that she might never see me again, but she knows what it means to love someone and to have no other will but to follow them wherever they might go.

My father embraces me as he leaves me at the harbour in Greenock, expecting a relative to meet me. He is still not happy at my decision but he assures me of his love and concern for my wellbeing, and I watch him depart with sadness in my heart that I might never see him again.

Oh, how busy everything is in Greenock. This is the largest town I have yet seen and it is noisy and dirty, and with so many people! Sailing ships come and go in the harbour and the smell of fish is in my nose. Children run about in ragged clothes and bare feet, the women around the harbour area are careworn, some with patched clothes, and I wonder what I have come to. I take my box and ask the way to my brother's lodgings at Charles Street.

"Wid that be Upper or Lower, lassie?" A rough, but kind enough woman asks me in a dialect I hardly understand.

"I think it's the Upper Street."

"Aye, well it's aw the same, anyways, in'it?" And she laughs and tells me the direction to take.

I walk a long way, thankful my box is not too heavy, and then I find the house. My brother lives in one of the flats in the building and I am surprised to find him at home, for I thought he would be at work and that our cousin would let me in.

"Mary, my dearest wee sister! How good it is to see you after all this time. Come away in the house."

I am relieved to find his accent has still a lilt like my own. "You're not working today, Robert?" Then I am worried. "You still have your work at the shipyard, don't you?"

He laughs at my frown. "Don't you be worrying yourself, Mary. Of course, I still have my work. I'm taking some time off today to be here for you."

I am only a little convinced. I do not think he would be allowed the time away from work, and why then did he not meet me at the harbour and carry my bag? No, there is something else that he's not telling me.

We catch up with our lives and I tell him all about my betrothal to Robert Burns, the poet farmer. He is happy that I love someone but he worries at the idea of me travelling so far across the seas, away from home. My brother is kind and thinks only of my happiness.

Our cousins welcome me to their home, and we while away the evening time with news of our families. It is when we retire that I hear my brother cough and I fear he may be unwell.

Amidst my fears, I lie and think of my dear, dear Robbie and wonder when he shall come for me. My brother is going to find out which ships sail for the Indies, and I shall imagine my love and I are soon on board one of them.

Chapter Thirty-Three

"Ae fond kiss, and then we sever;
Ae farewell, alas, for ever!"
(R. Burns: *Ae Fond Kiss*)

Eilidh paced up and down the room while she waited for Rory. She had covered the top of Kirsty's bed with every item of clothing she possessed, trying to choose something flattering but comfortable.

"Look, it's not your clothes they're going to be interested in, it's you they want to see," Kirsty finally told her.

"I know, but it's important to me that I feel my best."

In the end she picked out the skirt she had worn at the hotel with Lewis, as much to give her confidence and because he had liked it. She paired it with a simple, short-sleeved blouse and a light cardigan. Her low-heeled shoes would complete it fine.

"Goodness, you'd think I was going for an interview," she laughed at last.

"Aye, that's maybe not far off the mark. An interview to be the dragon's niece," Kirsty told her.

That remark did nothing to calm her already fraught nerves. Where was Rory? She started pacing again, checking the clock and her watch, until there was a ring at the door bell. Sure enough, her chauffeur had arrived.

"Relax and remember to keep breathing!" Kirsty shouted as they left.

Rory helped by talking all the way and reminding

her that his father might repeat things due to his illness. She wasn't looking forward to that either, as it probably would confuse the poor man more, having a stranger to dinner with them.

She didn't recognise the house, which proved how seldom she had been there, if at all. A low detached bungalow, it was fairly old like most of the property in the west end, with a small neat front garden. As she thought, it was not that far from the Esplanade.

Taking a deep breath, she waited beside Rory while he rang the bell.

"You'll be fine," he whispered.

She was grateful for his presence but not entirely reassured. Considering they were expected, they had been left on the doorstep a tad too long surely.

Then the door opened to reveal her aunt.

"Hello, Eilidh. It's so lovely to see you after all these years. Come in, please. Hello Rory." She allowed her son to kiss her cheek but didn't touch Eilidh.

"Hello, Aunt Elizabeth. It's been a long time. It's good to meet you at last." Eilidh was determined to be open and friendly, for now at least.

The woman wasn't exactly unfriendly and she smiled briefly, but hadn't held out her arms and welcomed the prodigal either. Oh well, Eilidh reasoned, they'd only just met. There was the barest resemblance to her mother, but Elizabeth was taller, slimmer, and sharper-featured with thinning lips. Her hair looked professionally styled and coloured to maintain a soft golden tone, while her two-piece skirt and cardigan seemed a little old-fashioned. In fact, everything about her suggested an earlier era. It also made her slightly formidable. Eilidh was used to the people here being casual and young in spirit, no matter their age.

"We're going to eat right away, if you don't mind. I like to maintain a routine for William. I imagine Rory will have told you of his little problem?"

"Yes, I was sorry to hear it." Although "little problem" wasn't quite how Eilidh would have described the onset of Alzheimer's. Quite the reverse. Maybe her aunt was in denial.

She showed them into a beautifully furnished living room. A cream, leather three-seater sofa, two armchairs, a medium-sized television screen, long mahogany and glass coffee table, and a modern marble fireplace with gas fire made up the bulk of the room. The walls were papered with a discreet pattern, and the deep-piled carpet was dark beige. Not the kind of room you'd want to bring children into.

"William, this is Eilidh, our niece from America."

Not the introduction Eilidh was expecting; it made it sound as though she had been born in the States.

Eilidh noticed her uncle's resemblance to Rory: once reddish hair now mixed with white, deep-set hazel eyes. He had been a handsome man, from Grace's photo, but was a little thin for his height. She noticed the gentle smile that constantly hovered around his lips, as though it was his natural expression, or perhaps he had forgotten some of his other emotions already.

She was surprised when he shook her hand right away with a firm grip.

"Eilidh." He played the name around his tongue and his smile seemed as genuine as it was possible to be.

"Hello, Uncle William." She liked him at once and received the impression he was pleased to see her. What a difference from her reserved aunt.

"We'll sit at the table, if you don't mind. Rory, will you come and help me bring in the potatoes and vegetables, please? I'll bring the casserole."

Eilidh wasn't surprised to be served a traditional type of chicken casserole, as her aunt seemed very conservative. But she felt a twinge of sympathy for Sarah as she noticed how Rory was treated in his childhood home. He glanced across and made a face when his mother was bringing in the plates. He obviously knew how it must look.

She was glad it wasn't a bigger table, as they each sat at one of the four sides. Her uncle was placed in between her aunt and Rory, and Eilidh presumed that was so they could help him if necessary.

Once the meal was served, her aunt chatted about the weather, the cost of food and fuel, the behaviour of today's youth, and the state of the world. Her uncle appeared to be listening but said not a word, while Rory smiled at him now and then. Only when they reached the pudding of fresh cream and strawberries did she ask about America, as though reluctant to mention it.

"And your mother? Does she still have that bookshop?"

A terrible silence descended as Eilidh realised she still had to tell this woman that her only sister was dead and buried.

Eilidh put her spoon down and began gently, "I'm afraid my mother died recently. That's why I came back. Breast cancer. I didn't know your address or I would have let you know."

As the silence continued, Eilidh was alarmed to see the colour drain from her aunt's face. "She's dead? Mary has died?"

The words seemed to cause a chain reaction. Rory

tried to speak to his mother, Eilidh started to apologise. But it was her uncle who surprised her most.

"Mary? Where's Mary?" he asked, and looked round as if expecting her to walk through the door.

It was too much for her aunt. She stood up and walked through to the kitchen, leaving them all aghast. Eilidh got up at once, ignoring the two men. Her aunt was gripping the kitchen sink and still looked deathly pale.

"I'm real sorry, Aunt Elizabeth, there was no easy way to tell you." There was nothing else she could offer, as it was as much her aunt's fault that she hadn't known her address.

"How could you? Blurting it out like that, in front of William. You can see how confused he is."

Something didn't seem quite right. She had thought there might be tears, or sympathy for Eilidh's loss, but this? Well, she wasn't going to take any blame, not now, or ever.

"Look, Aunt Elizabeth, I've apologised for telling you like that but you asked. And it's not my fault that I didn't know where to contact you." Then her own remembered grief took over. "If you didn't contact my mother when she was alive, I wouldn't have thought you'd mind not being at her death!"

There was another stunned silence, and Eilidh swallowed. She'd gone too far. Her aunt turned and stared at her, eyes blazing. Then just as Eilidh was going to look away, or apologise, she noticed the woman sag and the tears in her eyes. That only made her feel worse. This woman was obviously used to keeping herself under control.

"You have no idea how much I missed my sister. But too much had happened between us, and neither of us knew how to heal the hurt."

Eilidh was astonished at her words and had no idea what to do, or say.

Then Rory appeared at the kitchen door. "Everything okay?" He looked from one to the other, at a complete loss.

His mother stood up to her full height. "Rory, would you please take your father out for a while. Make sure he puts his warm coat on. I want to talk to Eilidh. We'll have coffee later."

Eilidh didn't know who was most taken aback, her or Rory. But he went to do his mother's bidding at once, obviously glad to escape. He glanced at Eilidh to make sure she was fine with it and she nodded.

Once the men had gone, her aunt invited her through to the living room and asked her to sit down. Although she was under control again, a suspicion of tears lingered under the older woman's eyelashes and Eilidh wasn't sure whether to say anything else. She kept quiet, intrigued as to why the woman wanted them to be alone.

"First, let me ask a question. Do you know the reason why your mother went to America and why we fell out?" Aunt Elizabeth asked, hands gripping the edge of her seat.

"Well, no. That's partly why I'm here. I actually know nothing at all about my life here, or who my natural father might be. I can't move on until I find out the answers. Mum refused to talk about the past."

Her aunt nodded as though she'd expected that reply. She stared at Eilidh, looked away as though wondering how to continue, then back again. She nodded, decision made. "I'm going to tell you a story, Eilidh, but you might not like everything you hear. None of us behaved well. But I can't keep it hidden away any longer. Especially now."

Her hands clammy and her heart beating faster than normal, Eilidh waited, not daring to speak.

"A crowd of us used to go around together in the seventies; boys and girls. Although your mother was five years younger than me, we still did some things together. William was part of the crowd, and your mother's friend, Grace, and her brother, Ronnie. Two other girls joined us sometimes and a couple of boys. We had good fun, although Ronnie was a nuisance now and then since he was so slow."

She paused. "Your mother was the most popular girl around, Eilidh. Sweet-natured, much better looking than any of us, and mischievous, even quite flirtatious at times."

Eilidh didn't like the way this was going.

"Anyway, when the Americans were based in the Holy Loch," she paused again, "you know about all that, don't you?" When Eilidh nodded, she continued. "Well, that was an exciting time. It affected Dunoon and that side of the river most, of course, but we had our share of the fun. Some of the companies here would organise dances and invite the sailors over. You can imagine how all of us girls loved that, a bit of Hollywood glamour on our doorstep. But the local boys weren't so happy. Why would they be, since most of their girls were more interested in the Yanks?"

Eilidh made some kind of assent; she could picture it all too well, especially since she'd heard little bits before.

"Sorry, I know it's not telling you anything yet but I want you to understand the background." She paused as though trying to find the right words. "Anyway, your mother and I were both keen on

William, although I was nearer his age. Then she got friendly with one of the Americans and William turned to me eventually. I was always a bit jealous of my vivacious young sister, and I made sure I grabbed him quick. We eventually got married. Ronnie also loved your mother in his own simple way, and he wasn't happy she ignored him in favour of her American sailor."

Eilidh knew Ronnie figured in the story somewhere but couldn't believe the way her mind was working and she listened hard.

"Soon we were all a bit older, and I was expecting Rory. Mary's sailor had gone back to America and she was free again. One night, there was another big dance in Greenock and everyone went except me, so I only heard about it afterwards."

Eilidh held her breath.

"Some kind of fight broke out near the end. I don't know if some of the local boys finally lost their cool with the Americans, but it turned a bit nasty. Ronnie didn't understand it all. He only wanted to be with your mother. In all the ensuing carry-on, William eventually found Ronnie outside trying to kiss your mother and she was fighting him off. Ronnie was very strong and didn't fully understand how much he hurt her. William found Grace and she took Ronnie home."

So, Grace *had* known more about it. Eilidh almost gasped aloud. But she didn't want to break the spell of revelation. She might never have another chance to hear the full story. She couldn't resist a question. "And Ronnie? He surely wasn't my father, was he?" It didn't feel right.

Aunt Elizabeth hesitated, then shook her head, lowering her eyes for a moment as though she couldn't continue. Then she took a deep breath and resumed her story, giving Eilidh one quick glance.

"William took care of your mother."

Something in the way she said it made Eilidh's heart jump. Her aunt was silent for a while and she didn't know whether to interrupt, her thoughts running widely in a different unbelievable direction.

"Some months later, it became obvious Mary was pregnant. Grace and I assumed it was that American she'd been seeing, but he had gone home by then and we hadn't worked out the dates at that time." She glanced back at Eilidh and her voice shook. "Then Mary came to see me one day and told me the baby was William's. That they had always loved each other, although they'd tried to deny it since he was married to me."

Now Eilidh started trembling, heart beating widely. It couldn't be true, surely? That would make Rory her half-brother.

Elizabeth looked straight at her, the tears now more noticeable.

"Can you imagine what that did to me, Eilidh? I was pregnant with William's child and my own sister was telling me she too bore his child and that he loved *her*, always had. All my suppressed jealousy gave vent to such terrible words. I refused to believe her and called her a tramp, and even worse. I honestly still thought the American was your father, that because he had gone she was jealous of my marriage to William. It was the end of our relationship."

Now that she'd spoken the awful truth, Elizabeth seemed more in control once more, while Eilidh sat in a turmoil of emotion. Then her aunt continued and Eilidh wondered what could possibly follow.

"I confronted William, of course, and he denied it

at first. But he's Catholic, and the enormity of what had happened got to him in the end. He couldn't be sure the baby was his, but the fact it was a possibility nearly destroyed us. I'd converted when we married, and in the end, he promised to stay with me and our legitimate child. He didn't believe in divorce and said he loved me. I had to believe that was true. I don't know if he truly loved my sister. I never asked. I didn't want to know."

My god! Eilidh smoothed the hair from her damp brow; this was not what she had expected to hear. Then her aunt inadvertently confirmed it by her next words.

"When we were younger, William used to joke about her being Mary Campbell. His middle name is Robert you see, and how they might have been Burns and his Highland Mary. But he stayed true to his word. I never saw my sister again until our mother's funeral, and once when she was going away. Since she was travelling to America, I still held onto the belief, hope perhaps, that your father must be the American.

"I still don't know until this day, and it has torn me apart when I've thought about it at times. William has been a good husband and father and I've never wanted for anything. But I lost my sister, and to some extent my mother, by refusing to see Mary again. And now you are here at last."

Eilidh put her hands up to her face and bowed her head. That letter hidden in the treasured book of Burns' poetry, it was in William's hand, using his middle initial to write to his Mary. She had no doubt that he'd loved her mother, but had chosen to stay with his wife and unborn son. There was nothing to be gained by telling her aunt about that.

There was one thing she still needed to know. If William was definitely her father, there was only one way she might find out, apart from DNA, which she had no intention of suggesting. She had tried to find out if birthmarks were hereditary and had studied mixed opinions, although she'd been interested to read on the Internet about actual cases of identical birthmarks between family members.

Eilidh stood up and took off her cardigan. "I have a little birthmark on my shoulder and it's not from my mother. Have you seen anything like this before?"

She unbuttoned the top of her blouse and eased it from her shoulder to show the small crescent.

Her aunt gripped her heart and let out a sob. "So, it was true! All this time, she had been speaking the truth. Rory has one exactly the same on his back. And William has a bigger one on his shoulder. They call it their silver moon."

Eilidh sat down, completely washed out by all these revelations. Her father was William, and Rory was her brother, not her cousin. It was too much.

"What are you going to do, Eilidh?" Fear shook Elizabeth's voice.

What could she do? Ruin everyone's lives because she wanted a father after all these years? She finally looked up.

"Thank you for telling me all this, Aunt Elizabeth. You can imagine it's a bit of a shock…"

What on earth should she do? Her aunt was right, none of them had behaved well, but her aunt was the one who had been cheated on. Eilidh had liked Rory's father at once…*her* father. Yet he was already disappearing into a world of his own that would soon be his only reality. Even now, nothing would be gained by trying to tell him who she was; he probably wouldn't understand anyway.

But there was Rory. She couldn't go through the rest of her life pretending to be his cousin. If he was a member of a Christian church, then he would be able to handle the truth and still love his mother and father. For surely the very heart of his faith was forgiveness.

She looked her aunt in the eye at last. "I want Rory to know the truth. That is the only thing I insist on. There have been enough secrets. I'll let you tell him whatever you want, as long as he knows we are half brother and sister. And I would appreciate it if you would allow me to see you and William now and then." She couldn't call him her father yet. "I don't have any other family and I'd like to feel welcome in this one. But William will never know who I am. I promise. I've only ever wanted to know my father's identity, as I always felt my roots were completely in Scotland."

Her aunt stood up, all trace of tears gone. "Thank you, Eilidh. As you can see, William is already losing his short-term memory. He probably won't even remember meeting you earlier. Eventually he'll need professional care. But I understand what you are saying. Rory has a right to know."

She smiled hesitantly, and Eilidh wondered if they might ever be friends sometime in the future.

By the time the two men returned, Eilidh and her aunt had cleared away the dishes and were making coffee. A certain amount of strain remained between them but Eilidh was also conscious of her aunt's efforts to speak to her normally. After all their emotion, they had to appear as normal as possible in front of the man who had no idea that his past had come back to confront him. And he never would.

"Hello there, we're ready for our coffee, aren't we, Dad?" Rory came into the kitchen and glanced briefly between his mother and Eilidh.

"Thanks for taking your father out, son, you know how he loves being in the fresh air."

"Hi, Rory. Your mum and I have been getting to know each other," Eilidh said, trying to sound natural.

She was pleased to see her aunt smile. Maybe the healing was beginning for Elizabeth after so many years of resentment, anger and jealousy, and always the uncertainty that she was the true love of her husband's life. Plus, the regret that she'd lost her sister. Now it was too late for them, but it wasn't too late for her and Rory.

Eilidh stood up to go after they'd finished their coffee. Both she and her aunt needed time to process everything. She noticed that William smiled over at her occasionally, and it twisted her heart that he'd never know she was his daughter, the result of his deep love for her mother.

Then, as she was about to leave, he shook her hand and said, "Is your name Mary, did you say? Like Highland Mary?"

"It's Eilidh, Uncle William. Mary was my mother's name."

She saw his puzzlement and squeezed his hand, wondering what was going through his cell-damaged mind. She didn't dare look at her aunt, until she filled the sudden silence.

"Goodbye, Eilidh. Come back and see us soon. You'll be made welcome."

Her aunt's words brought the first tears to Eilidh's eyes that night. It would be fine. They would all get through it and get to know each other all over again, without the shadow of the past.

As Rory drove her home, he was obviously puzzled by her silence. "I hope mother behaved. Was everything all right? I know she was upset when she heard about your mum."

"Everything's fine, Rory, and yes, your mother behaved very well."

She didn't mention that his mother would be speaking to him soon. Let him seek her out once he knew who she really was. They would cope. And it explained why she had felt a strong connection to Rory from the beginning. She had a brother. She really hoped he would be as happy to find out he had a sister.

Chapter Thirty-Four

1786

I am right to be fearful of my brother's cough, for soon I can see he has head pain and the beginning of a fever. When I go out to walk about the town and harbour, I am even more fearful for they say there is disease in some places. No-one can tell me what manner of disease it is but there are few that go away without leaving problems behind, or worse. He is complaining now of pain in his legs and back, and his cough is no better.

He is in a rash! My poor brother is too unwell to go back to his work and I am thankful I'm here to look after him. We think he might have the measles, because of the fever that comes with the spots. Then I hear something that chills my heart. They say that typhus is calling on Greenock.

Robert is no better, but not too much worse as each day passes, and I pray that his fever will break and he will smile at me again.

He is worsening. There have been deaths from the typhus. We are all worried now. I continue to nurse my poor brother, mopping his brow when he burns. But he does not recognise me at times and I fear he is slipping away from me.

He speaks such nonsense in the night. His mind is not his own and his heart beats less strongly. I weep already, for I know he will not recover.

He is gone. Dead in the dark of night. My poor, dear brother is in no more pain or distress. I weep into my pillow. Ma and Pa will be so sorrowful when they hear. I thank God that I was able to see him once more and to be able to care for him in his last hours.

I am so very tired now it is over. It is so many months since I left my love behind in Ayrshire and I do not hear from him since I came here. Where are you, my Robbie? For I have need of you beside me.

My head has begun to hurt these past days and I coughed last night. I can see the fear on the faces near to me, though they try to hide it.

I am too tired to rise from my bed. I know with each passing hour that my cough is worsening. It wracks my back and causes me pain. I pray that it is not yet my time to go on a different journey from the one I had planned with my dearest love.

The rash has appeared on my arms. I am so weak with coughing and sore in body and mind. Where is my Robbie?

The doctor has been, and I hear quiet voices. They do not tell me what he says. But I know. My body now burns with heat. I think longingly of that day by the cool brook when I discovered what it means to love…

Where are you Robbie? Our ship will sail without us…

The women mop my brow and sing to me. I hear a far-off voice calling me his Highland Lassie. Oh, he is coming for me at last...

I am in his arms and he is loving me. We shall be on our ship soon. Then the room shifts and he is not there...

My eyes are open and I see a great light. My brother beckons... but I cannot go to him. My Robbie is coming for me...

Chapter Thirty-Five

"Then gently scan your brother man,
Still gentler sister woman;
Though they may gang a kennin' wrang,
To step aside is human"
(R. Burns: *Address to the Unco Guid*)

After the trauma of the previous evening at her aunt's, Eilidh went out for the day without telling anyone where she was going. She needed time to think everything over before she faced Rory. She hadn't mentioned the devastating revelations, but would tell Kirsty and Jamie and Lewis eventually. Rory could tell Sarah. No-one else mattered.

But it could wait until after the hospice fund-raising ceilidh dance, as that should be a celebration of their friendship and joy. The hospice, although caring for cancer patients, also celebrated life with compassion and dignity, allowing space for families to be together in the end. And the event would serve as a fitting memorial for her own mother's fight against the disease.

Although a fresh morning, already a mist of rain was creeping over the distant hills. Eilidh didn't care and decided to walk until she was tired. Setting off round the pier, she passed the boat and the station without stopping, then on through the town and beyond the outdoor swimming pool. When she reached a bench by the narrow promenade, it was still dry and she sat down to stare out at the open sea.

Across the wide expanse lay Dunoon, where

Highland Mary eternally watched for her great love, Robert Burns. Where a small quiet seaside town had been infiltrated by thousands of American sailors and their families over a period of thirty years. Where her mother had flirted with and possibly loved one of those sailors for a short while. And it was that exciting, yet troubled time that had brought those sailors to Greenock, to a momentous evening when the local youths had rebelled. The night she most likely had been conceived, when two people could deny their feelings no longer.

She had come to terms with Uncle William being her father. She knew without doubt that he had loved her mother so dearly, perhaps more than his own wife and son. Who could say? But he had done the decent thing, whether from love or because of his religious beliefs, he alone knew. And her mother? She had lost the love of her life, Eilidh was sure of it, but she had treated her sister badly in her pursuit of that love. Eilidh couldn't think any less of her mother, because she now knew what it was to love like that, but she did think more of her aunt than she had before.

No doubt Grace had thought her poor, slow brother had hurt her friend; no wonder she didn't want to say anything, out of protection. Or perhaps she had known all along that Mary and William were in love.

Eilidh stood up and walked further on. It helped her to think. Rory would accept the situation, once he got over the shock; she was sure of it. She had seen the way he cared for his father. Their father. And he would see another side to his mother, one that might make him more sympathetic towards her. She was pretty sure the nonsense over the wedding venue was in the past. Now she understood why her aunt had clung to her adopted religion, as, in a way, it had possibly saved her marriage. But she would understand that Rory and Sarah deserved to live out their faith in their own way.

Kirsty and Jamie would probably live in the flat and have children as soon as possible, ensuring Jamie well and truly settled down. They would make wonderful parents.

And her own future? Eilidh wondered. She would soon move into her lovely new flat with her own view of the river and mountains, but she suspected it would never be truly her home unless Lewis shared it with her. She couldn't imagine her life without him now and knew he felt the same. She was going to be a Campbell with a happy ending.

She reached Lunderston Bay before she stopped again. The beach was quiet apart from one or two people walking their dogs by the shore. Striding across the grass, she sat down on the rocky outcrop above the shingle shore. The mist had cleared from the far-off hills and she could see the greens and browns and purples that spoke of this part of Scotland. Her home. She watched the yachts and the gulls and the pair of swans that swam down river towards her. And she listened to the gentle waves that constantly washed the dirt and sand away, making everything clean again.

On the way back, she called into the craft shop and bought the green and ivory hand-made African bracelet for Kirsty. It was some small measure of thanks for all her kindness, and everything she'd been to Eilidh over the weeks since she had come home. They truly were friends for life.

On the last Saturday in August, as the ceilidh band

took up their fiddles for the energetic Eightsome Reel, Eilidh took her lover's hand. They smiled into each other's eyes before joining their friends to make up the set. Lewis stood head and shoulders above the others and his highland outfit of kilt, white dress shirt, and broad black belt made her spirits dance with the music. For a moment she paused, hearing the echo of those past times, seeing the shadow of other reels and jigs when two women called Mary Campbell had danced with their own loves.

Then all thought was lost as Eilidh Campbell was whirled into the arms of Lewis Grant and she gave herself up to the music and dance and wherever it might lead.

Epilogue

"Oh, Mary! Dear departed shade!
Where is thy place of blissful rest?
See'st thou thy lover lowly laid?"
(R. Burns: *To Mary in Heaven*)

The small girl stood solemnly beside her mother and father, in front of the huge gravestone.

"Who's that man and lady, Mummy?"

"That's a very famous poet called Robert Burns and he loved that lady, Mary Campbell, very much," Eilidh replied.

"As much as you and Daddy?"

"Well, maybe not quite that much!"

Eilidh smiled at her little daughter and then up at her husband. Lewis took her hand on one side and his daughter's on the other, and he grinned with deep blue eyes that crinkled at the corners from a few more lines.

They had been visiting the family graves, and stopped as usual at Highland Mary's on the way down. Eilidh never tired of delighting to see that the moss-covered, dirty old stone of her childhood had been cleaned and given pride of place in a garden commemorating the Bard's lost love.

She had started her novel, and the lovers' tragic story still had the power to fascinate and move her. Even more so now. Her aunt had been able to provide some family history which William had started before his illness, and it seemed there was indeed a very distant connection to Mary Campbell's Greenock family. And Eilidh had found out a little more of the story.

When the council dug up Mary's remains in 1920 to move them to her new burial place, they had found a tiny coffin buried with her. Eilidh knew that opinion had been divided down through the years as to whether or not this was her dead child, brought to early birth through Mary's illness. Or, more likely, that it was the infant of a family member buried – as was often the case – in the same ground.

Eilidh didn't care either way. The fact remained that Mary Campbell died of the same typhus that had killed her brother. And Robert Burns had been too late to ever see her again, partly because his first book of poems was published and he had delayed his departure to Greenock.

It had taken Eilidh a while to forgive him for that, imagining that Mary had waited ever hopeful. Yet the poetry he had written thereafter showed that he could hardly forgive himself. He had never forgotten her. Even after his legitimate marriage to Jean Armour and their many children, he still wrote of his Highland Lass. Mary Campbell had remained in a small corner of his heart for all time.

Later, Eilidh read the faint printed copy of an article in the *Greenock Advertiser* of 1823, which said that several ardent letters from Robert Burns to Mary Campbell had been found in her wooden chest after her death. Having received no reply to his letters, Burns finally wrote to Mary's uncle in Greenock. And from him he learned the tragic news. It went on to report that one of Mary's family members had burned all the letters after she died. Eilidh had to accept that the couple were never destined to be together.

She understood more than most how much forgiveness could change people. She was glad she'd had the opportunity to know her father as much as was possible in his final days, and knew that her aunt now valued her friendship. Their lives were all the richer for it.

Now they had a celebration to attend; the birth of her new nephew. Rory and Sarah and her Aunt Elizabeth would be waiting to toast the newest member of the family. Eilidh smiled as she always did at the engraving of Robert Burns and Mary Campbell, captured in an eternal embrace. Then she turned away with her husband and daughter, Mhari Elizabeth Grant, to walk back down the hill.

Acknowledgements

My grateful thanks to the following people for their various support, help and enthusiasm during the journey of this novel from first idea to eventual publication:

Joan Fleming and her late husband, Archie, for lending me a modern scholarly book about Burns; Kathleen Hammond and her late husband, Albert, for the gift of a precious old book; My friend Liz for her excitement in this story, and Catriona for her endless encouragement; First writing mentor, Sheila Lewis, and her faith in my tentative idea for this story, and Maggie Craig for her valuable critique of the original first few chapters at the Scottish Association of Writers Conference some years ago.

The Romantic Novelist's Association New Writers' Scheme, where I received an excellent critique and huge encouragement to submit this novel to a publisher, and members of Erskine Writers for their support over the years.

Sandra Wilson at the Watt Library for finding relevant material from The Greenock Advertiser and for the leaflet on Highland Mary, and Margaret Kane at the Greenock Burns Club for access to some of their archive material.

My sister, Irene, for the inspiration for part of the setting of the novel; My husband, son, and daughter for their unstinting encouragement when I began writing this novel.

And thank you to my lovely publishing house, Crooked Cat, for an enjoyable experience and a wonderful cover, and to my editor, Christine McPherson, whose professional eye tweaked any clumsy sentences and caught silly errors that a writer's eye passes over.

I consulted, and was grateful for, many books, letters, and articles during the research for this novel including:

James Currie, *The Life of Robert Burns*, Chambers, 1838

Maurice Lindsay, *The Burns Encyclopedia*, Robert Hale, 1995

James MacKay, Burns: *A Biography of Robert Burns*, Mainstream Publishing, 1992

Andrenne Messersmith, *The American Years*, Argyll Publishing, 2003

Gavin Sprott, *Robert Burns: Farmer*, National Museums of Scotland, 1990

The Greenock Advertiser and *The Greenock Telegraph*

Inverclyde Initiative, Highland Mary Leaflet, 1987

As a born and bred Greenockian (now living in central Scotland), I've been fascinated by Highland Mary's story since childhood. I have since researched Mary Campbell's story but have not consulted any living descendants. This is a work of fiction and I preferred to use the research material to spark my own creative imagination.

As a result, I have fictionalised the meetings and conversation between Highland Mary and Robert Burns!

About the Author

Rosemary Gemmell now lives in central Scotland but grew up in Inverclyde. She is the author of historical and contemporary novels and tween books. She is also a prize-winning freelance writer of short stories, articles and poetry, many published in UK magazines, the USA, and online.

Rosemary is a member of the Society of Authors, the Romantic Novelists' Association and the Scottish Association of Writers. She has a Masters in Literature and History, and Diploma in European Humanities.

You can sign up to her newsletter on her blog or website for up to date news and occasional giveaway competitions.

Published Books

Highcrag
The Highland Lass
Return to Kilcraig
Dangerous Deceit
Midwinter Masquerade
Mischief at Mulberry Manor
Christmas Charade
Pride & Progress
Venetian Interlude

Aphrodite & Adonis Novellas
The Aphrodite Touch
The Adonis Touch
The Aphrodite Assignment

Short Story Collections
Beneath the Treetops
End of the Road
Two of a Kind

Non-Fiction Articles
Scottish People and Places

Middle Grade Children's Fiction
Summer of the Eagles
The Jigsaw Puzzle
The Pharaoh's Gold